D0204964

"A captivating story from the very first page until the end. The plot thickens like pea soup, and each character has a different spice to add to it. From the easy-to-re-create recipes in the back to its high-energy, ever-changing story line, this one is good enough to serve to the higher-ups. Ollie is definitely a character worth following. Great job, Julie Hyzy. Another all-around great read!" —*The Romance Readers Connection*

"Ollie Paras is at the top of her game in [*Buffalo West Wing*], as is Hyzy . . . Every White House Chef Mystery is cause for celebration. The daily schedule in the White House kitchen is trauma enough, but Hyzy always ratchets up the tension with plots and danger . . . Julie Hyzy's star shines brighter than ever with *Buffalo West Wing*." —*Lesa's Book Critiques*

EGGSECUTIVE ORDERS

"The ever-burgeoning culinary mystery subgenre has a new chef-sleuth . . . The backstage look at the White House proves fascinating. Recipes are included for Eggcellent Eggs." —*Booklist*

"A quickly paced plot with a headstrong heroine and some recipes featuring eggs all add up to a dependable mystery." —*The Mystery Reader*

HAIL TO THE CHEF

"A gourmand's delight . . . Julie Hyzy balances her meal ticket quite nicely between the glimpses at the working class inside the White House with an engaging chef's cozy." —*Midwest Book Review*

"The story is entertaining, the character is charming, the setting is interesting . . . Fun to read, and sometimes that is exactly what hits the spot. I've found all of Hyzy's books to be worth reading, and this one is no different." —*Crime Fiction Dossier* (Book of the Week)

"[A] well-plotted mystery." —*The Mystery Reader*

STATE OF THE ONION

"Pulse-pounding action, an appealing heroine, and the inner workings of the White House kitchen combine for a stellar adventure in Julie Hyzy's delightful *State of the Onion*."
—Carolyn Hart, national bestselling author of *Death Comes Silently*

"Hyzy's sure grasp of Washington geography offers firm footing for the plot." —*Booklist*

"[A] unique setting, strong characters, sharp conflict, and snappy plotting . . . Hyzy's research into the backstage kitchen secrets of the White House gives this series a special savor that will make you hungry for more."
—Susan Wittig Albert, national bestselling author of *The Darling Dahlias and the Confederate Rose*

"From terrorists to truffles, mystery writer Julie Hyzy concocts a sumptuous, breathtaking thriller."
—Nancy Fairbanks, bestselling author of *Turkey Flambé*

"A compulsively readable whodunit full of juicy behind-the-Oval Office details, flavorful characters, and a satisfying side dish of red herrings—not to mention twenty pages of easy-to-cook recipes fit for the leader of the free world."
—*Publishers Weekly*

More praise for the novels of Julie Hyzy

"A well-constructed plot, interesting characters, and plenty of Chicago lore . . . [A] truly pleasurable cozy."
—Annette Meyers, author of *Hedging*

"[A] promising talent with a gift for winning characters and involving plots." —*Chicago Sun-Times*

Berkley Prime Crime titles by Julie Hyzy

White House Chef Mysteries

STATE OF THE ONION
HAIL TO THE CHEF
EGGSECUTIVE ORDERS
BUFFALO WEST WING
AFFAIRS OF STEAK
FONDUING FATHERS

Manor House Mysteries

GRACE UNDER PRESSURE
GRACE INTERRUPTED
GRACE AMONG THIEVES

FONDUING FATHERS

JULIE HYZY

BERKLEY PRIME CRIME, NEW YORK

THE BERKLEY PUBLISHING GROUP
Published by the Penguin Group
Penguin Group (USA) Inc.
375 Hudson Street, New York, New York 10014, USA

Penguin Group (Canada), 90 Eglinton Avenue East, Suite 700, Toronto, Ontario M4P 2Y3, Canada (a division of Pearson Penguin Canada Inc.) • Penguin Books Ltd., 80 Strand, London WC2R 0RL, England • Penguin Ireland, 25 St. Stephen's Green, Dublin 2, Ireland (a division of Penguin Books Ltd.) • Penguin Group (Australia), 707 Collins Street, Melbourne, Victoria 3008, Australia (a division of Pearson Australia Group Pty. Ltd.) • Penguin Books India Pvt. Ltd., 11 Community Centre, Panchsheel Park, New Delhi—110 017, India • Penguin Group (NZ), 67 Apollo Drive, Rosedale, Auckland 0632, New Zealand (a division of Pearson New Zealand Ltd.) • Penguin Books, Rosebank Office Park, 181 Jan Smuts Avenue, Parktown North 2193, South Africa • Penguin China, B7 Jaiming Center, 27 East Third Ring Road North, Chaoyang District, Beijing 100020, China

Penguin Books Ltd., Registered Offices: 80 Strand, London WC2R 0RL, England

FONDUING FATHERS

A Berkley Prime Crime Book / published by arrangement with Tekno Books

PUBLISHING HISTORY
Berkley Prime Crime mass-market edition / January 2013

ISBN: 978-0-425-25181-2

BERKLEY® PRIME CRIME
Berkley Prime Crime Books are published by The Berkley Publishing Group, a division of Penguin Group (USA) Inc., 375 Hudson Street, New York, New York 10014.
BERKLEY® PRIME CRIME and the PRIME CRIME logo are trademarks of Penguin Group (USA) Inc.

PRINTED IN THE UNITED STATES OF AMERICA

10   9   8   7   6   5   4   3   2   1

ALWAYS LEARNING   PEARSON

In memory of my dad

ACKNOWLEDGMENTS

I love writing these White House Chef Mysteries. Having been able to create Ollie and her friends and to see them through all sorts of dangers as Ollie stirs up trouble provides me never-ending enjoyment. This sixth book in the series brings answers to questions Ollie's been asking all her life, and I hope you enjoy digging into the truth alongside her.

I tapped into many friends' expertise for authentic details and I'm grateful for their generous help. First up, Ellen Crosby. This talented author of the outstanding Wine Country Mysteries advised me where best to set a vineyard just outside D.C. Thank you, Ellen!

Many thanks to my blog sisters, The Cozy Chicks (www.cozychicksblog.com), and my friends at Cozy-Promo. It's wonderful to be part of such helpful and supportive groups. Thanks also to Facebook friends Diane Donceel McDonald and Jeanine Elizalde for helping me sort out a plot problem early on. Even though the story ultimately went a different direction, Diane's and Jeanine's enthusiastic help was appreciated nonetheless. Enormous thanks as well, to my good friend, David Eppenstein, for legal advice as I neared the climactic scene. His timely input prevented Ollie from making a very big mistake!

Maureen Corcoran Komperda has been one of my dearest friends since high school and I know I can always depend on her for guidance on medical issues. Thanks, Corky!

Reference librarian Jeanne Munn Bracken was happy to help, and her input earned her a brief mention in this story. Watch for it.

An Australian friend, Sarah Byrne, generously bid at a Bouchercon charity auction, winning the chance to name a character in this book. Keep an eye out for her, too.

My deep gratitude to James A. Tobias at the Historical Resources Branch of the U.S. Army Center of Military History for helping me get a key piece of paperwork just right.

And to the incomparable Judy Bobalik, who came up with the title, hugs and thanks!

These books would never come to life without the support and generosity of my fabulous editor, Natalee Rosenstein; her delightful assistant, Robin Barletta; and sharp-eyed copyeditor Erica Rose at Berkley Prime Crime. Thanks to Larry Segriff at Tekno Books, who has been an absolute pleasure to work with. And, of course, many thanks to my enthusiastic agent, Paige Wheeler.

Lastly, as always, to my family. You are my life. I love you all so much. Thank you.

CHAPTER 1

MY MOTHER PLACED A SERVING OF HOMEMADE panna cotta in front of Gav and tucked a spoon next to it. "Ollie told me she's served this very recipe to the president and his family," she said. "Can you believe that? Such a simple dish, and one she learned right here in my kitchen."

Her wide smile crinkled her eyes as she placed a helping in front of me. "I tell my bridge club the same thing every time I make this. I know they must be getting tired of me bragging about you being the White House executive chef, honey, but I can't help myself."

"Oh, Mom," I said.

She completed her circuit around the dining room, serving Nana and then herself, before resuming her seat at the table's head.

Gav lifted his spoon. "I don't know how I can manage even a bite of dessert after that wonderful dinner," he said, as always delivering the perfect compliment at the perfect time. "But I'll do my best." After a slow mouthful and a rumble of delight, he looked up at my mother again. "It's obvious where Ollie gets her talent."

Nana grinned. Mom beamed.

I pulled my own dish of panna cotta closer, savoring a little burst of joy from being surrounded by those I loved best. We had the windows open on this unseasonably pleasant Chicago summer night, and even though only a narrow gangway separated Mom's second-floor window from the two-flat next door, a gentle breeze managed to snake its way in. Carrying the scent of fresh-cut grass and the sound of neighbors chatting outside, it twisted around us, delivering a featherlight touch of bliss.

Mom seemed younger than when I'd seen her last. She'd been seeing a gentleman named Kap ever since her trip to D.C. a few years back, and the man's presence in her life was paying obvious dividends. As for Nana, she looked exactly the same, only smaller. Every time I saw her, she seemed to shrink a little bit more.

Not much had changed in the house since my last visit home. The dining room walls were still the same soft cantaloupe trimmed in white. The oak floor still creaked when I stepped on the threshold to the kitchen or walked near the windows. What had given me a surprising jolt, however, was the familiar almond fragrance of Liquid Gold that had hit the moment we'd first arrived. Back in my childhood, one whiff of that sweet scent and I'd known company was coming. It had taken me a moment to realize that this time, it was Gav and I who were "company." The unexpected insight was touching, and a little bit sad.

Gav and I had been here for two days, giving my family their first chance to interact with the handsome government agent I'd told them very little about up until now. I'd held back on details, not because I was afraid they wouldn't like him, but because I knew how much my mother worried for me. She respected me as an adult, but still feared my getting hurt—the way she had all my life. I knew that if she had any inkling as to how deeply I cared for this man, she'd be very worried indeed.

From the moment Gav and I had arrived here at my mom and nana's, however, it had been nonstop chatter among us all. I'd been delighted by the ease with which Gav had won them over, and thrilled that their zealous interest in details about our relationship hadn't scared him off.

My gaze lit upon the framed photo that held the place of honor at the center of Mom's antique oak buffet. The picture had been taken so long ago I didn't even remember the event. But I'd clearly been there, smiling big for the camera, my dark bob blowing in the wind as I wrapped chubby three-year-old arms around the backs of my parents' necks. Proof of an idyllic childhood moment during that brief time we were all together, when we were a complete and happy family.

I averted my gaze before anyone noticed me staring. The last thing any of us needed was to be reminded of the awkward moment last night when I'd broached a subject that my mother considered off-limits. I squirmed in my seat now, knowing I'd be bringing it up again and soon. Gav and I had made this trip specifically to get information, and because we were scheduled to return to Washington, D.C., tomorrow, I didn't have time to waste.

But not right this second. I didn't have the heart to spoil this sweet moment of contentment.

My mom, unfortunately, had other ideas. She steered the conversation to a subject I wished she realized was off-limits with *me*.

Turning to Gav, she said, "Ollie tells me that the president's children are just as charming in real life as they seem on TV. Do you like kids?" Clearly convinced she was coming across as nonchalant, she smiled and asked, "You don't have any of your own, do you?"

Gav cocked an eyebrow. "Not yet." He scraped up the

last of his panna cotta and popped it into his mouth. My mom flashed me a pleased glance, which I pretended not to notice. On the flight out here, I'd warned him that she might latch onto this topic. He'd told me not to worry. I did anyway.

Mom sat up straighter, pretending to concentrate on her spoon, maintaining her excruciatingly obvious just-making-conversation tone. "Oh, so you *do* hope to have children someday?"

He stared at her straight-faced, but I knew him well enough to detect a grin lurking beneath the surface. "Six or seven, at least. Maybe a dozen."

My mom shot me the evil eye. I laughed.

Nana guffawed. "Serves you right, Corinne," she said. "Let these young people take their time. They've got their whole lives ahead of them."

"It never hurts to be curious," my mom said, good-naturedly. She switched gears then. "Unless, of course, you're Ollie. I swear, honey, you get into such trouble with your nosiness. You need to be more careful."

Gav leveled a meaningful look at me, even as he directed his words to my mother. "Your daughter is smart, she's tough, and she has good instincts. Her curiosity—even when it isn't welcome—has done far more good than harm."

Just like that, my mother's face closed up. I knew why; we all did.

"Mom," I began. She gave a little head shake. I closed my mouth.

She put her spoon down and stared at it. Nana closed a thin hand around her wrist. "Corinne," she said in a voice so soft I barely heard her, "of course it's your decision, but remember what Tony asked of you."

I held my breath. I didn't understand what Nana was saying, but I knew she was on my side on this matter. While my mom had been in the shower this morning, Nana had come upstairs from her apartment and urged patience. "She won't shut you out forever," Nana had said, but when I pressed her for more she'd refused. "This is your mother's story to tell. Not mine."

The clock in the living room ticked, smacking at the silence with every measured step of its second hand. Each lonely beat twisted my heart and chipped at my resolve. Maybe this had been a terrible idea. Maybe I should come back another time on my own. Maybe . . .

Mom pushed back from the table, causing her chair to scrape against the floor. She stood, looking down at Nana, who narrowed her eyes, then nodded. With a glance at me— one that held both impatience and resignation—Mom stepped sideways, and without a word, crossed the dining room into her bedroom, where she closed the door.

Gav reached over and grasped my hand. "I'm sorry," he said, "maybe we shouldn't have come."

But before he could finish, Nana raised a finger in the air. "Wait," she said.

There were no words to describe the heaviness in my heart. I felt as though I'd caused my mother pain by revisiting old wounds. Worse, I'd somehow let her down.

When she'd been gone for more than five minutes, I could no longer stand the tension. "You're right," I said to Gav. "We should go—"

At that moment, Mom's bedroom door opened and she emerged wearing an expression that spoke less of anger and disappointment and more of resolve. Carrying a shoe box I could tell was almost as old as I was, she made her way back to the table and set the box reverently at her place.

Nana flicked a glance up at us, then turned her attention to her daughter.

My mom reclaimed her seat, taking great care not to make eye contact with me. Part of me wanted to scream, to ask why there was a need for such secrecy. The other part of me wanted to run from the room. After all these years, my mom was finally about to address the questions I'd asked all my life. And all of a sudden I didn't know if I wanted to hear the answers.

Placing both hands atop the turquoise-and-gray cardboard box, my mom spoke in a quiet voice. "You can't know how hard this is for me."

I held my breath.

She looked up now, meeting my eyes with a steady gaze and shaky smile. "You can thank your grandmother and Kap. They convinced me that this was the time."

"Kap knows?" The question sprang from my lips before I could stop myself.

"No specifics," she said. "No one knows specifics except Nana and me and a man who helped us out at a very difficult time in my life."

I wanted to ask a hundred questions but I knew to keep still. This was my mom's moment. She needed to do this her way. I waited.

"Your grandmother and Kap are right. I probably should have shared this with you years ago, but I couldn't. I was afraid of hurting you. I was afraid of ruining the image you had of your father." She smiled again, but her eyes were glassy wet. "You idolize him. And what I'm about to tell you could spoil that forever. It shouldn't," she hurried to add, "because I knew your father better than anyone. He was truly the best man I'd ever met. No matter what other people said."

My heart was beating so hard I could feel its reverberations in my chest. At some point I'd let go of Gav's hand—I didn't know when—and I clutched my fingers together in my lap, aching to hear what Mom was about to tell me, terrified of what she might say. How bad could it be? I wanted to look at Gav, to see support in his eyes, but I couldn't tear my attention away from my mother.

Outside, an ambulance siren wailed. A sad, solitary cry in the dark.

My mom took a deep breath. "I never wanted you to know the truth about your father's death," she said. "I wanted you to remain the little girl who worshipped her dad's memory. But you're an adult now and you deserve to know." She lifted the lid. "It's time."

CHAPTER 2

I DIDN'T KNOW WHAT I'D EXPECTED TO SEE, but I felt my anticipation deflate the moment the lid was removed. Inside were old papers folded in half and a few snapshots that tilted out from between the yellowed sheets. I couldn't make out the pictures from my angle.

"You've seen photos of your dad in his army uniform," Mom said. She waited for my nod of acknowledgment before easing one of the pictures out of the box, holding it with both hands as she studied it. "He was so proud of his military career. When we were first married, I used to joke that if it were between me and service to the country, I'd come in second place." Mom focused on me. "Once you came along, however, there was no contest. You were first in his world. First in mine."

She handed me the picture.

The faded color snapshot was old, taken with an inexpensive camera and printed on paper that had seen better days. The photo's corners were rounded, softened by age and by what I guessed were many stolen glimpses by my mother over the years. Despite the overall yellow-green cast, despite the fact that the lighting had been poor, I recognized my father immediately. Though not particularly tall, he stood erect and seemed far more imposing than the man to his left. Both were in full military dress, and both wore a fruit salad of medals on their chests.

When I looked back at my mom, I noticed she'd turned toward the window, lost in some private memory.

I chanced a look at Nana, who stared at her daughter with such intensity I wondered if she was attempting to transmit strength through her powerful gaze.

"Your father was a good man." Mom bit her lip, still looking away. "Correct that. He was a *great* man. He was strong, devoted, and compassionate. If he had a flaw, it was that he had such a finely honed sense of right and wrong. We all know the world is not black-and-white. I loved the fact that he could appreciate gray in the little things, but when it came to the bigger issues, there was no compromise. When it came to protecting this country, or to being a good citizen, he made no concessions." She fingered one of the folded documents in the box. "Which is why this almost killed him, years before he actually died."

Her hand shook as she handed me the sheet.

My eyes scanned the page, immediately recognizing my father's name, "Anthony Paras," printed on the government form. I read, then stopped myself. I reread what else was written there, my mind refusing, my whole being rejecting what was so clearly, so preposterously stated.

"This says—"

Mom's words were quiet. "Dishonorable discharge."

I glanced at Gav, who looked as confused as I was. "But this is wrong," I said. "Obviously."

"It's not."

"But," I began again, "Dad's buried at Arlington. You

can't be buried there with a dishonorable discharge. He had medals. He was a hero." My voice had risen and I had to tamp down a rising hysteria. My world tilted off its axis. I couldn't say it enough times: This was wrong. Did no one else understand that?

"He was discharged for insubordination," Mom said. "He never gave me the details. In fact, he told me he was so ashamed that he never wanted to speak about it. So we didn't."

"No," I said with force. "No. This is not right. There must be some mistake."

"No mistake," she said.

I grabbed my head with both hands, trying my best to stay calm. Failing. "You can't just get into Arlington because you *want* to," I said, trying to make my mother understand that she had to be wrong. "I've visited his grave there. You have, too. How do you explain that?"

My mom and Nana exchanged a look I didn't understand.

Gav had brought his chair closer to mine, a fact I didn't notice until he ran a hand down my back. "Let's hear more," he said.

I didn't want to. Not if it involved my dad being dishonorably discharged—the equivalent of a felony conviction. My father. It couldn't be true.

The pain on my mom's face was almost more than I could bear and in a moment of instant realization, I knew I was making this harder for her than it already was. Gav was right. I lowered my hands into my lap, making fists beneath the table my mom wouldn't be able to see. It took every ounce of my love for her to calm myself down. "I didn't mean to interrupt," I said, fighting the urge to run from the room. "Go on."

"The other man in the photo is Eugene Vaughn." The name meant nothing to me. "He was your father's commanding officer and very good friend."

I worked hard to not interrupt again.

"Eugene took care of getting your father into Arlington. He also made sure we received veteran's benefits after your father died."

That was wrong, on so many levels. Still, I held my tongue. The breeze that had tickled us earlier with its gentle touch now ran shivers across my neck.

"After the discharge, your father went to work for a company that manufactured dietary supplements."

"Dietary supplements," I repeated.

She gave a brief nod. "The company was called Pluto, Incorporated. They're located outside Washington, D.C. Your father originally wanted to move back here, but Pluto's offer was too good to pass up."

A tiny memory flickered in my brain. "Didn't they have a logo with . . . planets?"

"They did. Bigger planets surrounding little Pluto, back when it was still considered a planet." She sighed. "Things change in the most unexpected ways."

"I remember . . . We used to have a trophy or something. It had the solar system on it."

"I kept it out for a few years because I couldn't bear to put anything of your father's away. Every time I did, it felt as though I was losing him all over again." She smiled at me. "You have a good memory."

"Seems like an odd logo for a dietary supplement company."

Nana, who'd remained quiet up until now, spoke up. "That's what I always said. The ads made me think that if I took their pills I would see stars. No thank you."

The little bit of levity helped my mom continue her story. "Your dad worked in the management information systems department there, moving up the ranks to eventually become one of the vice presidents."

I wanted to ask how a felon would be hired for such a key position in the first place, and then how in the world he'd been able to move up, but again, I stopped myself. Back then, times had been different and maybe safeguards weren't as strong as they were now. What I said was, "That's quite an accomplishment."

"Your dad started coming home late," Mom began again. "I wasn't worried about him in that way," she said with wide eyes and a knowing expression. "Your father had problems he wouldn't talk about." She spread her hands over the contents of the shoe box. "But he was not unfaithful. He was having problems at work."

" 'Problems?' " I parroted, because I couldn't stand to not know the whole story. I wanted—no, needed—her to get through this quickly. This was like ripping off a bandage in super slow motion. I could barely endure the pain.

Gav must have felt my impatience because he gripped my shoulder in silent warning.

"Tony said there was a man at work who was giving him trouble. He wouldn't elaborate," she added. "He told me he was afraid of big problems with this guy."

"That's pretty cryptic."

"Your father was a careful man."

Not careful enough, I thought.

"I remember the day you told me that he died," I said gently. "You told me that he'd gone to heaven, but I didn't understand why he wasn't coming home to us. Years later, you told me that he'd had an accident." My mom's expression tightened as the memories washed over me. "What kind of accident was it?"

This was hard for her. I waited for her to swallow a couple of times. She pulled her lips in, biting down. I could feel the fear and sadness that threatened to reduce her to tears. After a moment she drew a breath. "He was murdered. Shot on the street."

I sucked in air. I'd been waiting to hear the truth all my life. When I did, it hit me straight to the gut. "Who killed him?"

She shook her head. "We never found out. Tony didn't come home that night. I called the police the next morning to report him missing. . . ." I watched her relive the moment. She swallowed again. "They said they had a John Doe they'd picked up. He . . . matched my description of Tony so they asked me to come down."

"And it was Dad?"

"And it was your dad."

She pulled out his death certificate and unfolded it before me. I'd never seen it before and only my mother's insistent entreaties for me to respect her wishes had kept me from trying to obtain a copy on my own. Shot in the back of his head, twice, the medical examiner had ruled it a homicide. I stared at this new piece of evidence. "And they have no idea who did this?"

"He was found in a rough neighborhood, far from our home and from Pluto's offices. No one knows what he was doing out there so late at night."

"Did you tell anyone about the trouble Dad was having at work?"

"Of course, but without the man's name, the police said it was like investigating a shadow."

"But they did investigate?"

"Of course. They believed it to be a robbery gone bad, though they never found a single lead. Everything was missing. His wallet, his watch, his . . ." She drew in a quick sob. "His wedding ring. All gone. That's why he was a John Doe. I had to go to the morgue to identify him."

I reached a hand out and grasped my mother's warm one. "That had to be so very difficult for you."

Her grateful glance wrenched my heart.

"It was the worst experience of my life," she said. "And then I had to contact Eugene Vaughn."

I picked up the photo again. "Why?"

"Your dad wrote me a letter shortly before he died. He told me he'd written it and made sure I knew where to look when the time came. I didn't want to hear any of that, but he made me promise that if anything happened to him, I'd read the letter before I made a single decision."

"He knew he was going to die," I said to no one. "He knew."

Mom pulled the last document from the box. "I have the letter here. I'll let you read it later because he talks about how much you mean to him and how much he knew he'd miss us. In it, your father asked me to contact Eugene Vaughn about burial in Arlington. I had the same reaction you did, Ollie," she said. "I knew that his discharge made him ineligible, but at that point I had lost my husband and this was the last thing he'd asked me to do for him. So I contacted Eugene and told him what had happened."

"He pulled strings to get Dad in?"

Mom and Nana exchanged a glance.

"Not right away," Mom said. "He asked me to trust him and then suggested that you and I move back to Chicago and I find a local cemetery with a mausoleum."

None of this was making sense. "A temporary entombment?" I asked.

"Eugene said that he'd be able to help, but that we needed to wait until the time was right. He coached me through the entire process and a year later, almost to the day, we had your father moved to Arlington." She sighed. "Sadly, there was no fanfare, no ceremony. Eugene warned that we needed to keep it quiet. But at least your father was finally laid to rest where he deserved to be. I don't know what I would have done without Eugene helping me through all the paperwork, all the heartache. He took care of everything."

"How did this Eugene manage such an impossible feat?"

She didn't answer me. "Things got worse."

I turned to Gav, who sat in rapt attention. I looked at Nana, hoping she would correct my mother. "How?" I asked.

"Pluto was very kind to us when your father died. They paid for our relocation to Chicago and took care of all funeral expenses. The owner of the company came to visit me himself to express his condolences. He handed me a check for fifty thousand dollars to put into trust for your education, telling me it was the least he could do."

That didn't sound like things getting worse. Mom squared her shoulders. "Months later, he contacted me again, this time by phone. According to information they'd discovered when clearing out your father's desk, they had reason to believe he was selling corporate secrets to other firms."

"What?" I exclaimed. "No way."

I barely remembered my father and was hardly in a position to vouch for his integrity. Yet I could feel how wrong this was, with every fiber of my being.

"That was my reaction," Mom said.

Nana raised her hand. "And mine, too."

"Craig Benson—that's the owner's name—asked me questions I had no answers for. Questions about what your father might have told me about Pluto and who your dad met with outside of work. Honestly, your father was always home when he wasn't working, so I had nothing to share with him." She frowned. "I was so taken aback by the accusation that I couldn't think."

"What did you do?"

"I almost told them about Eugene Vaughn, I was so upset. The only reason I didn't was because Eugene had warned me not to tell a soul that I'd contacted him. He said that if I did, Tony might never get into Arlington." She gave a sad shrug. "I guess I'm glad I kept my mouth shut."

I stared at the wall across the room, seeing nothing. My brain was reeling from overload. I'd always known there was more to the story of my dad's death, but I hadn't expected anything like this.

"It's a lot to take in all at once, isn't it?" Mom asked,

reading me so well. "There's one last thing you need to understand: I don't believe a word of it."

My attention snapped back and I stared at her. "You don't believe he was selling secrets?"

"*No.*" The word came out angry, decisive. "Nor do I believe he was kicked out of the army for a good reason. I believe he was set up. How else could Eugene have finagled his burial at Arlington? When I pushed him for answers, however, he refused. He told me that Tony had been a respected hero and that no matter what his record stated, he deserved a place of honor for all eternity. Does that sound like a man with a dishonorable discharge?"

"You didn't dig deeper?"

"I couldn't. Eugene warned me that if I made a fuss, I could jeopardize your father's last wish."

"Dad never said anything that made you suspicious? You never had an inkling of what was really going on?"

Her eyes grew soft with memory. "Above all else, your father wanted to keep us—you and me—safe. He warned that there would be details he couldn't share, but that any secrets he kept were only for our protection. He promised he would never do anything to hurt either of us. I believed him. I believe *in* him. To this day."

The living room clock chimed the hour and I looked down at my hands. I was squeezing them together with white-knuckled anxiety. I forced myself to relax my grip. "Mom," I said, "I've been pushing you for the truth and I'm sorry, truly sorry, for having forced you to relive this. I had no idea."

"I know you didn't," she said giving me her best motherly sigh. "Which is why I made you promise to wait and not dig into all this yourself. To be frank, I never wanted to have this conversation. I wanted you to live your life without this burden. But you aren't one to walk away without answers. Pandora's box is now wide open. Knowing you, you'll poke your nose into all this and try your best to sort it out. That's the biggest reason I held back all these years."

My mother did, indeed, know me well.

She held a hand out to Gav. "He's right about your curiosity. You've done a lot of good—for many people." Mom picked up the letter from my dad again. "Your father knew you'd want to look into this someday. There's no doubt that you are his child: brave, strong-minded, and a little foolhardy." She placed the letter back into the box and handed it to me. "It's your story now."

CHAPTER 3

MY MOM'S LIVING ROOM COUCH WAS PERFECTLY acceptable for a good night's sleep, but I found myself wide awake and prowling the floor at three in the morning. Gav and I were scheduled for a late flight out, so there was no need to be up and about before the crack of dawn. After last night's revelations, however, I couldn't force my brain to relax.

I picked up the shoe box of secrets and crept past my mother's room, where her soft, regular breaths rolled out as I tiptoed past in stealth mode.

I stopped at the middle room, my bedroom, the door of which hung slightly ajar. Teenagers—even the most well-behaved of them—crave real privacy. In a rush of memory, I recalled how much I'd hated the fact that my door had never latched completely. We'd certainly tried. No matter how many times we'd adjusted its hinges, my door never failed to fall open at the tiniest provocation.

But right now I appreciated that annoying glitch. I peered in at Gav, asleep on my twin bed with the pink-, green-, and purple-flowered comforter bunched around his long legs. He'd left the window shade open and there was just enough glow for me to appreciate his moonlight-blue profile in repose. My mom hadn't changed a thing in here since I left for college oh so many years ago, and I liked the fact that it always felt like returning to my personal cocoon. Gav being part of that cocoon made it even better.

He slept on his side facing the door, one arm under the pillow, the other draped over the edge of the narrow bed. When we'd first arrived he'd tried to insist that I take my bed and he sleep on the couch, but in the face of three opinionated females he never had a chance.

I sighed, contented beyond words to have him here with me.

He rolled over onto his back, throwing his free arm over his head, his lips pursing then relaxing repeatedly. A lock of hair fell across his forehead and he clumsily brushed it away, still sound asleep. A moment later, his face went slack, his arms relaxed, and he quieted once again.

As much as I wanted to wake him, to talk quietly about all we'd learned the night before, I turned away and continued to the back bedroom. Flipping on the light, I made my way over to the computer. I placed the shoe box on my lap and fired the machine up. Within moments, I was launching a browser and typing in my search terms.

I wasn't looking for anything in particular. After all, what possible information could I find online that would support or disprove allegations against my father? I knew I wouldn't find a description of his court-martial, nor would I happen across a link that read: "Click here for Evidence that Anthony Paras Sold Pluto Corporate Secrets to a Rival Firm." And if I couldn't find such information, how could I dream of refuting it?

I needed to start somewhere, however, and the Internet

was my best shot. I'd come to the realization that many of my best online discoveries had come from digging into details where I happened across bombshells, usually by accident. One never knew what secrets floated in the ether. Sometimes it was a matter of knowing where to look. Sometimes it was dumb luck.

Two hours later, I'd learned a little. Pluto, Incorporated was still in business. The small yet successful family-owned company operated outside Washington, D.C., distributing dietary supplements across the United States.

Craig Benson, the owner, the man who had come to visit my mother when my father died and who had subsequently accused him of corporate espionage, was no longer president. That position was currently held by his son, Kyle Benson, though Craig had retained the title of CEO. Their ages weren't listed, but photos on Pluto's website allowed me to guess. Craig looked to be five to ten years older than my father would have been. Kyle looked to be Gav's age.

Pluto distributed all sorts of supplements, mostly vitamins, minerals, and herbs. All these years later, I still thought their planetary logo was a peculiar choice. When I looked to the heavens, I very rarely thought of dietary supplements. The only part of the entire concept that strove to tie the two together was their tagline: "Trust Pluto supplements to discover *your* heavenly body."

Not exactly what I'd call catchy.

For a second, I wondered if Craig Benson would even remember my dad. A moment later, I'd answered my own question. There was no way I'd forget anyone I believed had betrayed me. Forgiveness was one thing, forgetting another.

I scrolled through information about vitamins that could boost my immunity, clear my skin, and make me less forgetful. My right leg bounced an impatient rhythm as questions raced like pinballs through my head with little *pings* of doubt. What if Benson was wrong? What if my father hadn't stolen his company secrets? What if incriminating information had been planted among my dad's belongings? The real culprit could very well have set him up. If I could determine who that "other man" at work had been—the one my dad had claimed had been giving him trouble—maybe I'd find real answers. Answers that would allow me to both expose the killer and clear my father's name at the same time.

I stopped and forced myself to remember that all this had happened more than twenty-five years ago. The chances of me being able to find pertinent information about any of this were slim. Less than slim, if I were being perfectly honest with myself. I refused to believe that my father was guilty, but there seemed to be little way to uncover evidence to the contrary.

I gazed out the small room's window at the morning moon hanging high above, flaunting its reflected light. I pushed against the blue melancholy that cloaked me with doubt. I knew better than most that the mind played tricks on people who couldn't sleep: Often what was no more than a speed bump in the full light of day felt like an excruciating hurdle when confronted in the depths of night.

I stared up at the moon again, thinking of my many treks to Arlington to stand before my dad's grave, to chat with the silent father I couldn't even remember. I'd put him up on a pedestal, the way daughters often do with their dads. Maybe it was time to admit he'd been a man, no better, no worse than any other man in the world. With flaws and weaknesses. With a dark side he tried his best to conceal.

Sadness and longing took up residence in my chest, squeezing my heart in its painful embrace. I tried to shake off the despair, reminding myself that the only truly effective cure for sorrow was time.

And work. Dragging my attention back to the computer, I widened my Internet search, hoping to find some oddity, a tidbit that felt out of place, a crumb to follow. I scribbled notes, but even as I did so, I realized these were probably brick walls and dead ends. There ought to be a link that led me to the truth, shouldn't there? Or was my sleep-deprived brain allowing fantasy to take over for good sense?

After more futile searches, and increasingly buggy eyes, I gave up on the Internet and turned to what had started it all. I opened the shoe box, gingerly removing the letter my dad had written to my mom. I'd already read it three times. I'd have it committed to memory soon. My mom had explained the gist of it well enough when we were all seated at the table. She hadn't detailed my father's many professions of love and the emotion that came through when he wrote about missing out on the lives of the two girls he loved most in the world. She'd skipped over those, I believed, because she'd wanted me to experience those passages for myself. They'd torn at my heart when I read through the first time, and even now my throat burned as I skimmed to reread the final paragraphs.

As I write this at our kitchen table, Corinne, I hear you reading to our little Olivia in the next room. What a miracle you and I brought into this world. Have you ever encountered such a bright, inquisitive child? She's kind and compassionate, determined and proud in a way that combines the best of us both. So beautiful, so luminous. I hope I can be here to watch her grow, to be the best dad in the world to her. To see the world through her innocent eyes.

Things, unfortunately, don't always work out the way we hope or plan. If situations develop the way I fear they might, I won't be here for her when she needs me most. I can hardly bear the thought.

I'm certain there will come a day when Olivia is older, when she demands the truth. I trust you to share this with her when the time is right. I know you believe in me, and I hope and pray that she will believe in me, too. No matter how dark things seem, there is always true light if you look hard enough for it.

He signed off then, with all his love to both of us.

I couldn't help but believe that through this letter he was reaching out to me, personally asking for my help. And I knew I couldn't let him down.

"You're up early."

I turned to see Gav standing in the doorway. Looking rumpled in a pair of cotton sleep shorts and T-shirt, he ran a hand through his bed-flattened hair. I noticed, belatedly, that the sun had started to come up. "What time is it?"

"Just about six. Have you been up all night?" He strode across the room and bent down to peer at the computer screen. "I should have guessed," he said.

His face was very close to mine. "You brushed your teeth," I said.

Planting a kiss on the top of my head, he laughed.

"How long have you been up?" I asked.

"Long enough to brush my teeth so I could come in and wish you a proper good morning." He glanced down at the open box on my lap. "Have you come up with any leads?"

"Leads?" It was my turn to laugh. "You make it sound as though I'm trying to solve a crime."

Crouching next to me, he placed a warm hand over mine, his gray eyes searching. "Aren't you?" he asked softly.

"I don't know what I'm doing."

He reached up to cup my cheek in his palm. "We'll talk more about this later, you know we will. But for now I need you to remember one thing."

"What's that?"

"Whatever you need, I'm here for you."

I leaned into him, our foreheads touching. I wrapped a hand around the back of his neck and whispered, "I know."

"Good morning," Mom said from the doorway, making us jump apart like two teenagers caught smooching. She, too, was still dressed in her sleepwear, but had pulled on a fuzzy pink bathrobe and looked wide awake. "Anybody want coffee?"

By the time coffee was ready, Mom had popped a cinnamon cake into the oven and was starting to fry up some bacon. "Go ahead," she said to Gav. "I can tell you want to jump into the shower. Plenty of time before breakfast is ready."

As he left the room, Nana came up from her flat downstairs, peering in through Mom's back door. "Smells good, got any extra for an old lady who's too lazy to cook for herself?"

I helped Mom by starting the hash browns and pulling out the eggs. "You know we don't usually eat this much in the morning," I said.

She sniffed. "When you're home, I get to spoil you. Is there a problem with that?"

Last night's heaviness seemed to have dissipated with the appearance of the sun on this bright new day. Nana poured herself a mug of coffee and sat at the counter to watch us work. "That Gav," she said, with a nod toward the washroom, where we could hear the water running, "he's a hunk."

"Thanks, Nana. I think so, too."

"I have to tell you, Ollie, I wasn't thrilled at first when you said you were bringing him here," Mom said.

This was news.

"Nothing wrong with him, nothing at all," she added quickly. "It's that I sensed you might push me this time. About your father, I mean. I wasn't sure I wanted to share all that in front of a stranger."

"I'm sorry," I began, "I never—"

"No, don't apologize. I had misgivings when I knew you were bringing him, but now that I've met him . . ." She let the thought hang as she turned pieces of bacon over. "I can't explain it, but I trust him."

I put an arm around her. "I'm glad. He's a keeper, Mom."

Mom smiled. "He's good for you, Ollie. Be kind to him. Try to stay out of trouble. For his sake."

"I always do."

She waved her bacon-flipper at me. "Don't fib. You're talking to your mother, remember."

I was about to protest when Nana interjected. "Does he have any nice grandfathers you can introduce me to?"

When Gav finally emerged from the bathroom, hair damp, in a fresh T-shirt and jeans, my heart gave a happy little lurch. "You look great," I said.

"And I smell bacon." He came around behind me and placed his hands on my shoulders. "Is there anything I can do to help?"

Mom and Nana exchanged a look of admiration Gav couldn't have missed, even if he weren't a highly trained observer. "Everything's ready. Have a seat."

After breakfast, Mom took her turn in the shower. The moment we heard the water stream on, Nana clasped both hands around her coffee mug and leaned forward, whispering. "I'm glad she finally told you." With a quick acknowledgment of Gav, she added, "You too. It's been a lot for her to bear alone all these years, and I know she thought she was protecting you, Ollie, but facing the truth is always best. Your mom needed to unburden herself. She waited far too long, if you ask me, but nobody's asking me, are they?"

I leaned across the table to pat her skinny arm. "You can spout off anytime you want," I said in a whisper, then added in a more normal tone, "I don't think we need to keep our voices down. There's no way to hear conversations going on in the kitchen with the water running." I winked. "Believe me, I tried lots of times when I was a kid."

Gav's eyes twinkled. "Some things never change."

CHAPTER 4

OUR FLIGHT ATTENDANT SET A WOBBLY GLASS of water in front of me and another in front of Gav. "Sorry about the turbulence," she said with a wide smile. "The pilot says we'll be above it momentarily."

"Thank you," I said.

I smiled and went back to paging through the in-flight magazine I'd pulled from the seat pocket, my mind barely registering all the unusual and expensive gadgets available to order. "When are we going to get to the good part?" Gav asked.

I turned. "Good part?"

"When you tell me precisely what you have planned," he said, pointing a finger toward my carry-on, where I'd stowed the shoe box. "You've been too quiet for too long."

I closed the magazine. "My first step will be to visit Eugene Vaughn, I suppose. That is, if he's still alive. I was able to find a couple mentions of him online, but they were from a few years back. There's no telling . . ." I sighed. "This could be an enormous waste of time and effort."

"And emotion," he said.

Although we were the only two people in our row and were talking quietly, I didn't want to get too specific when others might overhear. Gav knew that about me. It was one of my quirks he really appreciated. I smiled. Who was I kidding? He seemed to like all my quirks. He was so different from the arrogant man I'd assumed him to be when we'd first met.

"What are you thinking about?" he asked. "Your face completely transformed from a second ago."

I laughed. "You."

I could tell that my answer made him happy.

"I'll do whatever I can to help," he said. "Don't be afraid to ask."

"You know I won't."

"There's not much you can look into right away, is there?" he asked. Carefully avoiding any mention of the White House in case of eavesdroppers, he added, "I'm surprised they're asking you to come in to work this week. You deserve time off."

I waved his concern away. "If it weren't for their son," I said, avoiding Josh's name, "I wouldn't have agreed to come in during my vacation." I snugged an arm through his. "But he's tough to resist."

Gav shook his head. "You're a good person. They're lucky to have you there."

"It's nothing really. Just a few hours over a couple of days. Besides, if you and I had a whole week to ourselves with no interruptions, you might get bored with me."

He pulled my arm closer. "Not a chance, kiddo."

A thought occurred to me. I looked up at him. "You're eligible to be buried at Arlington, aren't you?"

He nodded. "I may not have ever known your father, but I can understand why that was important to him. For what it's worth, I believe in what you're doing—what you're about to do. No matter how I turn this situation, no matter how I look at it, it feels as though pieces are missing. Big pieces. I've never heard of anyone being 'snuck' into that cemetery. We're not getting the whole story. I'd bet on that much."

"Dietary supplements," I said, shaking my head. "My dad went from being a decorated hero to heading information systems at a dietary supplement company."

"A man with a family needs to put food on the table first. You don't know what Pluto offered him, what kind of pay or benefits. They may have been the best game in town."

"For a dishonorably discharged veteran."

He sighed. "Let's take one thing at a time." I liked his use of the word "Let's."

"What do you suggest?" I asked.

He glanced at his watch. "You have to be in at . . . your job . . . early tomorrow, right?"

"About nine. Not too bad."

"By the time we land, it's going to be too late to do anything tonight. I have a couple of errands I need to run tomorrow, so how about we agree to tackle all these big questions on Wednesday? We'll come up with a plan and get started first thing."

"I appreciate you, you know that?" I asked.

"Your mom thinks you need to appreciate me more."

"What do you mean?"

"While you were in the shower this morning, she and your nana asked me to keep an eye on you. Make sure you don't get into trouble the way you usually do. They were quite vocal about how they think you ought to heed my advice."

"You three talked about me behind my back?"

"Uh-huh. And if you remember, you, your nana, and I talked about your mother behind her back while *she* was in the shower." He gave me a very pointed stare and gestured "come on" with his free hand.

"What?" I asked.

"I took a shower. I took one every day, in fact. I can't imagine I escaped without a little 'shower gossip' going on behind *my* back." He narrowed his eyes, but I caught the twinkle of amusement in them. "Time for the truth. Cough it up, Paras. You're under interrogation."

"They like you," I was happy to tell him. "A lot."

"Really?" he asked, looking far more relieved than I would have expected. "I'm glad. I like them both, very much. You come from a strong family," he said. "They're amazing women, and so proud of you. As they should be."

I pulled away. "Back up a minute. They asked you to keep me out of trouble?"

"Yeah."

"What did you say?"

All humor left his expression. "I told them the truth. That I will keep you safe, even if it kills me."

OUR FLIGHT FROM O'HARE WASN'T VERY LONG, but by the time we'd landed at Reagan National Airport, I'd begun to doze. Gav nudged me as we taxied to the gate. "I slept through the pilot's announcement and landing?" I asked.

"You were up all night trolling the Internet, remember?"

"True enough."

Gav drove me to my apartment. Yawning, I asked him if he wanted to come up, promising to fix a late-night snack. He declined. "You have to be at the White House tomorrow, don't forget," he said. "Besides, I have a few things to do back at my apartment." He walked me to my door, kissed me good night, and made sure I got in safely.

I was wiped. Whether it had been the emotional toll the trip had taken, the fact that I hadn't gotten much sleep, or a combination of both, I didn't know. But whatever it was, I was happy to be home. I tumbled into bed and was sound asleep within minutes.

* * *

"HOW WAS THE TRIP?" CYAN ASKED WHEN I arrived the next morning. With her red hair tied back as usual, and purple contacts brightening her wide eyes, Cyan stood next to our giant mixer, watching the massive beater turn as she ladled in what looked like vegetable broth.

Gav and I had decided to keep our relationship under wraps for as long as possible, so my staff believed I'd simply gone home to visit my mom and nana.

"Great," I said. "How's the kitchen?"

Bucky had been standing at the stove with his back to me, one hand manipulating a frying pan over a high flame, the other perched on his hip. From behind, with his bald head, he always reminded me of a slim bowling pin. He had a tendency to gesticulate, and though he took pains to hide it, a heart of gold. He turned and grimaced, which for Bucky, was as good as a smile. "Your buddy Virgil has been prancing around here like he's the king. He's off right now . . ." Bucky swirled a hand in the air, ". . . doing his best to appear useful without actually doing any work." With a mischievous grin, he asked, "He doesn't know why you're back today, does he?"

"Nope," I said, pointing at them both in turn, "and I prefer to keep it that way."

Bucky turned the flame off and placed his frying pan on one of the cool burners. He gave his concoction an appraising glance, then turned to me, wiping his hands on his apron. "Why?" he asked. "Virgil never hesitates to rub his familiarity with the First Family in your face. They passed over him because they want *you* working with Josh. This is your chance to gloat. Why not enjoy it?"

"Tempting," I said, tying on an apron. But it wasn't, really. Even though Virgil got under my skin, even though I knew the look on his face would be priceless when he realized that I'd garnered some capital with this family, thereby intruding on what he considered his precious turf, I knew that "rubbing his face in it" wouldn't give me any true satisfaction. Did I want the First Family to prefer me over Virgil? Darned right I did. But while proclaiming "Nyah, nyah," might provide a quick giggle, it wouldn't do me any good in the long run.

I tried to take the high road where Virgil was concerned, convinced that someday it would pay off. Doing so *had* paid off—to a small extent—with Sargeant. After a recent skirmish we'd shared, he'd been better. Tolerable, even. If Peter Sargeant, our persnickety and easily aggravated sensitivity director could be tamed, there was hope for anyone.

"Virgil was uncharacteristically cheerful the entire time you were gone," Cyan said.

"Figures. He likes it best when he thinks he's in charge."

Bucky made a face at his frying pan and I couldn't tell whether it was because he was disappointed in its contents, or because of our topic of discussion. Ever since the new chef had joined the White House there had been some question as to how the reporting structure actually worked. Bucky had always been my first in command, but now the lines were blurred.

It didn't help that Paul Vasquez, our beloved chief usher, had recently resigned to deal with family concerns. Doug Lambert had taken over as interim chief usher, resulting in the near-universal consensus that Doug was in over his head. Until his permanent replacement was appointed, the kitchen—and other departments in the White House residence—would operate in a state of flux.

"What do you have planned for Josh today?" Cyan asked.

"Pumpkin cheesecake and a couple of salad variations. He's a smart kid and he's eager. Above all else, he enjoys the creative parts. If I can incorporate a few rules as we work, maybe I can make learning fun."

"You'll be great," Cyan said.

I glanced up at the clock. "I still have a few minutes

before I need to be up there. Anything else I need to know? Anything I missed since Thursday?"

"Not much," Cyan said. "I don't think—"

Bucky snapped his fingers. "Your tickets came in," he said. "I knew there was something I meant to tell you."

"For Saturday's Food Expo?" I asked. "Excellent. Marcel will be thrilled." Marcel, the White House pastry chef, known throughout the United States and his native France for his delectable treats, was scheduled to be a guest speaker at the Food Expo. He was nervous, yet delighted to have been invited to present and I'd promised him I'd be there for moral support.

"There's one problem," Bucky said.

Cyan held up two fingers. "Not just one."

I looked from one to the other. "What is it?"

Bucky made his way over to the computer desk, opened the drawer beneath, and pulled out an envelope addressed to me. "Here you go."

I took the proffered envelope and pulled out the letter and handful of tickets. The White House address must have inspired them to provide extras. "What's the problem?"

Cyan gave me a sheepish look. "I know I promised, but I can't make it after all. I have a meeting with my mom's doctors Saturday. They say she's been acting up these past few days and we need to discuss her meds."

"Bucky?" I asked.

He scowled. "I can't go either. Your buddy Virgil announced that he's taking Saturday off. Which means I have to be here. We've got two Service by Agreement chefs scheduled that day but we can't allow them to run around without guidance."

"Virgil's taking the day off?" I said, with a whine in my voice I hadn't expected.

"For all we know, he's going golfing with the president. Again." Rolling his eyes, Bucky went on, "He didn't share specifics with us, just declared that he won't be here. I suppose we should thank our lucky stars that he at least gave us a little bit of notice this time."

I sighed. "I suppose." To Bucky, I said, "If you want to go to the Expo, I can come in here instead."

He shook his head. "Marcel is counting on you. Go ahead and have a little fun. It's part of your vacation anyway." He stopped himself. "You've got quite a few tickets there," he said with a curious glint in his eye. "Is there someone you'd like to invite to go with you?"

Cyan's face lit up. "Is there?"

"Are you kidding?" I said, attempting to dodge the question. "Who would I invite to a foodie show besides you guys?"

I knew Cyan was completely in the dark where Gav was concerned, but I wasn't so sure about Bucky. His occasional needling commentary made me believe he was onto us—or at least suspected that I was seeing someone. I wasn't about to admit to anything. Not yet. I tapped the tickets against my lips. The event was a showcase for food and products that supported the food industry. There would be equipment manufacturers, cooking demonstrations, giveaways, and plenty of innovative ideas to explore. I wasn't going solely to see Marcel's event. I hoped to get a glimpse of new gadgets coming our way. Maybe Gav would want to go.

Okay, that was a stretch of crazed proportions. Gav wouldn't be interested in the least, though that didn't mean he'd refuse to come along. I could ask. It certainly wouldn't hurt.

I glanced up at the clock. "I'd better get my ingredients together, they're expecting me upstairs."

CHAPTER 5

JOSH RACED INTO THE FIRST FAMILY'S PERSONAL kitchen, breathless and wide-eyed. "Am I late?"

The kid was so cute. Of all the kids I'd encountered at the White House, Josh was my favorite by far. Earnest, eager, with boundless energy and a smile that lit up a room, he'd taken a liking to me, too. We'd bonded several months ago, and I'd been caught unawares by dormant maternal instincts that had bubbled up since then.

"Good morning, Josh. You can't be late. Today is our day, remember?" I said. "We've got a lot—"

Josh's mother, Denise Hyden, First Lady of the United States of America, came around the corner behind him. Tall and serene as always, she offered an indulgent smile. "Good morning, Ollie," she said warmly.

"Good morning."

Despite the fact that I was the executive chef at the White House, I felt like an intruder up here in the president's personal kitchen. Significantly smaller than our space on the ground floor, it could have been featured in any middle-class suburban sitcom. While our ground-floor work area was all stainless steel and tile, this kitchen had wooden cabinets, flowered wallpaper, and utensils like those I used at home.

Up here, the family moved about freely without Secret Service escorts. This was where they entertained guests, watched TV in their pajamas, and spoke without fear of being overheard.

"What are we doing today?" Josh asked.

When Mrs. Hyden had first approached me about spending time with Josh, I'd been under the impression that it would be he and I working together in the family kitchen. I hadn't expected that she would be joining us as well.

"I have a few ideas," I said.

Mrs. Hyden and I had gotten off to a rocky start when her husband had taken office and the family had first moved in, but a tense situation involving Josh—one that I'd had a hand in seeing to a safe conclusion—had put this mom firmly in my corner.

"I was thinking about pumpkin cheesecake, would you like that?"

Josh was already digging through the supplies I'd brought up with me, admiring the gingersnap cookies and toasted pecans as he pulled them out. "Are these for the crust?"

"They are."

"I love cheesecake," Josh said. "Did you know that I made the fried chicken strips from the recipe you gave me? That was the most fun homework I've ever had, plus it was super easy," he said, beaming. "It turned out great."

"I have no doubt."

Mrs. Hyden hadn't moved from her perch in the doorway, and although she smiled as her son bragged, there was a pensive look on her face. I wondered what was on her mind. "Okay, Josh," I said, "how about we get started? Why don't you break the cookies into smaller pieces while I pull out the food processor?"

"Ollie." Mrs. Hyden took a hesitant step forward. "Do you have a minute to talk?"

"Of course," I answered. "Josh, will you be okay on your own with that?"

He gave a good-natured eye roll. "I've done stuff like this before, remember?"

"An excellent job, as I recall," I said to him before following Mrs. Hyden through the adjacent corridor and into the West Sitting Hall. She stood before the half-moon window there and turned to face me. "What can I do for you?" I asked.

Her mouth worked itself into a smile, but her eyes tensed. "I know I can count on you to keep what I'm about to say confidential."

"Of course."

Slim fingers writhing, she took a breath. "Josh," she began, her eyes lighting up as she spoke her son's name, "is a wonderful boy."

"He really is," I said sincerely. "I'm thrilled to know he's interested in becoming a chef and I can't tell you how much it means to me to be able to work with him."

"That's what I wanted to discuss. My husband doesn't . . ." Her hands, ever moving, belied the calm she strove to keep on her face. "He believes there's more for Josh." She quickly added, "Not that there's anything wrong with aspiring to be a chef. You must understand I'm not suggesting that."

Eyes wide, her face was pained and earnest. The First Lady of the United States was worried about offending me? Self-conscious as I confronted this unique situation, I responded kindly, "I'm sure you don't."

"Truly not. What I mean to say is that my husband has dreams for Josh. He desperately wants him to go into public service. He thinks that . . ." Her words trailed off in obvious agony. Collecting herself again, she continued, "You, Ollie, have become the best of the best." Clearly on firmer footing now, she went on, "You've proven yourself, not only in the kitchen. But even you have to admit, you're one in a million."

I opened my mouth to protest, but she cut me off.

"You've earned a position that is arguably the top chef spot in the country. Maybe even the world. You've also gained a great deal of notoriety for your, shall we call them, extracurricular activities?" She smiled at that. I did, too.

"Josh is talented," I said. "He has a great personality and a strong work ethic that shines through, even at his young age. There are millions of talented people in the world, and I have no doubt there are many who are much better than I. Hard work, perseverance, and an open mind are what separate the good from the great."

Ack! Had I just called myself great?

Mrs. Hyden didn't seem to notice the gaffe. She nodded. "I believe Josh will be successful at whatever he puts his mind to. He is only nine years old. When I was his age, I wanted to be a movie star." She gave a rueful laugh. "Kids change and grow. As their horizons expand, so do their plans. I understand that this interest in becoming a chef may be a phase. Regardless, I want to encourage Josh. My husband isn't completely against it, but he prefers our son be exposed to other opportunities as well."

"Have you talked about this with Josh?"

"A little. He's not happy."

I didn't expect he would be. "How can I help?"

Suddenly uncomfortable again, she splayed her hands. "When you work with him, don't sugarcoat. Not that I think you would, but, as I said, you're at the top of your game. Most would-be chefs never reach your level of achievement. My husband wants Josh to be sure he understands what kind of life is ahead of him—all of it: the hard work, the disappointments, the pressures—before he falls in love with cooking for a living."

I ran a hand through my hair. "I may not have children,

but I was a kid once. I knew I wanted to be a chef from the time I was about ten years old." I gave a wry smile. "Of course, back then I wanted to be Nancy Drew, too."

"I'd say you've succeeded on both counts."

I felt blush creep up my cheeks and returned to the main topic. "You're not asking me to discourage Josh?" I phrased it as a statement but ended it as a question.

She hesitated.

I took the opportunity to plunge forward. "Josh is so bright, so inquisitive. If I suddenly started dwelling on only the negative aspects of the job, he'd see right through me."

She sighed. "I just ask that you present a balanced picture."

I had no problem with doing that and said so.

"Thank you." Visibly relaxed now, she and I returned to the kitchen. We heard scuffling and bumping, much like the sounds a nine-year-old would make to avoid being caught eavesdropping.

Mrs. Hyden took the lead. "Josh," she said in a commanding mother's tone, "what have I told you about listening in on adult conversations?"

I bit my lip, thinking of the countless times I'd lingered in doorways. A bad habit I'd never been able to shake.

He stood at the small kitchen's center island, crushed cookies in front of him, innocent face staring up at us as we walked in. I could tell he was working hard to keep emotion at bay, but his dark eyes were big and his lips turned down. The bottom one didn't quiver, but I thought that was just a matter of time. Depending on what Mrs. Hyden said next.

"Were you listening at the door?" she asked.

He nodded.

She gave a little huff of impatience, but when she looked at her son her gaze softened and she continued gently, "You know you're not supposed to do that."

His fingers gripped the edge of the countertop. "I thought Dad liked the food I made for him."

She was quick to comfort, crouching to put her arms around him. "Of course he does, honey. That's why we talked to Ollie about working with you. We believe in you. She does, too." She sent a pleading look my way.

"You're talented, Josh," I said sincerely.

He rubbed his nose with the back of his hand.

I took a step closer. "I mean that. I knew I wanted to be a chef at about the same age you are right now."

His eyes brightened but he remained skeptical, giving me the you're-just-saying-that-to-keep-me-from-crying look I'd seen on kids before.

"If you heard everything your mom said," I went on, hoping to stave off tears, "you know that your parents believe in you. They believe you'll be great at whatever you choose to do. Your dad might have other plans, but that doesn't mean that his are right and yours are wrong." I was treading choppy waters here, but Mrs. Hyden's pointed look encouraged me to continue. "It doesn't mean that there aren't other options out there that you might love as much or more than being a chef. What we're doing here"—I held my arms out expansively—"is experimenting to see if this really is what you want to do with your life. Your mom asked me to show you all of it—even the negative parts—and she's right to do that. The more information you have, the better choices you'll make."

I feared I'd talked too much. Josh had squirmed out of his mother's hold and begun cracking the cookies in half again. After a few moments, he looked up. "I want to know the negative parts, too. I want to know all of it." He got a superior look on his face, one that I found adorable. "I never said I thought everything would be easy."

I smiled. Mrs. Hyden stood. "Then we're all in agreement," she said with relief. "You know that your dad is always proud of you. I think the problem comes when he expects you to like everything he likes."

Josh snickered. "He picks basketball over football. Everybody knows football is better."

Crisis averted for now, Mrs. Hyden whispered her thanks, and left the two of us to get started.

About two hours later, as Josh and I were cleaning berries for one of the salad choices, I heard a familiar voice boom, "Something smells wonderful."

President Hyden strolled into the family kitchen, his wife right behind him. I could tell from their body language and from the apprehensive look on Mrs. Hyden's face that she'd engineered this little impromptu visit.

"Good morning, Mr. President," I said.

At the interruption, Josh burst into a detailed account of all we'd done, and although he was animated and cheerful, I could detect a wary look in his expression, as though gauging how his father might respond.

For his part, President Hyden appeared in control yet slightly uncomfortable. "I understand you're getting lessons from the best of the best," he said with a nod to me.

I wished he would forget social niceties for a moment, ignore my presence, and concentrate on Josh, but he continued addressing me, saying, "Denise and I thank you for the time you're spending with our son. We understand you're giving up your day off to be here."

"It's my pleasure," I said.

Josh eagerly directed his father's attention to the cheesecake, now cooling on a nearby rack. While President Hyden said all the right things and patted Josh on the shoulder as the boy explained the steps we'd followed to create it, he did so distantly. I could sense Josh picking up on his dad's distraction.

Talking louder and faster, Josh tugged at his father's hand and finally the president seemed to push himself into the moment. It wasn't as though he was being a bad parent, he just came across as a man with too much on his mind. As the leader of the free world, I imagined he had plenty of urgent topics competing for attention. Taking even these precious minutes to spend with Josh must have involved a logistical nightmare.

He was doing his best. Josh was doing his best. Unfortunately, it didn't seem to be enough for either of them. As a non-family bystander, there was nothing I could do but watch.

Nine-year-old boys might not be as savvy to another person's mood as political leaders were, but they sure demanded as much effort and attention, if not more.

"We're almost done for the day," I said when President Hyden asked what we would be doing next. "All that's left is to set up our next lesson."

"How about tomorrow?" Josh asked.

His mother intervened. "We're going to visit your cousins tomorrow, remember?"

Josh's face lit up. "I forgot. We're coming back Friday, aren't we? Can we do it then?"

Mrs. Hyden opened her mouth, clearly to argue.

"Or Saturday," he said, determined to not let me leave without a commitment. Turning to me, he asked, "Can you come back Saturday?"

"Saturday is the Food Expo," I said. "Marcel is speaking there and I promised I'd come listen. My tickets just arrived in the mail today, as a matter of fact. I'd planned to take my team, but that isn't going to work." I didn't want to tattle about how Virgil's spur-of-the-moment day off was messing up plans, but I sure felt like it. "It looks like I may be going alone." Or with Gav, if I could talk him into it.

Josh's eyes lit up. "Can I go with you? That sounds like it would be a lot of fun."

The president's expression hardened briefly. He was behind Josh, so the boy didn't see it.

"I don't know," I said, glancing up at his mother. "It's not up to me."

She held her hands out and turned to her husband for his

opinion. President Hyden squinted, then ruffled his son's head. "Tell you what, sport, I'll talk to the Secret Service. You know how tough it is to arrange these things and Saturday doesn't give us much lead time."

"Please, Dad? I know this will be awesome." His big round eyes widened. "I'm sure there will be a lot for me to learn there. All the fun stuff and even the negative parts as well."

Who said this boy wasn't an effective negotiator?

The president glanced at his wife, then turned to me. "Would this be all right with you?" he asked.

"Of course," I answered enthusiastically, even though that killed the idea of bringing Gav.

With a practiced smile, the president said, "If there's one thing we know we can count on, it's that our son is safe with you." Ruffling Josh's hair again, he excused himself.

"This is great!" Josh said as soon as he was gone.

"Don't get your hopes up, honey," Mrs. Hyden said. "You don't know what the Secret Service is going to say about this."

"Dad said it was okay. That's all that matters, right? They have to say it's okay, too!" For a second time, he exclaimed, "This is great!" and as his mother sighed, he went back to cleaning berries.

CHAPTER 6

WEDNESDAY MORNING DAWNED WELL BEFORE I woke up, which was unusual for me. I liked to get into the White House no later than seven in the morning, most times even earlier than that. Today being a day off, and, in fact, one of several in a row, provided the delightful luxury of sleeping in. I rolled over, guessing by the level of sun pouring in through the window that it had to be around eight A.M. A peek at my alarm clock confirmed it.

Positively decadent.

An hour later I was fed, showered, dressed, and I'd spent enough time online to map out my route for the day. I called Gav and left a message, telling him that I'd be out for a while, but that I'd try again when I returned. I'd called him last night. His phone had gone directly to voicemail then, too.

When he'd finally gotten back to me last night, I'd been half-asleep. He'd sounded tired and had been vague about where he'd been and what he'd been doing. That wasn't like him. The only times he ever hedged on the truth were when national security issues were at stake. I didn't believe that was the case here, but I wasn't about to spend time worrying.

Gav inspired trust. It was amazing to me how freeing and how wonderful life was when you truly trusted another person. I knew he would bring me up to speed whenever he could and I expected it would be soon. We were both on vacation this week and he'd made it clear he intended to spend as much of that as possible with me. We'd taken a long time to finally cement our relationship and that meant we had a great deal of catching up to do.

I made it outside without being waylaid by either Mrs. Wentworth, my nosy neighbor, or James at the apartment building's front desk. I'd chosen to wear a bright green sleeveless shirt over cotton cargo pants, and as I made my way across the already warm asphalt to my little car, I was happy I'd chosen such cool clothing. It would be a hot one today, no question about it.

Although the Metro ran to Bethesda, Maryland, I would have had to take a train into D.C. and then transfer to get there. My destination was off the beaten path, and I wanted the freedom to move about. Plus, I liked driving. What with my hours at the White House and the little downtime I'd had in recent months, I didn't often get the chance to do much of it.

Twenty minutes later, I was exiting 495 North following a long ramp that led me into a lovely area with sprawling homes, tree-lined streets, country clubs, and tennis courts. I took the turns MapQuest had suggested and followed a small road almost to its end. I double-checked the address. There it was: Eugene Vaughn's home. The retired army general, the much-decorated man who had been so kind and yet so mysterious in my mother's hour of need, was definitely still alive.

Whoever he was, I thought as I shut the car door and

made my way up, he'd done well for himself. The home was a colonial-style redbrick, boasting huge gridded rectangular windows with black shutters and a shaker roof with three small gabled windows that promised cozy attic bedrooms. The garage was attached to the west of the home and I parked on its driveway, making my way eastward along the path to the front door.

My heart pounded as I lifted the brass door knocker and banged it, announcing myself. I knew little about this man. I had no idea how I would be received. No idea if he would recognize my name.

A woman answered. Taller than me, she had a wide forehead, blonde hair down to her shoulders, and carried an extra forty pounds. She wore pale blue cotton pants, gym shoes, and a bright patterned top cut in unmistakable healthcare provider couture. "May I help you?" she asked.

"Hi," I said, at once worried that I might be intruding on a sick man. "I don't mean to bother you, but I would like to speak with Mr. Eugene Vaughn, if that's possible."

Her eyes dimmed, her jaw set almost imperceptibly, but she maintained a friendly tone. "Is he expecting you?"

I took a deep breath. "No," I admitted. "Believe it or not, I could find his address but not his phone number."

She crinkled her nose. "It's unlisted."

"I know. I was surprised to even find his address." Truth was, I'd pulled a couple of strings to get my hands on it.

We'd been talking for less than thirty seconds and already I'd exhausted her patience. "My name is Olivia Paras," I began again. "Mr. Vaughn knew my father a long time ago. He—Mr. Vaughn, that is—helped my mom a great deal when my father died."

She relaxed slightly, probably relieved I wasn't there to sell anything, sway Vaughn's political opinions, or attempt to convert him.

I took advantage. "My mother recently told me about

Mr. Vaughn's assistance and I wanted to talk with him myself, if that's possible."

She nodded thoughtfully. "Eugene doesn't get a lot of visitors," she said. "I'll ask him. Fair enough?"

"Absolutely," I said, hoping he wouldn't turn me away.

She had me repeat my name and provide my dad's. "Wait here a minute," she said and shut the door.

I didn't know how much time to give her, but the point was moot. She was back before I could compose a text to Gav. Opening the door wide, she said, "Come on in."

The entrance hall smelled of lemon wax, coffee, and disinfectant. "My name's Roberta. I'm one of Eugene's caregivers." As she led me into the living room, she added, "Here you are."

Seated in an oversized burgundy chair, Eugene Vaughn stared at me from beneath bushy eyebrows. With his wild, tufted hair, he reminded me of Albert Einstein.

He blinked several times, working his mouth. "What's your name again?"

"Olivia Paras," I answered, wondering why I'd been granted an audience if he didn't know who I was. "Anthony Paras's daughter."

"Anthony Paras," he said, squinting into the distance. "There's a name I haven't heard in a very long time. Come closer. Let me have a look at you."

I crossed the long, sun-filled room. Taupe walls, white wood trim. Two of the tall windows I'd passed as I'd made my way to the door flanked the white-paneled fireplace. Cinnamon filled the air in here. An expansive ruby rug covered most of the hardwood floor. The sofa was camel colored and sported a multitude of throw pillows in various patterns featuring garnet, beige, and yellow. Lit candles—the source of the cinnamon aroma, no doubt, and effective chaser of sickroom smells—were perched here and there. Accessories and coffee table books, showcased everywhere, completed the tableau.

There was no television in the room. Eugene Vaughn sat with a book open on his lap. He held it up when he saw me take notice. "*Fahrenheit 451*," he said. "Good book."

"Yes, it is."

He wagged a finger toward Roberta. "She tells me I've read it before." He shrugged, then leaned forward and placed the volume on the low table before us. "I remember parts of it."

"I'm very glad to meet you, Mr. Vaughn," I said stiffly.

He peered at me. "For goodness' sake, child, take a seat. And call me Eugene. None of this Mr. Vaughn nonsense." He pointed a gnarled finger at a nearby wooden chair with red-and-white-checkered cushion. "Pull that up."

I complied.

"Tony's daughter, you say? The last time I saw you, you were a little pipsqueak. Grown up a bit, have you?"

"A bit," I said.

Eugene faced his caregiver, who'd remained in the doorway. "Roberta, dear, do we have any sweet tea to offer our guest?"

She smiled. "I'll go check."

I was about to tell her not to bother with anything for me, but thought better of it. Mr. Vaughn's apparent willingness to spend time talking was exactly what I'd come for, wasn't it?

"Thank you for seeing me," I said.

"Hah!" he barked as though I'd said something funny. "It was just a matter of time. Good thing you got here before I kicked the bucket. According to my doctor, that could be any day now. How is your mother?"

"Doing well, thank you."

He got a wistful look in his eyes. "She had a rough time of it when your father died."

"Yes," I said, encouraging him. "She told me a little bit about how you helped her."

"I did, didn't I?" he asked rhetorically. "You look like her. Look like your dad, too."

Steering back to the topic, I said, "My mom told me a bit about everything that went on when my dad was killed. It seems there's more to the story than she knows."

I waited for him to agree. Instead, he grunted. "And you're here because?"

"Because I hope you'll tell me the rest of the story."

"Rest of what story?" he asked.

Though frustrated, I wasn't ready to give up. I wondered briefly if he was toying with me. His colorless eyes were alert, probing. Though they were clouded with cataracts, they bore into me with shrewd assessment.

"You managed to get my father into Arlington," I said. "After a dishon—"

"Stop right there." He sliced the air with his hand, a commanding motion rendered all the more poignant by the quivering of his fingers. "You're moving too fast for this old man. Taxing my limited memory." I had my doubts about that. "I want to talk about you, first. Quite the reputation you have there, little girl."

Taken aback, I said, "What do you mean?"

"What, you think because I live alone and have nurses hovering over me that I don't keep up with the world? You've made a name for yourself. Gotten into a few scrapes along the way, eh?"

I could barely form words. "You know . . . me?"

"Been following your career ever since you came to D.C. as an assistant chef. Your mom would write me once in a while to tell me where you were studying or where you were working."

"Oh," I said, flabbergasted. "She never mentioned that."

"Nope," he said, utterly unsurprised by my proclamation. "Your father, your mother. Trustworthy people. Ask them to keep a secret, they keep it." He waggled his eyebrows. "You haven't been booted from your position, despite all the trouble you've gotten into, so I have to assume you inherited that trait, too."

My hands came up to my forehead. This was almost too much to take in at once. "Why haven't you ever contacted me?"

"Why should I? You don't know me."

Roberta returned with two tall glasses of iced tea and set them down on the low table before us. "If there's nothing else," she said, "I'll head upstairs to read."

Mr. Vaughn lifted a skinny wrist, from which a bold-faced watch dangled. "The tall girl is on duty next, right?"

She nodded.

He turned to me. "I'm not crazy about that other girl." To Roberta, he said, "Go on. Skedaddle out early. Go see those kids of yours. I've got company, I'll be fine."

"But—"

"Go on," he said with authority. "Olivia and I have much to discuss. I'll see you tomorrow."

Her face lit up. "If you're sure," she said. "I've got eight kids coming after school for a birthday party. This will be a huge help."

Within moments she was gone, and as soon as the front door clicked shut, he turned to me and chuckled. "Decades of security concerns make me unwilling to share tales in front of others. Even kindhearted women like Roberta."

I waited for him to continue. He didn't.

"Please go on," I said.

He blinked elfin eyes. "What were we talking about?"

I hesitated. "You're putting me on," I said, ignoring my polite tendencies and trying to catch him off guard. "You're trying to fake me out."

"You are a little troublemaker, aren't you?"

"Not intentionally." I took a sip of the sweet tea. I wiped my fingers, wet from the glass's condensation, on my pant legs. "I'm hoping you'll be able to fill in a few gaps in my mother's story."

"Tell me what *you* know," he said. "I need the refresher."

With my best attempt at patience, I explained everything

my mother had told me, finishing with a question. "How could you have pulled strings to get him into Arlington? That isn't right."

"Do you read the newspaper? Watch television?"

"Yes."

"Then you know how often things happen that are not right."

"But . . ." I said, about to argue.

He interrupted. "Do you always get a firm answer? An explanation as to why the guilty are released and the innocent incarcerated?"

"No, of course not."

"Yet you expect me to have all the answers."

"You do have the answers," I said. "How did my father get into Arlington?"

"Ah," he said, his eyes growing bigger and brighter. "That one is easy. He belonged there."

"Explain."

His eyes lost focus for a moment. "I can't." He turned toward the fireplace and was quiet for so long, I worried he'd forgotten I was there. "They don't let me build fires anymore," he said finally. "The nurses won't even build one for me. Say it's too dangerous." He made a noise deep in his throat before raising his voice. "I was commanding troops when they were still in diapers." He took a deep, wheezy breath and said, "Your father was a hero. He served his country well. And honorably."

"I believe you," I said. "You were his friend back then. Why the dishonorable discharge? Mom said it was for insubordination."

"Insubordination," he repeated still facing the fireplace.

"Mom also said that in addition to being his friend, you were also his commanding officer. You had to know the specifics about his discharge."

He chewed the insides of his cheeks, but didn't answer.

"My mom asked you that too, didn't she? Back when—"

"Young woman," he said, "all matters regarding your father's discharge are classified."

"It's been more than twenty-five years."

"Has it?" he whispered, blinking as though I'd surprised him. "Classified is classified." He shot a pale glance at me. "I know that much."

"Without breaking any laws, then," I said carefully, "what can you tell me that I don't already know?"

"Not much."

"How were you able to get him into Arlington?"

"Does it matter?" he asked.

"Of course it does."

"Listen, child. You were just a tiny thing when all this happened. You have no idea what was going on behind the scenes."

I tried to keep the impatience from my voice. "I would know if you'd tell me."

"I can't do that."

"But you're my only hope."

"How do you expect me to recall details from a quarter century ago? The answers you seek are beyond your grasp. Very likely beyond mine, too."

"You said the details were 'classified,'" I reminded him. "Clearly you remember. I think you're hiding behind your memory issues to throw me off."

"Nonsense."

"Don't you think it's unlikely that after twenty-five years anything about my dad is still protected?"

"I have not been advised otherwise."

He must have read the look of determination on my face because he glared at me with as much fervor as he could muster, lifting a finger to shake near my face. "Here is truth for you: Documentation or not, your father was an honorable man. He was not only one of my best friends, he was a man I trusted with my life."

"But now he's dead," I said, stating the obvious. "Gone for a very long time. He can't be hurt any longer."

Eugene surprised me by saying, "Others might be."

"Who?"

He shook his head. "Ramblings of an old man. Forget I said that."

Not a chance.

"Your father understood what was asked of him," Eugene said. "He didn't like it, but he understood. The world would be a better place with more men like Anthony Paras. That's all you'll get from me."

Eugene's voice had risen, his back had straightened, but as soon as the words were past his lips, he slumped, looking small in his oversized chair. "Give me that cover, will you, girl?" he asked, pointing.

A woven afghan had been thrown over the side of the nearby sofa, its cherry-and-cream design yet another perfect accent in this room. I brought it to him. He lifted both hands in the air and I tucked the fabric around his legs. "Thank you," he said.

The subject was dead. Clearly. I sighed my exasperation. Eugene didn't comment.

I considered taking my leave and thought about the best way to do so when Eugene mumbled, "Tony. Terrible loss for all of us."

Encouraged by this unexpected remark, I continued in a low tone. "A man at work was giving him trouble."

Eugene stared at the floor saying nothing.

"Pluto, Incorporated," I continued. "They worked together."

"Tony," he said.

I waited, but nothing.

"Pluto," I began again. "They make dietary supplements."

Eugene laughed, but not happily. "I take fiber pills every day. Don't know what brand. I should check that, eh?"

"This other man," I said, "he was trouble."

Eugene appeared to have gotten lost in his own musings. I wasn't sure he heard me, but I knew I'd kick myself later if I didn't at least try to press him further with the questions that burned in my brain.

"What do *you* know about this other man?" I asked slowly, hoping my question would sink in before continuing. "The company, Pluto, believed my dad had been a corporate spy. Selling secrets." I bit my lip. "That wasn't true, was it?"

Eugene's cheek twitched but he didn't answer.

"Those accusations came later," I said, "after my dad had been killed. Maybe this 'other man' was the real thief. Maybe he killed my dad and framed him to cover his tracks."

Eugene drew in a deep breath through his nose. His head came up and he turned to me again. I was astonished by the change in him. Suddenly alert, he said, "Interesting hypothesis."

"Is that what happened?"

"I have no comment."

"Mr. Vaughn—"

"Your parents and I are old friends. Call me Uncle Eugene."

I'd never do that, but I couldn't miss out on his sudden coherence. "If you were my dad's best friend, you must have known about this other man. What was his name?"

"Why would he have told me?"

"You were his best friend."

"Your mother was his best friend."

"He worried about putting my mom in danger. This 'other man' was obviously capable of doing us harm. You, on the other hand, were not only a trusted friend, but a big shot in the U.S. Army. You had power. He would have consulted you."

"Sounds very logical, the way you present it."

Despite the fact that I had nothing but gut instinct

screaming that I was right, I plowed forward. "My dad would have told you about this guy. I know it. What was his name?"

Eugene's graying tongue ran lightly over his lower lip. I could read in his face that he knew exactly who I was asking about. "That I can't tell you."

"Why not?"

He waved a pale hand in the air as though casting a spell. "We can't put more lives in danger."

"But don't I deserve to know if he's the man who killed my dad?"

Eugene was quiet for a long time, focusing again on the fireplace. When he finally looked up, he stared through clouded eyes. "Where's Roberta?"

CHAPTER 7

GAV'S APARTMENT WAS SMALLER THAN MINE, by quite a bit. Carved out of a much larger space when the building underwent renovation, it was barely bigger than a studio. Because of its retrofit design, once a person entered, they were required to take about fifteen steps through a narrow hall past the lavatory to finally reach the living area. Tiny but serviceable, the area was decorated in deep reds with a few accent colors here and there for interest. What had grabbed my attention the first time I'd been here and every time since, was the gorgeous and expansive view over D.C. from this twenty-first-floor vantage point.

I leaned on the waist-high sill, staring out the window.

"You planning to keep all the details to yourself?" Gav asked from the galley kitchen. He held up two bottles. "Red or white tonight?"

I pointed to the claret we both enjoyed. "I'm feeling dark."

He set to work opening the bottle.

I turned back to the window. Although the sun wouldn't set for a few more hours, I looked forward to evening and the beautiful glow of the city at night, with the tall obelisk of the Washington Monument proudly taking center stage. "This is the most amazing view."

"You say that every time."

I laughed. "I do, don't I? I've never asked: How long have you had this place?"

He twisted the corkscrew. "Since they opened it for new tenants," he said. "Ten years, give or take."

A half-wall of glass-block windows separated the tiny living and dining room combination from the sleeping area, which was little more than a mattress and box spring on a raised platform with a miniature dresser wedged in near the windows. Except for the bathroom and a closet, there were no doors in the apartment. The entire place was awash in reds and I laughed softly.

"What?"

"Eugene Vaughn's place was decorated a lot like this," I said. "He's got a more traditional vibe going; you're more contemporary. But red is the color of choice for both of you. I'm wondering if that's a military thing."

"Or patriotic."

I glanced around, pointing to the blue throw pillows on the couch. "Good point." I faced him. "And your kitchen is about as white as you can get. White appliances, white cabinets, white floor. Nothing out of place."

"My kitchen stays clean because nobody cooks in it," he said, bringing me a glass of wine.

"We need to work on changing that."

"Next time," he said. "I don't mind going out." Truth was, I didn't mind either, and we'd had a lovely dinner at a restaurant within walking distance. We clinked our glasses, toasting nothing in particular, and sipped.

"Delicious," I said.

"Mm. Very good." Looking around his apartment as though seeing it for the first time, he said, "Maybe your friend Vaughn and I used the same decorator."

I nearly spit my wine. "You hired a decorator?"

He gave me a lopsided frown. "Something wrong with that?"

Tapping my lip to catch the dribbles, I said, "Of course not. Surprised is all."

"When I knew I'd be out of the country for a couple of years and needed to sublet, I figured I'd have a much better chance of finding a tenant if the place looked halfway decent."

"Did your decorator design your bathroom, too?"

"Why do you ask?"

"No reason," I said, taking another sip of wine.

"You're lying, Paras," Gav said. "What's wrong with the bathroom?"

I shrugged, but the look on his face told me he wasn't about to let the topic drop. "It doesn't fit with the rest of the place," I said carefully.

"Define 'fit.' "

"Your decorator likes reds and deep colors. Your bathroom is white and beige. It looks like it's never been painted. And that shower curtain . . ."

"What's wrong with the shower curtain?"

"Not a thing," I lied. "Let's change the subject."

He laughed. "I'm giving you a hard time. I bought it on sale, if that makes any difference. Found it in a 90-percent-off bin."

"That explains a lot."

"What? You don't like balloons?"

I loved it when his eyes twinkled. This man, the real Gav, was so different from the man I'd first met. "We'll shop for a new one soon," I promised.

He and I sat on the couch. "Your day," he said. "Spill, because I've got a lot to tell you about what I've been up to."

Although we'd already shared a little about our respective days at the restaurant, we'd kept personal topics to a minimum. The table we'd dined at was mere inches away from its neighbors, and as always, we opted to err on the side of paranoia where security was concerned.

"Not nearly as much to tell as I would have hoped," I said. "Eugene Vaughn is a nice old man with a memory that ebbs and flows. The thing is, when it's flowing, he's not always willing to talk." I provided a detailed accounting of the rest of the visit.

We sat facing each other on the couch. As I talked, Gav reached forward and fingered a few strands of my hair, staring at them as he did so. "So, he's holding back. What do you plan to do about it?"

"I have an idea," I said. "Even though Pluto, Incorporated is a privately held company, there have to be records somewhere, don't you think?"

He nodded.

"I figure the library is my best bet. I can go down there tomorrow morning and ask the reference librarian for help."

"Reference librarians are the best," he said.

"You know it. If there's a way to gather information about the company, they're going to be able to tell us."

"Us?" he asked. "You plan to include me? Don't you usually traipse off on your own for your investigations?"

He was teasing, but the question gave me pause. "This is different," I said. "I don't usually know I'm investigating until I'm right in the middle of it. This is really the first time I'm actively seeking information. And this time, too, it's just for me. I'm not trying to 'save the world' the way they mock me in the media. I'm on a personal quest this time. It's different. I'd love your help."

"I can't think of anything I'd rather do on our vacation," he said without any sarcasm whatsoever.

"Really?"

"As a matter of fact." He leaned forward, placed his wine-glass on the coffee table, and stood. "I had a feeling you might need a little assistance, and since matters of national security don't appear to be at stake . . ."

He returned to the kitchen and opened a cabinet next to the refrigerator. "Another reason why I didn't want you put-tering around in here tonight. Knowing you, you'd have stumbled across my secret stash before I could stop you."

I put my wineglass down and sat up straighter. "What kind of secrets?"

He returned to the couch, sat next to me, and placed a manila file folder of papers on his lap. "You know how I told you I was busy yesterday and part of today?"

"You wouldn't tell me what it was about."

"For good reason," he said. He gave me a sidelong glance. "You want to know what's in here, don't you?"

I inched a little closer. "What gives you that impression?"

"Remember that test I gave you in the Brady Press Brief-ing Room way back when we first met?"

I'd never forget. "Of course."

"You should have seen yourself searching for that hidden bomb. Determined, fearless, unwavering. You get that same look in your eyes far more times than is acceptable to the White House Secret Service. You've got that look again right now."

"I'd better work on that if I want to pursue my next career as an undercover agent."

He made a so-so motion. "You're able to hide your emo-tions when you need to," he said, "but right now you're unguarded." His eyes were soft when he added, "I like that." Back to business before I could get mushy, he said, "I have a couple things to share with you." He held up two fingers, still not opening the file. "Mind you, neither may give us any more information than we have right now."

I was as antsy as I'd ever been. We'd both completely

forgotten about our wine as Gav opened the file folder. "I spent the better part of today with Jeanne Bracken, one of the finest reference librarians on the planet."

"You did?"

"I knew that, at a minimum, we were going to need basic information on Pluto. Not necessarily the information one can find online, but what the company was like a quarter-century ago. Who worked there, what their financials looked like. . . ."

"You were able to get that?"

"Not everything. But enough, I think."

Because he was delivering the news slowly, I knew it must be good. "What did you find?"

He ran his fingers along the side of the stack of papers. There were at least fifty sheets there. "I made copies of whatever I could find on Pluto, from about five years before your dad worked there until about five years after. I included recent company information as well. I didn't know what might pop, which is why I bracketed the years and took a 'more is better' approach."

I scooched close enough to Gav to spread the files across our laps. Before I dug in, I remembered. "You said 'two things.' "

"The second thing may not materialize in to anything solid."

I waited.

"While you were at the White House yesterday, I drove out to meet someone," he said. "His name is Joe Yablonski. Joe was to me what I sense Eugene Vaughn was to your dad: my commanding officer for many years, and now my good friend. Joe works for . . ." Gav hesitated. "Let's call it the Department of Defense."

"Interesting wording," I said. "What does he do for them?"

"Even if I had specifics . . ."

I finished it for him. "You couldn't tell me."

"What's important is that he's connected. Very connected. I don't know anyone who wields as much influence as he does behind the scenes. And he counts me as one of his close friends. I asked if he'd be willing to meet with you."

"He must have agreed," I said.

"We have an appointment with him tomorrow."

"That's why you were so secretive yesterday," I said, understanding now. "You were afraid of getting my hopes up and having him refuse."

"Are you interested?"

"Are you kidding? Of course! I have no idea how to begin this kind of search into my dad's past. If there's opportunity for help—not just having doors opened, but to even find out which doors *exist*—I'm all for it." I wrapped an arm around his neck and kissed him. "Thank you, Gav." I was lucky to have this man in my life. "You know how important this is to me."

"I do," he said. "I also know how persistent you are about uncovering truth. I figured if I help you find the answers you're looking for, it might save us both a lot of time and trouble."

"You sweet talker, you."

"We'll drive out there tomorrow."

"To the Pentagon? Why not just take the Metr—"

"Not to the Pentagon. It will be better for all of us to keep this meeting on the QT."

"Sounds very cloak-and-dagger," I said.

"Joe is connected," Gav repeated. "No sense jeopardizing that."

"How would meeting with him cause any problems?"

"You're a force, Ollie. Whether you like it or not, you have a reputation. Better to keep Joe out of it in order to protect his."

Although Gav had spoken in an admiring tone, I wasn't

quite sure how to take his words. "You really believe I could hurt his reputation?"

"I know it."

Something in his voice made me ask. "Have I hurt yours?"

He hesitated.

"What did I do?" I asked. "What has happened that I don't know?"

"Nothing of consequence."

"Tell me."

Gav flexed his jaw. "During your last adventure, there was talk that I might have become too emotionally involved."

"Who—?"

"Doesn't matter."

"What happened?" Sounding like a nervous fifth-grader, I asked, "Did you get into trouble?"

"Not trouble," he said.

I waited.

He sighed. "There was a plum assignment that came up. I would have been considered for it, but I was warned not to apply."

"I'm so sorry."

"I'm not. It would have taken me out of the country. For two years."

"Oh." I stared up at him. "Did you want this assignment?"

He put an arm around me and pulled me tight. "Any other time of my life, yes. Not right now."

"Do a lot of higher-ups know that we're involved?"

"Only those who need to know," he said.

"I don't want to be trouble for you."

"You're not. I mean that." Reacting to the look on my face perhaps, he said, "Don't sweat it, Ollie. I'm exactly where I want to be. Let's put that aside for now and see what we can discover in Pluto's paperwork."

Although I wanted to know exactly what kind of impact I might be having on his career, he seemed so eager for me to dive into the information he'd uncovered that I took his suggestion and let it go.

Gav had been thorough in his investigation, and I realized as we sifted through all the information he'd uncovered that he'd pursued this thread exactly in the manner I would have. He'd pulled together all the pertinent information about Pluto that he could find, and after about an hour of reading reports, newspaper articles, and company newsletters—which were a magnificent resource—we decided to put together a time line.

That took another hour. When I looked up, the sky was dark, the city glittering. I stood up and stretched, making my way to the windows. "I won't say it again," I said, "but this is so amazing. I could stay here forever."

He came up behind me, placing his hands on my shoulders. "It's a little small for two people. Permanently, I mean . . ." He stopped.

Gav was seldom at a loss for words, but I understood. After suffering tragedies early in his life, he still had difficulty thinking and talking about the future. I placed a hand atop one of his. "We've got plenty of time."

"I hope you're right."

Our faces were reflected back in the dark glass and I wished I could wipe the sadness from his eyes. The man was unflinchingly courageous in matters where he was required to put himself at risk. When it came to me, however, he fought powerful demons to keep fear at bay.

I turned to face him. "I'm not going anywhere."

He held me at arm's length and studied me for a long time. "Do you promise?"

"Promise. Your worries of being a jinx are over. We can take our sweet time about the business of you and me."

He pulled me tight and I drew in a deep breath of his

heady, manly scent. His chest rumbled as he spoke, "I don't know, Ollie. Wherever you go, trouble follows. You get my heart racing. In more ways than one."

"I'll behave," I said, laughing. "I mean, really, how much danger can I get into looking at old company reports?"

CHAPTER 8

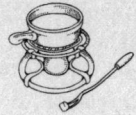

GAV STILL HADN'T TOLD ME EXACTLY WHERE we were headed when we set out the next morning in his silver Honda Civic. We were both dressed casually, wearing sunglasses to shade the sun's blistering brightness. We headed north and west, and were about twenty miles out of D.C. when I looked up from the notes I'd been making on the time line we'd created the night before.

"So what's this Joe Yablonski like?" I asked.

Gav kept his eyes on the road. "I can tell those Pluto papers have you enthralled."

"They get repetitive after a while," I admitted. "I started adding names to the time line," I said. "Employee of the month, retirees, etc. Trying to get an idea of who actually worked there at the same time my dad did." I exaggerated my blinking. "Reading in the car makes my eyes go wobbly."

"Joe's unique," he said. "I think you'll like him."

"How much farther?"

"A while."

"Great," I said, "plenty of time to get dizzy."

I resumed reading for about five minutes. "Hey!" I said.

Gav lowered his sunglasses long enough to glance over to me. "That sounds promising."

"Maybe. About three weeks after my dad died, one of the company vice presidents was hurt on the job, and badly. He's in a wheelchair and homebound."

"How does that help you?"

"It doesn't. But Harold Linka, the man who was disabled, still works for the company. He has an office at home." I pointed even though Gav kept his eyes forward. "Maybe he'd be willing to talk to us."

"If we really believe that your dad was shot and subsequently framed by a man he worked with, then you risk opening up old wounds."

I frowned at him and waited for him to notice before I spoke. "I wouldn't go in there all gangbusters. I'd be careful. Even if this Harold Linka didn't know my dad well, he might know who his friends were back then."

"Don't lose sight of the fact that memories shift over time. Twenty-five years can skew recollections."

"My visit to Eugene Vaughn made that clear," I said, scribbling "Harold Linka" into my notes. "That doesn't mean I won't try."

I glanced up again, taking in the surroundings. "I haven't been out this far in a long time. You drove out here Tuesday?"

"Joe and I met at a different location. A bit closer to home."

"Because meeting with you isn't going to hurt Mr. Yablonski's reputation?"

"Something like that."

"Hmm," I said, not thrilled about the name for myself I'd apparently cultivated. I'd have to do my best to impress this Joe Yablonski. "I hate to miss all this lovely scenery, but I still have plenty to read. Let me know when we get close."

"You've got a while yet."

WHEN WE CROSSED INTO LOUDOUN COUNTY, Virginia, Gav let me know that we would arrive at our destination in about ten minutes. Perfect timing; I was nearly finished with my analysis. "I came up with one other name," I said. "I think this Michael Fitch could have been at Pluto the same time my dad was." I waved my hands over the uneven piles of pages and notes spread across my lap. "Except for the owner, Craig Benson, it looks to me as though the place has suffered a lot of turnover through the years. Check this out." I held up a newsletter and read a paragraph about how Pluto had welcomed their newest employee as executive secretary.

"So?"

"Three months later, there's this . . ." I read aloud another passage that was word-for-word the same welcome. "Same position, different woman." I shuffled the pages into a neat pile and placed my notes on top. I tapped the straightened pile. "The only two viable candidates are Linka and Fitch, the ones I mentioned. I hope we get lucky."

"Here we are." Gav turned onto a gravel road. We bumped and jostled along for at least another mile until he pulled into what could only loosely be described as a parking lot, adjacent to a group of one-story whitewashed brick buildings all with blue roofs.

The structures were nestled into this low area amid rolling hills, surrounded on all sides by trellises of grapes growing in long, lovely rows almost as far as I could see. Nearby, next to the largest of the buildings, three worn wooden picnic tables sat beneath a cluster of trees.

There was one other car in the sunny parking lot, and a

butterscotch lab had found shade under one of the picnic tables. Otherwise, the place seemed utterly vacant.

"A vineyard?" Leaving my paperwork behind, I got out of the car and stretched in the late morning sun. "Gorgeous day to be outdoors. Does your friend live all the way out here?"

Gav didn't answer. He shut his door and came around to my side. Wearing jeans, a T-shirt, and the sunglasses he'd pushed atop his head, he looked more like a handsome tourist than a government agent, although his alertness and ramrod posture threatened to give him away.

After we'd alighted, I'd expected him to lead me to the rustic two-story home about fifty feet farther up the gravel path, but instead he placed a gentle hand at the small of my back, guiding me toward the nearest building. "They're only open limited hours," he said. "Closing at noon today. Let's do a tasting."

I glanced at my watch: 11:30. "Sure." Each of the white buildings sported blue metal doors and paned windows trimmed in blue. "I missed the vineyard's name on the way in."

He spoke very close to my ear. "Follow my lead."

I gave him my best you're-just-teasing-me look, but he missed it.

"This way," he said. We went around the building's corner where one of its blue metal doors was propped open with a cinder block. WINERY ENTRANCE was hand-lettered in gold, next to the door.

Coming in from the sun, I stopped after three steps to allow my eyes to get accustomed to the dark room. Although well-lit, the windows had been covered with wooden-slat blinds, helping to keep the place cool and maintain a cozy air. And cozy it was. From the nondescript exterior, I'd expected little more than a countertop and a few bottles on display, but this room was welcoming and friendly. Small, no bigger than twenty-by-twenty, its corners were warmed by the soft glow of Tiffany lamps.

The floor was concrete, the ceiling high and industrial, but the walls were painted in muted jewel tones with quality artwork on them, placed around and above wine displays. Directly across from the door, the room's bar took center stage. A young couple browsed the wine selections. An older gentleman leaned heavily on the bar's far right flank. Wearing overalls, a red plaid shirt, and studying us with undisguised interest as we made our way in, he had to be Joe Yablonski.

A middle-aged woman behind the bar gestured us in. "Welcome to Spencer's Vineyards. Free tastings." She graced us with a cheerful gap-toothed grin. "We offer them free because we know you're going to love our wines."

"We'd like to do a tasting," Gav said. "I've heard great things about this place."

"Where you from?" She pulled two glasses up from behind the bar and placed them before us. She then drew out two printed sheets and two pencils. "Here's for making notes. My name's Ermengarde, but everyone calls me Erma."

"We're just down from Frederick for the day," Gav answered. "Visiting friends and we thought we'd bring wine. What's good here?"

She straightened the neck of her apron with unabashed confidence. "Everything."

She poured our first wine, describing it far more eloquently than I would have expected. As we took our first sips and I marveled at the wine's smoothness, she said, "Say, would you folks be interested in a tour?" She cocked her head toward the young couple, who'd selected three bottles of wine and were waiting for her to ring them up. "It only takes about fifteen minutes." She leaned toward the young couple. "You liked the tour, didn't you? Think it was worth it?"

They looked at one another and then at us. "We enjoyed it."

Gav turned to me. "What do you say, honey?"

Honey? I gurgled my mouthful of wine. "Sounds great," I managed.

The old guy leaning at the bar pushed himself off and ambled out the door. I glanced up at Gav, but he'd already begun jotting notes about the wine Erma had poured for us. "Wonderful," he said, pointing to the printed sheet where the description and its price could be found. "Not terribly expensive either."

This was some charade, I thought as I sipped.

We'd made it through two more wonderful wines before the young couple departed and we heard them pull away. As soon as they did, Erma grinned. "How you been, Gav?" she asked, coming around to the front of the bar to give him a hug. "We sure miss you around here." Before he had a chance to answer, she turned to me. "And you must be Ollie."

I was completely nonplussed. "You know me?" I said in about as lame an exclamation as I'd ever uttered. "I'm sorry, you really had me there."

"We've sure heard a lot about you," she said, wrapping me in a full-body hug. "Gav just goes on and on."

His cheeks reddened. "I missed you, too, Erma," he said. "Thanks for letting us use your place here today. Joe's already here, I take it?"

"Bill's gone to get him." She gave Gav an appraising glance. "You're looking mighty fine, son." To me, she said, "I think you're good for him."

This was a lot to digest at once. Gav had told me about his childhood, mostly spent in foster homes in the Midwest. I didn't know how Erma and Bill figured into that equation, but I assumed I'd find out. "You sure were quiet about all this on the drive up," I said to Gav.

"I didn't know if there would be anyone else here," he

said, gesturing toward the door. "And if there was . . . Hey!" This last exclamation came as the man who had been leaning on the bar when we arrived—obviously Bill—returned with another man. Gav strode up to both of them, giving Bill a vigorous back-slapping man hug, before gripping Joe Yablonski's hand in a sturdy, joyful shake. Gav was as happy as I'd ever seen him and I found myself smiling, too.

"This is Ollie," he said, bringing the two men forward. "Ollie, this is Bill." He stepped back as I shook the man's hand. "Bill and Erma have been part of my life . . ." A shadow flitted across Gav's features for the briefest of moments. "For a very long time. They're family."

Bill and I exchanged pleasantries though I got the feeling the older man still hadn't finished assessing me.

"And this," Gav said, bringing me closer to the second man, "is the inestimable Joe Yablonski."

Joe Yablonski looked exactly as I'd expected, only bigger. Taller than Gav, he was wider, too, with broad shoulders, a massive chest, and a neck that draped over his collar. I guessed him to be in his mid-fifties. He looked the type who would be far more comfortable in a dress uniform than in the civilian Dockers and polo shirt he was wearing. "It's very nice to meet you," I said.

He wrapped a meaty hand around my smaller one. "The pleasure is mine, Ms. Paras."

"Ollie, please."

All business again, he turned to Gav. "Shall we find a comfortable place to chat?"

Erma was immediately solicitous. "Of course!" she said, "I know your time is limited. Bill will go set out the closed sign at the front gate and you all can have this entire room to yourselves."

Gav stood back, hands clasped. He didn't seem surprised when Yablonski shook his head. "I think I would much prefer we walk. You have no objection to our wandering through the vineyard, do you?"

"None at all," Erma said without consulting her husband.

Bill grunted. "I'll go set up that closed sign anyway."

Yablonski led us back out into the sunshine. He took five long strides along the gravel path, then stopped and stared to the left. Several seconds later, he stared right. Extending his arm, he pointed. "That way."

We'd traveled about a hundred yards farther up the gravel path, past the house, when Yablonski noticed me lagging slightly behind. Although I did my best to keep up, it took me twice as many steps as it did them to cross the same distance. He stopped. "My apologies," he said.

He continued at a more leisurely pace. Open land and trellis rows surrounded us on all sides. The air was quiet, the sky clear. "I like this," Yablonski said, glancing around. "Good place to have a serious conversation."

Personally, I thought it was overkill.

"Has your friend Leonard told you much about me?" he asked, as though Gav wasn't standing right there. It felt strange to hear Gav referred to by his given name. I knew how much he hated "Leonard" and I took pains never to use it.

"I know you were his commanding officer. I know he considers you a friend."

"Anything else?"

"He told me you work for the Department of Defense."

"But?" he asked, clearly reading my expression.

"I have my doubts."

I could tell I'd surprised him. "Fair enough. Let's keep it at that, shall we? From what I understand from your friend here"—he indicated Gav—"and from what I've read in the newspapers, you have a tendency to get involved in matters of national security even when you're instructed to stay away. What do you have to say about that?"

I glanced at Gav for help but his look told me I was on my own. I got the distinct impression that if this Yablonski could help me, he wouldn't do so unless he believed he could trust me. "Like everything you read or hear, there's a kernel of truth," I admitted. "The idea of the White House chef getting involved in conspiracy plots, bomb threats, terrorist actions . . ." Hearing myself, I stopped, then began again. "It does sound ridiculous. I admit that. If you knew the whole story behind each of these circumstances, however, you might understand how I got involved in the first place."

He watched me as I talked. "You sincerely believe I would condone your involvement?"

"Condone?" I laughed. "Hardly. I wouldn't expect that from anyone, even Special Agent Gavin." The look in Gav's eyes encouraged me. "But I think, given the facts, you might actually understand how situations evolved." I pulled myself up to my full height. "I take national security seriously, if that's what you're asking. I'm not reckless. I keep the Secret Service apprised of all my activities. Ask Gav."

"Leonard's opinion may be compromised at this point," he said. "But there are others who corroborate these assertions of yours. You have friends in high places." He held up a chubby finger. "That doesn't mean I want to be seen in your company. No offense."

"Or overheard in my company, apparently."

His lips spread in a sly smile. "Or overheard. Your young man here is calling in a very large favor by asking for my assistance." Again the fat finger. "I'm willing to do so, on the condition that you tell no one of my involvement and that you keep me updated on your progress. From what I've heard thus far, nothing involves national security or classified information. If I discover differently, you will cease your investigation immediately."

"All I want to know is what really happened with my dad."

Gav remained silent.

The big man commenced walking again, remembering to take shorter strides. The ground here was hilly but he didn't seem to be out of breath. At the top of a small rise, we could see more trellised vines stretching out ahead of us, and the rest of the vineyard below.

Yablonski took a deep breath through wide nostrils. "Invigorating to be out here," he said apropos of nothing. Fixing me with a penetrating gaze, he asked, "I need a definitive answer. Do you agree to cease your investigation on my command?"

"As long as you agree not to issue such a command without providing me an acceptable reason." I adjusted my jaw. "That's as definitive as I can go. If that means you refuse to help, so be it." The words tumbled out, raw with emotion. "Investigating my father's murder is important to me. I plan to follow any leads as far as I possibly can. I won't make promises I can't keep, even if that means losing you as a resource."

Yablonski shifted his attention to Gav, who flashed an "I told you so" look.

"Your terms are acceptable," Yablonski said. "If you haven't already deduced, I am a careful man. I'm willing to help because I respect Leonard and owe him more than I can ever repay. I don't anticipate running into any difficulties, especially given that your father's death occurred so long ago."

I felt my shoulders relax, realizing at that moment how tense I'd been. If this had been a test, which it seemed to be, I'd passed. I would be grateful for any help this man could provide. For his part, Yablonski appeared to relax, too.

Now that we'd established ground rules, Gav spoke up. "I knew you two would hit it off."

I stifled my reaction. I'd hardly call this "hitting it off."

"Joe and I talked yesterday and I brought him up to date on everything," Gav said. "Except the details of your meeting yesterday, of course. You hadn't told me about that yet. You may want to bring Joe up to speed, too."

"Sure," I answered.

But Yablonski had other ideas. "After meeting with Gav, I did a little digging on Pluto," he said.

"You did?" I asked. "Why?"

He shook his head. "I remember hearing the name come up several times over the years, but whenever it did it was in regard to situations in which I had no oversight. I didn't pay close attention. In my line of work, we respect chain of command and boundaries."

That sounded like a chastisement, but I let it slide.

"What did you find out about Pluto?" I asked.

"Not much, unfortunately. But what I didn't find is far more telling. The file on the company—we have one because they do a lot of overseas business—had missing pieces. Critical documents I would have expected to see weren't there. In their place were memos directing me to contact other parties for further information."

"Who?"

"That I can't tell you."

"Fair enough."

"What I do know is that the owner, Craig Benson, has retained the title of CEO, a role that allows him to act on the company's behalf."

We already knew that but I let him continue.

"His son, Kyle, is running the company now and from what I understand, the younger man is doing well."

"What do you think any of this has to do with my dad?"

"Perhaps nothing at all." He seemed to be baiting me, waiting for me to question why he'd wasted so much time looking at Pluto.

I didn't oblige him. Instead, I smiled. "Thank you."

His eyes sparked with an energy that could have been interest or antagonism. "I am always thorough," he said finally. "In order to put a complete story together—in this case, the story of why your father was murdered and by whom—I prefer to do surplus research rather than not enough. Now, tell me about your meeting yesterday with your father's commanding officer."

"Eugene Vaughn wasn't especially helpful." At my mention of the name, Yablonski's eyes registered recognition. Enough for me to press. "You know him?"

"I know of him. It was never my privilege to serve with the man, but I wish I had." His attitude changed from one of admiration to one of patent curiosity. "With regard to your father's burial at Arlington," he began, "you claim that Eugene Vaughn was instrumental in facilitating that event?"

Now we were getting to the key part. "That is my understanding."

"What did he tell you?"

"Not much. Mr. Vaughn is elderly and can't always track the conversation. Either that or he's fooling me completely. One thing he was adamant about, however, was that my father belonged in Arlington, no matter what."

Yablonski lifted his chin and stared down at me. "What Gav has told me is highly unusual. I'd go so far as to say it's impossible. You're certain of the facts in this matter?"

"I've visited my dad's grave," I said. "And my mom showed me the dishonorable discharge papers."

He made a thoughtful noise. "There's no chance you've been visiting a grave for a man with the same name as your father?"

"With the same birth and death dates? I don't think so."

"I suppose not," he muttered. "Tell me something: Why look into this matter at all? If I uncover evidence that proves your father was erroneously buried in one of the most sacred places in our country, I will do whatever is in my power to see that situation rectified. Do you realize that?"

My turn to hold my head high. "Of course I do."

"And yet you persist?"

"My father belongs there. I plan to prove it."

"And what if you're wrong? Are you willing to put your mother through that kind of heartbreak?"

There was the crux of it. I swallowed. "I'm not wrong."

"How can you be so sure?"

I broke eye contact long enough to take in the hills around us, the warm scent of summer, and the sky above, so blue. There are things a person knows deep in her heart, her soul—things that had to be true, because if they weren't, the universe, and everything in it, was wrong. I looked at him again. "I know me," I said. "I know who I am, who my parents are, and were. My mother could not have loved my dad if he were anyone else. Remember, my father was a hero. That's documented."

"His dishonorable status is documented, too."

"There's been a mistake. I can feel it."

Yablonski studied me. "And you're willing to risk all because of this certainty."

I'd be lying if I said the thought of hurting my mother didn't make me weak in the knees, but I was right. I knew that more strongly than I'd ever known anything before. "I am."

He gave the briefest of nods. "It was a pleasure meeting you, Ms. Paras. I will be in touch via Special Agent Gavin." Yablonski smiled. It was perfunctory, not warm. "Leonard will meet you in a moment back at the car. He and I have a few matters to discuss first."

Thus dismissed, I made my way back the way we'd come, frustrated and unsure. Why hadn't Gav said very much? I had a few matters of my own to discuss with him, too.

CHAPTER 9

I CHECKED MY PHONE AS I WALKED TO THE car. One missed message from the White House. I dialed the interim chief usher's number immediately. "You called me?" I asked as soon as he picked up.

"Yeah, Ollie." Doug sounded overwhelmed as ever. Despite the fact that he'd been in the position for almost two months now, he still hadn't found his groove. "Hang on, I have notes around here."

As he shuffled through papers, I turned, gazing back up the hill. Gav had moved closer to Yablonski, and from their body language, it seemed as though they were having a far friendlier conversation than the one I'd experienced. I was too far away to hear anything, but to me it looked as though Yablonski was laughing. He didn't strike me as a man with a particularly keen sense of humor.

"Here we go," Doug said. "The First Lady asked that you come in tomorrow."

"Tomorrow?" I knew my voice betrayed my disappointment. "Has something happened?"

"Nothing earth-shattering," he said. "I guess you mentioned a food convention to her?"

"The one Marcel is speaking at," I said, confused. Doug should know this. "That's on Saturday, not tomorrow."

He sighed. "Yes, Saturday. It seems the Secret Service has been ordered to arrange for Josh to accompany you to this convention."

"It's on?"

"Surprised the heck out of me, too. The First Lady said Josh has been talking nonstop about the event ever since you invited him."

I hadn't exactly invited Josh. I'd brought up the subject and he'd run with it. I'd been certain the suggestion would be shot down by his mother, his bodyguards, or both. Doug continued, "Secret Service wants you here tomorrow to prepare. On such short notice, with limited opportunity for reconnaissance, they are extremely uncomfortable with the president's son out in public at such a well-attended event."

"They want me in tomorrow to talk about it?" I asked, still not understanding.

"Better than that," Doug said, sounding amused. "Because the Service hasn't had the chance to fully prepare, they want you and Josh to go incognito."

"You mean wear disguises?"

"A consultant will be here tomorrow morning at eleven to outfit you."

"Wait," I tried again. "Are you serious? A disguise?"

"Tomorrow. Eleven A.M."

I sighed. "Got it."

Erma and Bill must have been watching from their home, because the moment I closed my phone, they hurried over. That is, Erma hurried; Bill ambled. "I suppose you'll be taking off soon," Erma said. She reached out to grasp both my arms. "I packed up a few bottles of wine for you. They're already in your car." She hesitated, then continued, almost shyly, "We're so glad to see Gav happy again. He deserves it after all he's been through."

I glanced back up the hill. Gav and Yablonski were making their way down, and they still seemed pretty darned cheery. "I'm very lucky," I said, meaning it. "You've known him for a long time?"

Erma slid a glance toward Bill.

"Gav's a good man," he said gruffly. "We're right proud of him." With that, he turned and headed back toward the house.

Yablonski and Gav were still a ways off, but Erma stepped closer as though afraid they might overhear. "Gav told you about . . . his past?"

Maybe it was the way she said it, maybe it was the pain in her eyes; I suddenly knew who these people were. "Oh," I said, reaching out to grab Erma's hand. "I didn't put it together. Your daughter . . ." Gav had been engaged twice before. Both women had died tragically. Erma was undoubtedly mother to one of them, but there seemed no way to tactfully ask which.

"Jennifer," she supplied, sparing me further awkwardness. "We were devastated when she—" Erma took a breath. "After all these years, it still hurts to think about." She dug a tissue out of her apron pocket and held it tight in her fist. "But your Gav never forgets. He's like a son to us. We were so happy for him when he got engaged again. And then . . ." Her words trailed off.

"I'm so sorry."

She forced a smile. "Gav doesn't bring anyone around for us to meet unless he's serious. And I can see by watching you two together that you're good for each other. You've got that way about you."

As the two men drew closer, she leaned forward and hugged me tight. "He's your Gav now," she whispered.

"I think maybe," I whispered back, "he's both of ours."

She released me, looking embarrassed by her show of emotion and said, "I'd better be off. Don't be a stranger."

Hurrying away, she stopped Yablonski and Gav in front of her house and talked to them for a few moments before reaching up to give Gav a hug. I was touched by their evident affection. Up until now, Gav's past had been only what he'd told me. Meeting Erma and Bill brought his life into sharper focus, allowing me to see the three-dimensional flesh-and-blood individuals who'd helped shape him.

I wondered if that was how he'd felt meeting my mom and nana. Given his foster care upbringing, Erma and Bill could very well be the closest thing to Gav's parents I'd ever encounter.

Gav left his friend in front of the house and jogged over to meet up with me. I waved good-bye to the well-connected yet mysterious government man. "Isn't Yablonski leaving now, too?"

"Yablonski?" He laughed. "You can call him Joe. No, he prefers we go ahead so that no one notices us leaving at the same time."

"This guy is careful," I said.

Gav held the door open for me, an amused expression on his face. "How old do you think he is?"

"I don't know." I waited for him to shut the door, walk around the front of the car, and get in. "I'd guess fifty-eight?"

"Sixty-seven," he said. "At least thirty of those years were spent in deep-covert operations across the globe. Being careful has saved his life. Literally."

We pulled out, the gravel pinging under the car's carriage as we bumped along. "Bill didn't say much, but I liked Erma. She's great."

Gav glanced sideways. "She tell you who she is?"

"Yes," I admitted. "I had an inkling, though."

"I thought you might." He nodded. "They'd lived in Maryland all their lives. That is, until Jennifer was killed.

After that they couldn't stay there anymore. Too many memories. Relocated here."

"You've helped them, haven't you?" I asked. "Having you in their lives is like holding on to their daughter."

"Does that make you uncomfortable?"

I thought about it. "No. They love you, Gav. You're family to them."

"As they are to me."

"What about Morgan's family?"

Sadness settled over the car, but these were conversations we needed to have. "I keep in touch. But not like this. It's different. You may meet them someday, too," he said. "You may not."

We were silent for about four miles. "So . . ." I said, "this Yablonski fellow . . ."

Gav laughed. "You didn't like him, did you?"

"I don't know what to think about him."

"He likes you."

"Does not."

Gav mulled for a few minutes before starting again. "What's important is that he'll do what he can. And for a man in his position, that's a real coup."

"You were pretty quiet while he and I talked."

Gav acknowledged my comment with a nod. "You two are more alike than you realize. He wouldn't commit to helping until he got to know you. And you . . . you don't trust easily either. You needed to assess the man before you'd accept what he finds out for you."

"True enough."

"The good thing about you, Ollie, is that you don't equate nice with trustworthy."

"What do you mean by that?"

He smiled. "I saw the snide looks you gave me when I showed up at the White House a few years back. You despised me."

"I did not."

"Sure you did. But you recognized that I was there to do my job as you were there to do yours. You trusted me."

"Eventually."

"Eventually. But you didn't like me one little bit. That came later." He looked at me over the tops of his sunglasses. "At least, I assume it did."

"After today, I'm not so sure," I teased. "That Yablonski made me jittery."

"You held up well under his scrutiny. I can tell you from personal experience that not many people do."

We'd driven about halfway back to D.C. when I remembered to tell Gav about having to report to the White House in the morning. He wasn't as shocked by the notion of donning disguises as I'd been. "You've seen how life is there. Photographers hound the First Family, capturing every expression they make. Waiting for them to make a mistake so they can exploit it for personal gain." He huffed. "Put a photo up on the Internet and it becomes instant fodder for interpretation. You've seen the one with President Hyden not saluting when the two army officers flanking him are?"

I hadn't. "There must be some mistake. Or a good reason he wasn't saluting."

"Curtain number two. Turns out the photo was snapped as the Marine Band played 'Hail to the Chief.' Presidents don't generally salute themselves at that point." Anger made his sarcasm all the more pointed. "And yet this photo went viral with captions purportedly proving that President Hyden isn't patriotic. It's all about spin."

"You didn't vote for President Hyden, did you?"

"No," he said, glancing my way again, "but truth is truth. If you have a gripe against a man, fair enough. Don't make garbage up."

"Well said."

We drove awhile longer, chatting more about Yablonski—who I would probably never feel comfortable calling Joe—and our conversation eventually turned to Pluto. I pulled up all the copies Gav had made, along with my notes. "I'd like to visit this company," I said.

"What would you hope to accomplish?"

"I don't know."

"Walking in and announcing that your father used to work there and was accused of corporate espionage may not garner you the warmest of welcomes."

That earned him a laugh. I looked out the window at the landscape speeding by. I glanced down at the company's address and read it aloud.

"Any idea where we'd find Planetary Parkway?" he asked as I looked the information up on my phone. "Beside the fact that it's in Fairfax?"

"Isn't Pluto being studied again? I'm talking about the heavenly body, now. Aren't they trying to have it reinstated as a planet?"

"Could be," he said, "I don't keep up on that as well as I should."

The website loaded that moment. "Got it," I said. "It's not far off 66."

"Want to take a detour?"

"You know I do."

Less than thirty minutes later, we arrived at Pluto, Incorporated. An uninspired U-shaped building, it tried its best to stand out among its look-alike neighbors, but even the lush evergreens and multi-colored annuals softening its foundation did little to differentiate it from the surrounding rows of blandness.

The company parking lot sat inside the U, the building's wings acting like arms enveloping employees' and visitors' vehicles. "Probably nice in the winter," I said. "I bet there's not a lot of wind." Gav looked at me and I shrugged. "Making conversation, that's all."

"Why? Are you nervous?"

I didn't answer. "Let's drive past the front door."

Other than having a spacious modern reception area of

white and chrome with sage modular furniture, there wasn't much to be deduced.

"Well?" he asked when we'd pulled out of the lot.

"I have a feeling that I'd understand more if I could get in there."

"How do you intend to do that?"

"Drive around again," I said. "Let's stop."

Gav's face registered surprise. "What do you plan to say when you get in there?"

"I don't know," I said. "I'll come up with something."

CHAPTER 10

"WELCOME TO PLUTO, INCORPORATED," THE young girl behind the glass-and-chrome desk said as we walked in. She had a slim build and a full moon–shaped face. Her dark hair, worn tightly pulled back, only emphasized the extreme roundness of her head. Crater-deep eyes took us both in with polite curiosity. "May I help you?"

I made quick introductions, smiling and keeping my eyes wide, my manner unthreatening. There was no reason to behave otherwise, but if I wanted to meet and talk with anyone at this company, I'd have to play extra nice. "My dad worked here," I said, "a very long time ago. We were in the neighborhood." I sent a doe-eyed look toward Gav. "We thought we'd stop by to see if the company was still around."

"Sure," she said. "Your dad worked here? When?"

I told her.

Her eyes widened. "That's before my time," she said.

"Before I was born, in fact." I could see questions forming in her eyes. "And you wanted to visit, why?"

"My dad died when I was very little," I said. "This was the last place he worked." I shrugged, maintaining my innocent demeanor. "It's probably silly for me to even stop by here, I mean, what are the chances that anyone would remember him?"

"Not silly at all," she said, her manner changing instantly. Solicitous now, she said, "I'm sorry to hear your dad died so young. What department was he in, do you know?"

"Management information systems," I said. "What we'd call the IT department now. According to my mom, he was a vice president."

Oh, I deserved an award for my acting. Gav looked like he was having a tough time keeping a straight face.

I wasn't sure where to take this next, but the girl spared me by asking, "You mentioned your dad was one of the executives?"

"That's what I understand."

"Maybe Mr. Benson remembers him."

"Craig Benson?" I asked.

"He's here today. That's unusual in itself because Kyle runs the place day to day now. But what a wonderful coincidence isn't it? I'm sure he'd love to meet you. He's such a nice man." She picked up the receiver before I could respond. "Mr. Benson?" She smiled up at me as he answered. "I have a woman at the front desk whose father used to work here a long time ago. She says she'd love to meet you." She was still smiling as she hung up. To us, she said, "Why don't you have a seat? Mr. Benson said he'd be delighted to come out and say hello." Her round head swayed like a bobbing balloon. "He's such a nice man."

Was she trying to convince me?

Gav and I glanced at the two sage sofas, which faced each other across a glass-and-chrome coffee table offering industry magazines for our reading pleasure. We exchanged a look, silently agreeing that we'd both prefer to remain standing. "Have you worked here very long?" I asked the young woman.

"I started in May right after graduation," she said with a self-conscious shrug. "I majored in economics, but this is the only job I could find." She blinked, as if hearing how that came out. "Not that I'm complaining. They've been very good to me here."

"I'm glad," I said.

Gav took over the idle conversation while we waited, asking her where she went to school. I was grateful to be able to take a backseat because my mind was leaping like a startled gazelle. This unexpected opportunity to meet Craig Benson—a man who had known my dad very well—could be an enormous boon if I only knew what to ask or how to approach him. This could be such a coup. I didn't want to blow it.

"What do you do for a living?" the girl asked Gav.

Smoothly, he answered, "I'm in insurance."

Her pale brows rose, but he didn't elaborate.

"Can you see yourself making a career here?" he asked, and I went back to pretending to listen.

I didn't have long. In the distance a door closed with a solid *clunk,* echoing in the sterile lobby and halting all conversation. A moment later, an older gentleman came into view. The girl at the desk looked very proud of herself as she said, "There he is."

I crossed the distance between us, extending my hand. "Mr. Benson," I said. "Thank you for taking time out to meet with me."

In an instant, I knew I wouldn't have the same concerns I'd had with Eugene Vaughn. Though the two were close in age, my father's elderly friend was in poor health and seemed to rely on a brain that slipped away whenever he tried too hard to clutch at a memory. Craig Benson carried himself with confidence. In his double-breasted navy blue suit and shiny wing tips, he gave the impression of being a lot taller than he was. I put him at about five foot eight. With a narrow band of graying hair encircling his otherwise bald pate and eyes that were rimmed dark from worry or lack of sleep, he wore a well-fed look of money. He reminded me of Uncle Fester from the old *Addams Family* reruns I used to watch as a kid, except better dressed.

"Erica didn't give me your name," he said as we shook hands. He glanced over my shoulder, spotting Gav. I watched curiosity take hold; Benson spent an extra few seconds assessing him.

"My name is Olivia," I said, "my dad worked here a long time ago. Maybe you remember him?" I waited a beat for Benson to give me his undivided attention. "Anthony Paras?"

Instant recognition jerked his head ever so slightly. "Tony?" He gave Gav another quick glance, as though looking for answers there. It took Benson less than a heartbeat to collect himself, but he did so admirably. "Oh, my," he said, bringing a hand to his mouth. "Oh, my."

Out of the corner of my eye, I noticed Erica's panicked reaction. I'm sure she was worried that she'd committed some egregious error by putting the boss in an uncomfortable spot. Her concerns were laid to rest almost immediately, however, when Benson continued. "It's been so long," he said. "You were just a little thing." He stepped sideways and extended an arm. "Come back to my office. Let's talk."

We started back the way he'd come, but Benson stopped Gav before we'd gone very far. "I fear I've been rude," he said, extending his hand. "I'm Craig Benson. And you are?"

Gav shook the man's hand. "Len Gavin," he said. "I'm with Olivia."

"I see," Benson said, leading us through a back corridor to a silver door. Pulling it open, he said, "This way."

In here, the décor changed. Sleek gray-blue walls with framed black-and-white photographs of Washington, D.C., landmarks lined a long corridor that ended in a T.

"Beautiful," I murmured, taking it all in. An effulgent urn of fresh flowers sat atop an antique table under a brilliant spotlight, looking out of place yet exactly right in this modern design.

"We had a professional redecorate our space about two years ago," Benson said. "My son's idea." From the askance look, I got the impression Daddy wasn't impressed. "It shows well enough."

We took a left at the T and passed through a door, where Benson welcomed us into his private office. His mouth twisted up and his eyes crinkled. "You can tell I didn't allow the decorator in here."

This office probably hadn't changed since my dad had worked here. The carpet was navy blue with gold braid running a narrow crisscross pattern throughout. The walls were cream colored, the furniture oak, most of it antique with the exception of a massive mahogany desk that took up almost 10 percent of the room. Every wall except one was covered with photographs of Craig Benson, glad-handing other men. There were a few notable politicians represented and even a celebrity or two, but most of the pictures were of people I didn't recognize. One wall had a door carved into it. I wondered if it led to an executive washroom, or to the office that sat to the right of the T.

An American flag stood in one corner next to the windows, a flag for a foreign country in the other. Between them was a second desk, antique oak, this one with at least a dozen framed family photographs atop it. As Benson invited us to sit, he noticed me looking at the flag. "My parents were born in Cabriga. I promised to never forget my roots, so I keep the flag here to remind me every day."

"I'm sure they'd be very proud."

"I'd like to think so." He settled himself. "Now, what can I do for you, Ms. Paras? May I call you Olivia?"

"I'd be delighted if you would."

He waited while I took a deep breath. "I know my visit

here comes as a surprise, but Gav and I were back visiting my mom last week—"

"Your mother!" he said, bringing a hand to his forehead. "Of course. How is she?"

"She's doing well," I said, shifting in my seat.

He laced his fingers across his chest. "And you? Do you live here in D.C.?"

"As a matter of fact, I do."

I was about to bring the conversation back to my dad when he said, "Indulge an old man. Tell me a little about yourself. I remember how proud your father was of you. What do you do for a living?" A smile, this time for Gav. "You seem to be well settled."

His questions were throwing me off my trajectory.

"I'm a chef," I said, hesitating before adding, "at the White House."

His eyebrows jumped, then furrowed. "Oh," he said, peering at me with greater intensity. "I never put that together. Forgive me. You're the executive chef, aren't you? Your photos in the newspaper and on TV don't do you justice." He shook his head in disbelief. "You certainly take after your father. I should have realized." As if suddenly remembering his manners, he added, "Congratulations on your prestigious position. I'm sure it took a great deal of hard work and no small measure of talent for you to reach such heights."

"Thank you."

He eyed Gav. "So is your friend here with you socially, or is he your armed escort?"

"Socially." This conversation was not going the way I'd hoped. I veered back. "Until last week, my mom hadn't told me much about my dad's time here at Pluto, nor about the circumstances of his death."

"Ah," Benson said, closing his eyes for a moment, "I understand now."

"Do you?" This had been one of my more impulsive

decisions. "I'm not sure I understand why I felt the need to come."

He leaned forward, elbows on the glass-topped desk, all attention focused on me. Up close, the bulging circles around his eyes were fat bags of purple. I wondered if they hurt when he blinked. "Of course," he said gently. "You're looking for closure. Completely understandable."

"I'd like to hear what you remember about that time," I said, "if you don't mind."

He glanced at Gav, whose face showed no emotion whatsoever.

"I can handle it," I said, bringing his attention back to me, "if that's what you're wondering."

"Yes, I imagine you can." He sat back, laced his fingers, and dropped his hands to his lap. "I'm aware of your involvement in national affairs. You've had some close calls."

I bit the insides of my mouth. "I'm not here to talk about myself," I said softly.

He studied me, eyelids low. "I take it your mother told you about what we uncovered after your father's death?"

"If you mean evidence that he was selling secrets to a rival, yes."

"Then," he said, raising his hands in supplication, "there isn't much I can add that you don't already know."

"I don't know who killed him," I said. "I'd like to know that."

"You're very direct," he said. "Your mother must have told you that the case was never solved. I make it a point to contact the police every year to find out if there have been any leads." He spread his hands out over the desk. "There never are, but I call nonetheless, so that no one forgets."

"That's extremely thoughtful of you," I said, "considering you believe he was stealing company secrets."

Benson leaned back again, coolly studying me. "Why do I get the impression that this isn't just a friendly visit after all?"

I could have bitten my tongue. "I'm sorry. I have a tendency to question things I don't understand."

"You and I share that trait, then." To Gav, he said, "You're very quiet."

Gav's voice was low. "This is Olivia's story. I'm here in a supportive role."

"All right, young lady." Benson leaned forward again. "I'll give you what you want. To be perfectly frank, I appreciate your no-nonsense approach. No sense dancing around a subject unnecessarily. Yes, I do call to see if there has been a break in your dad's murder case. Every year. You're right: It isn't just because I'm a nice guy, though I believe I am. I'm also a shrewd businessman. Anyone will tell you that. Of course, I want your father's killer apprehended, but I also want to set my own mind at ease. I want to know for certain that this was a robbery gone bad and not something more malicious."

I felt myself grow warm with anticipation. "So you think it's possible he was killed by someone he knew."

"Don't put words in my mouth," he said. "I'm telling you that I don't care for loose threads. An unsolved murder would qualify as one of the loosest, wouldn't you agree?"

"Who might have wanted my dad dead?" I asked. "I mean, among the people who worked with him here?"

He pointed upward with both index fingers. "If I believed for a moment that anyone on my payroll was guilty of such a monstrous crime, I would deal with that individual quickly and incisively."

"Even though you believed my dad betrayed you and Pluto by selling secrets to a rival firm?"

"Yes, even though."

"And by dealing with that individual, do you mean turning him in to the authorities?"

He hesitated for a fraction of a second, tilting his head as he regarded me. "What are you getting at?"

"Nothing at all," I said. Time for damage control. "Mr.

Benson, that all came out wrong. You can understand, I'm sure, my need to find out all I can about my father's death. Like you said earlier, I'm looking for closure."

His gaze softened. "We here at Pluto were devastated when your father was murdered. We offered a reward for information leading to the arrest of the killer. Please appreciate how hard it is for me to speak so frankly. You're his daughter, you deserve the truth, but we're talking about a dark time in Pluto's history."

"You truly believe my father was guilty?"

Benson smiled sadly. "I understand you want to believe otherwise, I truly do. I dearly wanted to as well."

"But—"

He gritted his teeth, speaking slowly, "I wish to heaven your father had not been killed. There's nothing that can be done about that now. It's best you leave the past behind and continue to live your own life, looking forward."

The look on his face, the finality in his tone told me that Benson had nothing more to share. Not willingly, at least. I stood and said, "Thank you," because politeness came naturally to me. "We appreciate your time."

"I'm sorry," he said. "You must understand that."

I didn't.

Back in the car, I stared out the window as we pulled away. "Well, that was depressing," I said.

Gav squeezed my arm.

CHAPTER 11

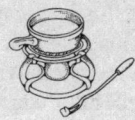

"FOR SOMEONE WHO'S SUPPOSED TO BE ON vacation, you sure spend a lot of time at work," Cyan said when I showed up in the White House kitchen the next morning. She had a pile of fresh basil leaves next to her and was in the process of seeding tomatoes.

"What can I say? I miss you guys. What are you making?"

"That goat cheese and mushroom bruschetta we've been wanting to try. Except I'm substituting fresh basil for the dried and I'm seeding the Romas first."

Bucky turned from his perch in front of the computer to greet me. "You missed out working on breakfast," he said with a glance at the clock. "Lunch is under way and we've got it covered. Don't tell me you're just here for a social call?"

Leaning against the stainless steel counter in the room's center, Virgil raised his attention from the notes he was writing to balefully follow the conversation with his eyes. "No," he said drily. "She's here for another session with Josh." Directing his focus to me, he asked, "Am I right?"

"Sort of," I said. After learning the hard way that Virgil had a tendency to blab, I didn't think it a good idea to mention that Josh and I planned to attend the next day's Food Expo together. "I have an appointment with Doug first," I said.

Cyan smirked and Bucky turned back to the computer with a shake of his head. Lucky for me, Virgil didn't notice. He kept his attention in his notes but addressed me. "I know you think that the more you get in with the Hydens the more likely you'll get me fired, but I warn you, it won't work."

Virgil was a broken record where his relationship with the Hydens was concerned.

I was fed up with Virgil's oft-repeated laments. "I've told you before," I said, "we appreciate the fact that you've taken over the family's daily meals. With the number of official dinners this administration hosts, we're already stretched thin." I leaned across the counter to look him straight in the eye. "Sorry to disappoint you, buddy, but I value the efforts of everyone in this kitchen, you included. I am not about to try to get anybody fired."

He made a face and returned to his work.

Was it always to be this way, Virgil trying to outmaneuver me because he thought I was outmaneuvering him? This was not my idea of an ideal working relationship. "What time is your appointment with Doug?" Cyan asked, doing her best to lighten the mood.

"In about five minutes."

"Sounds intriguing," she said with a mischievous grin.

"What does?" Peter Everett Sargeant strode into the kitchen, for once his question coming out inquisitive rather than intrusive.

I turned. "Good morning, Peter."

"You're here early, I see," he said, "good. Doug told me about your outing tomorrow with Josh."

Virgil looked up. Cyan and Bucky turned to face us. Oblivious, Sargeant continued. "I have to admit, I was surprised when he told me you'd be donning a disguise."

The center of attention now, I held out my hands. "I was a little surprised, too." Turning to my team, but focusing on Virgil, I added, "This is confidential. Do you understand? No one is to know that we're doing this."

"You're taking him to the Food Expo?" Virgil asked as though I hadn't said a word.

"You hadn't told them." Sargeant stated the obvious, looking chagrined. He pursed his lips as he addressed me. "You always tell your staff everything. How was I to know . . . ?"

"No worries, Peter," I said, staving off his denial of culpability. I was loath to jeopardize our fragile truce. To Virgil, I said, "Yes, Josh and I are going to the Food Expo." I was careful to repeat my warning, "But I expect you to keep that information confidential." To Sargeant, I asked, "Why did Doug tell you about Josh attending the Food Expo? That doesn't seem to fall within your purview."

"It doesn't," he admitted. "But the First Lady apparently requested my input. I confess to be mystified as to why, but one doesn't argue with the First Lady."

"True enough."

"Additionally," Sargeant continued in a more animated fashion than I was used to seeing from him, "it seems our interim chief usher believes you would welcome my presence." He affected a flabbergasted air, addressing the group as though performing for an audience. He splayed his hands against his chest. "Seriously?"

"Peter," I asked with a smile, "is that . . . humor?"

"Certainly not." He clasped his hands in front of his waist and adopted a more familiar, chastising tone. "Once again, Ms. Paras, you have drawn an erroneous conclusion."

"My mistake."

He narrowed his eyes at me, but there was no longer hostility there. "You should strive to be more careful."

Cyan watched our banter with a look of utter disbelief. She'd been bugging me for weeks to explain what had happened to soften the lines of war between Sargeant and me. Although the encounter itself wasn't any big secret, I'd found it hard to put into words exactly what had transpired. All I'd been able to tell her was that once two people faced death together, animosity lost its appeal.

"Doug is upstairs right now, Ms. Paras." Sargeant tapped his watch. "Let's not keep him waiting. He doesn't possess the abundance of patience I do."

This time, I laughed out loud. "Let's go."

We walked upstairs to the Entrance Hall and made our way to Doug's office. The chief usher was looking harried as usual. "There you are," he said with relief as though he'd been searching all over for us. I allowed myself a surreptitious glance at my watch. A minute before eleven. We weren't even late.

"Good morning," I said, gently reminding him not to forgo niceties. Placing my hands up near my face, I added, "I'm ready for makeup."

He didn't smile.

"You okay, Doug?" I asked.

Sargeant nudged me with his elbow but I couldn't interpret what he expected me to glean from it.

"The kids are home," Doug said. "Both of them meet with tutors daily to keep their studies up, but Abby's turned into a real teenager." Doug's derision couldn't be missed.

"I've interacted with Abby quite a bit over the past few weeks," I said. "She's as delightful as ever."

"Except for the fact that she doesn't want Josh hanging around her."

"I'm missing your point."

Sargeant took a step back, as though to distance himself

from the conversation. Oblivious, Doug's voice rose. "All of a sudden she's too busy for him. She has her friends over all the time. Either that or she's out at her friends' houses."

"These things happen between siblings," I said, shocked that he'd be talking about one of the First Family in this manner. "Now that it's summer and they both have more free time, it's natural that Abby branches out."

"Well, guess whose problem it becomes? Every day, Josh is stuck here by himself, asking me when he can go visit his dad. Do you have any idea how difficult it is to tell one of the president's kids that his dad is too busy? Every single day?"

I didn't have answers for Doug. Moreover, it was obvious he didn't want any. He wanted to vent.

Changing the subject, I asked, "Where am I meeting this consultant?"

"She's set up in the Solarium."

I couldn't contain my disbelief. "The Solarium?" I'd expected to be shuttled off to a little-used office in the East Wing. The sunroom on the third floor of the family residence was, and had been, a refuge for many of the First Families who'd occupied the White House. "Are you sure?"

Doug sent me a withering glance. Standing next to me, Sargeant continued to study a painting on Doug's office wall. "Yes, I'm sure," Doug said. "Did you always question every directive Paul gave you like you do with me?"

I took a breath before answering. "Sorry, that was just surprise speaking."

Doug glanced at one of the three digital clocks on his desk set to different time zones, and continued in a more controlled tone. "I didn't know where she planned to set up until a few minutes ago myself," he said. "You'd both better get up there, pronto. I promised you'd be in her chair by 11:15."

I didn't bother to ask who "she" was; I'd find out soon enough. One more question could very well send Doug over the edge.

Sargeant and I started up the stairs. When we were out of earshot, he leaned toward me and whispered, "The chief usher position does not agree with that young man."

"You know it."

We trekked up to the third floor, keeping an even pace. Sargeant, not one to make small talk, surprised me by asking, "Aren't you supposed to be on vacation this week?"

"You know how it is," I said. "When the White House calls, you come in."

He nodded. "How is your young man?"

"I . . ." Speechless, I coughed, trying to figure out an appropriate response. "Agent MacKenzie and I haven't been a couple in a very long t—"

"I'm not talking about Agent MacKenzie," Sargeant said smoothly.

I stopped at the landing. "Then who?"

He met my gaze now, one eyebrow arched. "Don't forget, Olivia, I *am* the sensitivity director," taking me aback with the use of my first name. "With everything that happened here a few weeks ago, your affections toward"—He glanced up and down the empty stairwell to ensure we were alone—"toward a certain Special Agent in Charge were not missed."

He started up the stairs again, but I caught him by the arm. "Wait."

Lifting my hand with two fingers, he removed it from his sleeve. "My, my. Did I inadvertently hit a nerve?"

The look in his eyes was unreadable. Sure, we'd forged a truce, but at this point I wasn't certain how permanent this state was. Humor and Sargeant weren't words that usually went together and even though I'd been certain he'd been teasing in the kitchen, now I wasn't sure how to react.

Gav and I were not ready to open our relationship to public scrutiny. Having Sargeant, of all people, in possession of such a secret was not good news. I didn't bother denying, however. Telling him he was wrong could only buy me trouble. "Who else knows?"

He didn't answer, but started up the stairs again. I followed. "Your secret is safe with me," he said.

"Is it?"

He faced me, again with that unreadable expression. "Does my awareness of this relationship make you nervous?"

"Truthfully? A little."

We reached the top floor and took a left, making our way across the central hall toward the Solarium. "I could get used to this."

Again I grabbed his sleeve, stopping him. "To what?"

"Making you nervous for a change."

"When have I ever made you nervous?" I asked.

"Let's go," he said, heading up the narrow corridor ramp into the Solarium. "They're waiting."

Frustrated, I frowned at his retreating back and then hurried to catch up.

"Ollie." Josh rushed up as Sargeant and I walked in. "Isn't this great? We get to wear real costumes. You should see all the noses we can pick." His face lit up with nine-year-old humor. "Get it? Picking noses?"

I laughed. "Good one."

He grabbed my hand and pulled me forward into the aptly named rooftop room. First Lady Grace Coolidge had called it the "Sky Parlor" because of its expansive view. The Truman reconstruction had brought bigger windows, providing the sunny, spacious area for First Families to relax in.

Four people watched us as we entered and I did my best to avoid looking ill at ease. Mrs. Hyden sat on a low-slung flowered sofa, her legs crossed, back to the gorgeous southern view. Three tall director's chairs sat empty in the room's center, as though waiting for *Dating Game* contestants.

As Josh pulled me toward the small group gathered there, I said "Good morning," to Mrs. Hyden and then turned to the others. They stood in a small cluster just behind the director's chairs, surrounding a high-top table on which sat what looked like a fishing tackle box filled with pots, jars, pens, and brushes.

"Hi, I'm Ollie," I said to the strangers. Two were in their mid-twenties, one female, one male. They both were dressed head to toe in black and both had dark hair and pale skin. I wondered briefly if they were brother and sister. The third of their group was a much older woman who regarded us with friendly curiosity. "This is Peter Everett Sargeant," I continued, holding a hand out toward my companion.

"Lovely to meet you both," the woman said.

Strikingly tall, she was in her mid-sixties wearing head-to-toe black as well. The monotony of her ensemble was broken up, however, by the flowing swoop of the over-sized purple, pink, and turquoise shawl that covered most of her torso. Small-boned despite her ample height, she wore her smile lines with powerful pride. All I could think as she introduced herself was that I hoped I'd look that good when I was her age.

She came forward with a graceful economy of movement, grasping my hand with both of her warm ones. "My name is Thora." She favored Sargeant with a delighted laugh as she greeted him. "So nice to meet you too, Peter."

He blushed. "Very nice to meet you, Ms. Thora."

She let go of his hand and turned, her shawl picking up the movement and billowing out capelike around her. "Oh my dear, please. None of that artificial 'Ms.' business. I'm Thora. And these two lovely young people are my assistants, Zoe and Adam."

Neither of them proffered a hand, but both glanced up long enough to make eye contact and nod a greeting. Josh practically danced with impatience. "They came from a real disguise company," he said. "We even get costumes."

Mrs. Hyden's amused look was unmistakable. "Remember, these aren't superhero costumes, Josh. Our goal is to make you blend in, not stand out."

"But—"

"Josh." She said it firmly, gently—enough to make his shoulders slump.

Thora ran an arm around the little boy's back. "That doesn't mean we aren't going to have fun, though," she said.

Josh looked unconvinced.

Sargeant took a few steps toward the door. "I will leave you to your business," he said. "Good day."

"Oh, no, you don't," Thora announced, pulling away from Josh and striding toward a bewildered Sargeant. At least a foot taller than our sensitivity director, she nonetheless tucked a hand into the crook of his elbow and urged him back into the group. "Even though you're not often recognized outside the White House, I have plans for you as well."

Sargeant looked at me. I shrugged.

Mrs. Hyden spoke up. "I would like you to accompany Josh and Ms. Paras to the convention, Mr. Sargeant."

The room fell silent. Sargeant stammered, "I don't understand."

Sargeant's discomfort was obvious to the rest of us, but the First Lady continued as though unaware. "I've come to understand that I may have been mistaken about you, originally," she said, referring oh-so-delicately to recent events. Fortunately for Sargeant, we had been able to discover another staff member's underhanded agenda before our sensitivity director lost his job. "I would like to give you a chance to expand your horizons a bit. To increase your level of responsibility. Let's see how this goes."

Sargeant's chin came up. He straightened to his full height. "Yes, ma'am," he said.

"Additionally," she added, "my husband is eager to expose Josh to all levels of diplomacy. This seems like a good opportunity to have him watch you both in action."

She didn't add that the president's wishes stemmed from his desire to diminish his son's interest in cooking, but I knew that had to be what was powering this new wrinkle.

"You and Ms. Paras proved to be a formidable team on

your first joint assignment," the First Lady continued. "It would be silly not to put you both together again."

Was she kidding? Judging from her serene smile, apparently not.

Mrs. Hyden must have misread our expressions because she hastened to add, "Don't worry, I wouldn't allow Josh to accompany you if I believed there was any danger. The Secret Service will be with you the entire time."

"I'm sure we'll be safe," I said. Then, remembering our conversation in the kitchen, I decided to voice a concern. "That is, unless Virgil says something to the press. You know he's been less than tight-lipped in the past."

Her brows came together. "He knows Josh is going with you?"

"He does," I said, omitting the fact that it was Sargeant who had spilled the beans.

"I will talk with him."

"Thank you."

"Enough chatter," Thora said, clapping her hands. The two young people watched her, bright-eyed and ready to move. "Today we plan. Tomorrow we execute!" She thrust me into the center chair, Sargeant into the one to my left, while Josh scrambled up into the one on my right. "And now, we begin!"

TWO HOURS LATER, MUCH TO JOSH'S DISMAY, we hadn't picked any noses. We hadn't picked any ears, or eyebrows, either. Nevertheless, that didn't mean we hadn't been transformed.

Awestruck by our changed appearances, I looked at Josh for the dozenth time and couldn't help repeating myself. "I would never recognize you."

He ran over to a full-length mirror at the end of the room. His mother stood behind him. "Unbelievable," she said.

Josh grinned at his reflection. "This is cool!"

The little boy didn't look at all like himself. Of the three of us, his makeover was the most drastic. Thora and her team had provided an undergarment that added about twenty pounds to the boy's slim frame. They'd also brought along baggy pants and a green-and-white-horizontal-striped T-shirt to cover this new body. They didn't add any prosthetics to his face, but they did use makeup in a way that truly gave him a pudgy look. I was amazed. A pair of scuffed gym shoes, a baseball cap featuring the Washington Redskins logo, and a pair of dark-rimmed glasses completed his ensemble.

I couldn't help from exclaiming, "You look like a completely different kid!"

He was laughing, but took time to point at me. "You don't look like yourself, either."

"I must agree with the young man," Sargeant said, shaking his head. "Ms. Paras, your metamorphosis is astounding." He held his hands out. "As for myself, I do not care at all for this hat."

Sargeant wore a baseball cap that matched Josh's except for the fact that Sargeant's was newer and cleaner. Josh's rim was more curved, more frayed. Like a boy's cap might be.

"It looks good on you," I said.

He wasn't amused. "This is a foolish addition." He turned to Thora. "What good is a hat when I'm required to remove it whenever I'm indoors?" he asked. "The moment we step inside the convention, I'll take it off."

"You'll leave it on," Thora said.

"That's a severe etiquette breach."

Thora patted him on the shoulder. "There are exceptions for public places. We'll decide that this is one of those public places, shall we? Security seems to be a fair reason to make an exception in this case."

"I don't like it."

Thora watched him with an amused look on her face.

"Do you like the mustache?" she asked, effectively changing the subject.

He picked up one of the handheld mirrors and studied himself. "It's trim, at least," he said. Thora had darkened and thickened Sargeant's eyebrows and had given him a five o'clock shadow.

"It would be better if you grow one naturally," she said, "but we don't have time for that. I'll ask you not to shave tomorrow morning."

"Not shave?" he gasped.

She squinted, ignoring his apoplectic response. Tapping a thoughtful finger against her lips, she tilted her head. "Do you usually shave at night, too?"

By his horrified and aghast expression, you would have thought she'd asked the sensitivity director about his choice of underwear. "My heavens, woman," he began.

"You appear to have a heavy beard. I'd prefer you not shave tonight or tomorrow, yes? And be sure to wear the clothing we picked out. I'd prefer you try it on now, but since you insist otherwise, I'll bow to your wishes. Tomorrow, however," she wiggled her fingers toward the outfit hanging over the back of Sargeant's chair, "it's dress-up time." Without waiting for him to respond, she turned to me. "He's so cute, isn't he?"

It took me a moment to realize she was talking about Sargeant and not about Josh, who was preening in the mirror.

"Cute," I repeated with a wide grin. "Yes, most definitely cute."

Sargeant gurgled and turned away.

"What about you?" Thora asked. "What do you think?"

Josh piped up before I could answer. "You look like a schoolteacher."

"I don't know about this," I said. Josh moved out of the way so that I could get a full-length look at myself. I held a hand against my mouth and spoke hesitantly through my fingers. "I've never been blonde before. I don't usually wear clothing like this."

Thora had outfitted me with a shoulder-length blonde wig that looked surprisingly natural. I fingered the wavy tresses like they were some sort of alien thing. Not me. Not me at all.

"You'll get used to it," Thora said with a confident lilt. "I daresay Josh is right. But I think you look more like Reese Witherspoon *playing* a teacher."

Mrs. Hyden, who had been quiet through this discussion, chimed in, "No, I think more like Julie Bowen from TV."

"But with glasses," Mrs. Hyden and Thora said together.

I didn't see myself as either of the actresses they mentioned. I did, however, see the schoolteacher look. I had to admit, I was able to empathize with Sargeant on this one and understood his discomposure. Every day we look in mirrors and see ourselves exactly as we expect. Today the three of us saw new people gaping back at us. Josh thought it was funny, but to me it just felt weird.

The outfit Thora had chosen for me—I'd learned during the process that she'd been given size information for all of us ahead of time—was as different from my personal style as I could get. "I don't understand," I said, "if we're traveling together—Josh, Peter, and I—shouldn't we all be dressed similarly?" I grabbed at the side of the pink V-necked dress she'd picked out for me. There was very little give because the dress was so form-fitting. The sleeveless print fabric ended above my knees, showing a great deal of leg over the matching heels.

I was glad I hadn't eaten lunch yet. One more ounce of fat on me and I risked bursting through the seams. "This is dressy and they're so casual."

I took another look in the mirror. The pink outfit, long blonde hair, and strappy heels really did make me look like Reese Witherspoon from *Legally Blonde*. But only if you didn't look too closely. She was much prettier.

Thora was unfazed by my complaint. "We're staging Peter as your father, Josh as your son."

"What?" Sargeant exclaimed. "I'm not old enough . . ."

Thora slid an arm around him, cutting him off. "No, dear, of course you're not." She winked at me. "We're all just playacting."

I went to rub my eyes, forgetting about the glasses until my knuckle hit frame. I took a look at those now, too. Stylish and oversized, they pegged me as a person who took great pains with her appearance before walking out the door every day. So not me. "Playacting," I repeated.

I wished I'd never mentioned the Food Expo to Mrs. Hyden.

CHAPTER 12

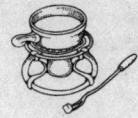

"YOU READY FOR THIS?" GAV ASKED LATER THAT afternoon.

"As I'll ever be."

We sat in Gav's car outside Harold Linka's home, planning our strategy for questioning the man. Linka lived about fifteen minutes from Pluto's headquarters in an upmarket subdivision that couldn't be more than twenty years old. "He may refuse to talk with us, you realize," he said.

"I know. We still have Michael Fitch on our list, too." I tapped the pages in front of me. "Doesn't it feel as though all we're doing lately is talking to people?" I ticked names off my upraised fingers. "I talked with Eugene Vaughn. Then it was you and I visiting Joe Yablonski. Now this guy." I sighed. "There's very little forward motion here. Are we just spinning our wheels?"

Gav chuckled.

"What's so funny?"

"You," he said. "Think about it. Ever since I've known you—wait, since *before* I've known you—you've been involved in uncovering conspiracies, or finding bombs, or solving murders."

I started to protest that I hadn't intended to get involved in any of those, but he kept going.

"This is the first time you're actively investigating a crime on your own. It's not just *any* murder this time, it's the murder of your dad. You want answers because this time it's personal. You're also investigating his dishonorable discharge, which you believe was either erroneously imparted or purposely done to harm his reputation. Have I missed anything so far?"

I didn't answer. I didn't have to.

"In the past, you've been targeted by international terrorists, bad guys with bombs, and assassins eager to shut you up. Through it all, you've been preparing state dinners for the leader of the free world." He paused. "Still with me?"

I nodded.

"Talk to almost any law enforcement professional and you'll hear the same story. A cop might never fire his or her gun in an emergency situation over an entire career. Secret Service agents spend all their time preparing so that there is no need for gunfire, so that threats are diminished before they ever unfold. Investigations involve a lot of legwork and require even more patience. What you've experienced thus far—the excitement, the fear, the terror—is an aberration."

"Aberration. You've used that word before as it relates to me."

He smiled but didn't comment. "This"—he pointed to Harold Linka's house—"is what investigations are really like. Tracking down leads, not knowing when something will pop. Staying with a thread until the story unravels and begins to make sense. I sense your impatience and, to be frank, I understand it. You're used to a speedier time line."

"You make it sound as though I'm complaining that life has settled down and become more normal."

"Let's take this one step at a time," he said. "We're moving slowly but methodically. Remember, all this happened more than twenty-five years ago. I'd say we're making strong headway."

"You really think so?"

"I do."

I'd written pages of notes, all of which I intended to leave in the car. I wanted to take a pen and paper with me, but the last thing we wanted was to make Linka nervous. Then we'd be shut out for sure. "I have to hope our friend Harold is eager to relive his early years at Pluto with us. People like to reminisce, don't they?"

Gav gave me a look filled with skepticism. "It's not like you're here to provide him an opportunity to share his glory days. You're looking for a clue as to who killed your father."

"I know."

"The fact that you're showing up at his door makes your motive transparent."

"I need to trace down every single lead," I said. "Even if nothing leads anywhere. Even if I wind up knowing no more than I do right now, I need to at least try to find answers." I heaved a sigh and looked up at the bright blue above. It wouldn't be dark for a few more hours. "Once I believe, and I mean truly believe, that I've done my best, only then will I be able to let this drop."

"Will you really?" he asked.

I rubbed my eyes. "I won't have much choice."

"No," he said. "You won't." With a glance at the townhome's front door, he added, "Let's go."

He started to open his door, but I grasped his arm. "Wait."

He turned, piercing me with his gaze. "You aren't getting cold feet. I know you better than that."

"I wanted to say thank you. For all your help, for all your

support," I said, emotion making my words come out choppy and rough. "Knowing you're with me through this makes all the difference."

At once, the look in his eyes softened. "For you? Anything."

We were halfway up the walk to Linka's front door, taking the short flight of stairs instead of the wheelchair ramp. "He's expecting us, right?"

Gav nodded. "I told him we were coming to talk about his work at Pluto."

"But you weren't specific?"

Gav reached forward and rang the doorbell. We heard the muffled chimes through the door. "He tried to push back a little, but I kept it vague. Danced around a bit."

"I guess that's—"

The front door opened. A woman in her late fifties smiled at us. Attractive, wearing yoga pants and a pink tank top, she had her blonde hair pulled back into a tight chignon. "You must be Leonard Gavin," she said smoothly. She glanced at me as though expecting Gav to make introductions. He remained silent. "I'm Harry's wife, Kate. Come right in. He's expecting you."

Politeness dictated that she lead us through the single-level home, but we could have easily found our way. The open, contemporary space had few walls and featured plenty of wide pathways. The walls were pastel, the lines clean. We took in the living room, dining room, and kitchen area all at once. Barrierless, this was an ideal home for a person in a wheelchair. Across the expansive teak floor, past a hallway that led to the more private areas of the home, Harold Linka sat in the family room, watching our approach.

Even though he was seated, you could tell he was a tall man, blonde like his wife, with a full head of hair despite his advanced age. He had his back to French doors that overlooked the couple's small yard where colorful petunias burst from flower boxes around a tiny patio.

A fluffy white dog lay across the man's lap. "Good afternoon," Linka said. For a man who had spent the last quarter-century in a wheelchair, he had a surprisingly strong voice. "I rarely get visits from strangers these days. Your phone call gave me pause."

He stared up at us with a bright, shrewd expression. Gav stepped forward and shook the man's hand, saying, "Thank you for agreeing to meet with us."

I nodded hello and stepped forward to shake hands, too.

Harold Linka's brows came together and he gripped my hand, hard. "You have me at a disadvantage," he said. Before I could respond, he said, "Mr. Gavin, you haven't introduced your lovely companion. Is this your wife?"

"Not yet, sir."

Not yet? My head snapped to face Gav.

He gave a little smile and shrug. "Allow me to present Olivia Paras."

Linka gripped tighter. "Olivia Paras?"

"Yes," I said.

He didn't let go. Glancing toward Gav, he narrowed his eyes. "You're not here to interview me for an article, are you?"

Gav took in a breath. "I never said I was."

"Hmm," Harold said. "No, you didn't. I inferred that. But you let me." Turning his attention back to me, he finally let go of my hand. "Let me look at you, child. You're Anthony's little girl, aren't you?"

It took me a moment to find my voice. "I am."

His wife had been standing behind us. "Who's that, Harry?"

"A friend of mine. From a long time ago." He waved a hand toward the front of the house. "You've got your class tonight, dear. Now that you see for yourself that these two young people don't intend to do me any harm, you can be on your way."

She had her arms folded across her chest. "Trying to get rid of me?"

He smiled up at her. "Yes. Now go. I'll fill you in later."

She gave us a smile, said, "It was nice meeting you," picked up her purse, and left.

"Sit," Harold said, waving a long finger toward a pale orange sofa. As we complied, he began stroking the dog's fur.

"Olivia Paras," he said again. "Your father used to talk about you all the time."

I was overcome with the desire to beg him to share everything my dad had ever said about me. I didn't know if it was like this for all children who'd ever lost a parent, but here I was, an adult who barely remembered her own father, meeting a man who'd known and worked with him. I wanted to crawl into Linka's brain, his heart, and examine every imprint my dad might have left there. I'd begged every story out of my mother countless times. But this man, unlike Eugene Vaughn with his ostensibly failing memory, might be able to give me more. I opened my mouth to ask him to please, please share everything he knew, but all I could manage to say was, "He did?"

"He was so proud of you." Harold's face creased into a smile. "I take it that's why you're here. You're not interested in Pluto; you're interested in what I can tell you about your father. Am I right?"

I was interested in both, but I nodded. "I'm glad you remember him."

"Tony? Of course." He settled more deeply into his chair and studied me. "You look like him, you know. I didn't see it initially, but I do now."

Pleased that he'd relaxed, I remained perched at the edge of the sofa. "What can you tell me about him, Mr. Linka?"

He waved a sturdy hand. "Call me Harry. Even though

I'm clearly old enough to be your father, that Mr. Linka stuff makes me feel old. Everybody calls me Harry."

"Harry," I said, smiling. "I can't tell you how great it is to meet someone who actually knew my dad." I shrugged. "Other than my mom, of course."

"Your dad talked about her all the time, too. Quite the family man, your father. How is your mother?"

My heart stirred, beating a little harder, a little warmer. Gav pressed a hand on my knee, and I understood its significance. We were here to investigate my dad's murder and his history with Pluto. As tempting as it was to get lost in stories of the past, I needed to maintain focus.

"She's doing great, actually." I'd been about to tell him about how my mom and nana lived in the same building in Chicago, but Gav's gentle reminder quieted my glibness.

Taking charge of the conversation's direction, I said, "I know you didn't expect us—me—here today, and that my friend Gav probably led you to believe we were curious about your work at Pluto before your accident." I waited for him to nod. He did, a quick flash of perceptiveness back in those bright eyes. "We do want to ask you a bit about that. After all, Pluto is how you knew my dad."

Harry stared down at the pooch in his lap, gently petting its small head with his giant hands. The dog's big brown eyes stared out at us from behind pristine white fur. With its tiny pink tongue clamped between its teeth, it looked more like a stuffed animal than a real one.

"Barney here is a Maltese," Harry said, apropos of nothing.

I wasn't sure where to go with that. "He's adorable."

Harry looked up again. "Your father talked about you and your mother, but I never met her. I can't imagine that she would have known me, and I certainly don't believe she would have been aware of my accident." I didn't have a chance to respond before he asked, "How is it that you know about it?"

Gav's grip on my knee tightened ever so slightly, but I resisted the urge to look at him. I decided to tell the truth. "We did our homework."

Harry blinked, watching me with eagle eyes. "And why, pray tell, did you feel the need to do so?"

I shifted in my seat. My intention had been to ask the questions, not answer them. Remembering that the best defense is a good offense, I feigned an abashed air. "You caught me. I'm nosy by nature. It's just who I am."

"An inherited trait, if I may be so bold," Harry said.

I wasn't sure if he was slamming my father or simply making an observation. Better to just plow forward to keep the lines of communication open. "My mother never told me how my dad died. Not until very recently, that is."

Harry's expression tensed ever so slightly.

I couldn't read him, so I went on, "I think she was trying to protect me from the truth. I mean, my dad was murdered in cold blood on an unfamiliar street in a neighborhood far from home."

"That's true."

"My mom said that weeks after my dad was buried, he was accused of being a corporate spy. That Pluto found evidence that he had been selling secrets to a rival firm. Pluto believed that the rival company was responsible for the killing."

As I spoke, Harry ceased petting the dog.

Now, in the heavy silence that followed my pronouncement, Barney looked up at his master, decided nothing good was forthcoming, and leaped to the floor, pattering into the kitchen where he noisily lapped up water.

Harry stared at me. "Craig Benson told your mother that?"

"Years ago, yes," I said. My pulse quickened, hoping his skeptical tone meant that he doubted the company's claims. I waited for him to shake his head in disbelief, dismissing the idea as ludicrous.

"I'm surprised," he said. "Craig generally keeps information like that quite close to his vest."

"It can't be true," I said.

Was that pity in Harry's eyes? Scorn? "Unfortunately, my dear, it is."

My knee-jerk reaction was to snap at his condescending tone, but I tamped down the rush of anger as much as I possibly could. "It can't be," I said again, this time less forcefully. I hated myself for the tendril of doubt that had crept up the back of my throat, wobbling my words.

Harry sighed. "I understand how you must feel, but I was there when they uncovered the betrayal. I'm sure your father never intended anyone to see what he'd gathered . . . I'm certain he planned to dispose of evidence that could be used against him, but, as we all know, he never got that chance."

"Who killed him?" I asked before I could stop myself. "You know who did it, don't you?"

He adjusted his shoulders. "I don't know for certain. I wasn't there."

"You're hedging," I said, so eager to press for answers that I didn't care how abrupt I sounded. "You may not have seen it happen, but you know."

I watched as he tried to work up a kindly smile. "This is very hard for you, I understand that," he said. "Especially since you've only recently found out about this terrible tragedy. You want the truth. It's your father we're talking about, so I will tell you as much as I know. But . . ." He paused long enough to run his tongue along the inside of his cheek. "I need to exact a promise from you first."

I sat up straighter. "From me?"

"You have a reputation, young woman," he began. "I've read your name in the newspapers and heard all about your exploits at the White House. While I applaud your verve and your energy, I feel it my duty to warn you, as a man who has lived long enough to learn a few hard lessons, that what we want to believe isn't always what we should believe. I'll

tell you the truth if you promise me to let the matter die
here."

"I can't promise that."

He held up both hands. "Then I can't help you."

"Wait," I said, inching so far forward on the sofa that one
more centimeter would land my back end on the floor, "that
makes no sense."

"You want your father to be innocent. He wasn't. You
want to know who pulled the trigger. You'll never find that
out. I'm willing to share what I remember about him in the
hopes you'll return home with your young man here and
allow the past to stay where it lies."

He sounded just like Craig Benson.

"Mr. Gavin." Harry turned to Gav before I could say a
word. "I may be relegated to this chair, but I am not without
other faculties." He winked. "I deduce that you are not only
entranced by this young woman, you seek to protect her. If
I were to hazard a guess," he raked Gav up and down, assessing him, "I would imagine you are either a college professor
or a member of law enforcement. You clearly come from a
military background. Olivia has made a name for herself,
getting involved in situations that are beyond her control. I
don't believe it's in her best interests to pursue this matter
beyond tonight's conversation. She is angry with me right
now." To me, he said, "Don't deny it. I see it in your eyes,
your body language. I may have lost use of my own body,
but I am an astute reader of others'."

Me? Angry? Furious was more like it. Livid with rage.

To Gav again, he said, "Tonight, perhaps tomorrow,
you'll be able to talk her into a better frame of mind."

I didn't trust myself to speak.

Gav did it for me. "You are absolutely right about one
thing." He got to his feet and offered me his hand. I stood
up next to him. "I *am* thoroughly entranced by this woman.
And if she wants to pursue this matter to learn more about

her father, I will do my level best to help. With or without your assistance."

Harry frowned. "Please don't be upset."

"Too late," I said. "How dare you treat me as though I have no right to the truth? How dare you wink and smile, suggesting that I can be talked down to—suggesting that you know what's best? You don't know me. And I don't believe you have anything of value to share with us."

We started for the door. Barney scurried next to us, barking. Whether it was encouragement to stay or enticement to leave, I didn't care.

As we stepped outside, making sure the little dog didn't escape, we heard Linka shout, "I'm only trying to help."

"Yeah, right," I said when Gav pulled the door shut behind us. "Trying to help. Give me a break."

He let me mutter all the way down the walkway. Gav and I weren't particularly demonstrative. In fact, we tended to eschew all public displays of affection. Thus, when he pulled me tight and soundly kissed the top of my head, I looked up in surprise.

"You are so strong." He beamed with pride. "God, I love you."

My heart swelled, and though my anger still burned, it simmered beneath the surface as I looked up at him. I snaked an arm around his waist and tugged close. "Me, too."

CHAPTER 13

SATURDAY MORNING FOUND ME IN MY BATH-room putting the finishing touches on my disguise. I was to meet Sargeant, Josh, and our assigned cadre of Secret Service agents at the White House at 10 A.M. I watched myself adjusting the blonde wig in the mirror, at odds with my reflection. This was so not me.

"How much longer are you going to take in there?" Gav asked from just outside the door. I hadn't even given a hint as to what my disguise might be, preferring instead to read his reaction when he experienced "the new me" for the first time.

"One more minute."

"You said that ten minutes ago."

I laughed in spite of myself, then marveled again at how the woman looking back at me in the mirror could have all my emotions and none of my looks. Sure, the nose and mouth hadn't changed much. Except for the fact that Thora insisted on me wearing a much heavier application of makeup than I usually cared for, my face was the same. And yet, not. The glasses made a striking difference. Coupled with the bubblegum-pink lipstick—"It matches the dress perfectly!" Thora had exclaimed with glee—they might have been enough to allow me to pass unrecognized. But the wig was truly the pièce de résistance.

"Hang in there," I called.

"I'm hanging."

He was. So patient, always. He'd listened to me rant the entire drive back the night before and had agreed with me when I told him I thought Harry was hiding something. I'd asked him if he had any idea what that might be. "Not yet," he'd said.

I looked at my reflection again. "What could I have done differently?" I asked the woman in the mirror.

She didn't answer.

"Gav told me that he watched Harry closely the whole time. He's convinced Harry was studying my reactions. He didn't like it."

The woman in the mirror arched an eyebrow.

"Yeah," I said. "I find that interesting, too."

From the other side of the door, Gav asked, "Who in the world are you talking to?"

"Someone I'd like you to meet." I took a deep breath, pasted on a wide smile, and threw open the door. "Here she is."

Gav was probably the most unshockable person I'd ever met. He remained calm, controlled, and unflappable almost all the time. Not now.

As I placed one strappy-heeled foot onto the carpet outside the bathroom door, and held my hands at the hips of my bright pink dress, I had to laugh because Gav's immediate reaction was to look behind me. As though I might be hiding behind this blonde person.

His jaw went slack. "What did they do to you?"

"Pretty weird, isn't it?"

He made a slow circuit around me. "This is . . ." He closed his mouth and scrunched up his face. "You're not . . ." Stepping back, he folded his arms and resumed a less animated expression. I'd shocked him all right, but in-control Gav was back in a flash. "The disguise is effective," he said. "I wouldn't recognize you." He brought his face down to my level. "Unless someone knew you were traveling incognito and they were looking for you specifically, there's no way. I think you're going to be fine today."

He straightened but continued to stare.

"You don't like it," I said.

His face remained impassive. "Not in the least."

I laughed. "Why not? They say blondes have more fun."

The man was not amused. "What time will all this be over?"

"It's just a costume. They told me I look like Reese Witherspoon."

"She should be so lucky." He shook his head. "I'll be in the living room. Let me know when you're ready to go."

Part of me was taken aback, but I liked it. Deep down, his reaction had warmed my soul. As much as I knew Gav and I were good together, it was nice to have reminders every so often that he truly didn't want me to change.

When I joined Gav in my living room, he shook his head again. "Don't get me wrong, you look great no matter what. It's just not you."

I grabbed the gym bag that held my change of clothes, then tucked my free hand into the crook of his arm. "Thanks."

AT THE WHITE HOUSE, SECRET SERVICE AGENT Rosenow, a woman I'd worked with before, escorted me into the back entrance from the gate where Gav dropped me off. There was no way I'd be able to make it in alone with just my ID, not with my Reese Witherspoon disguise on.

"Good morning, Ms. Paras," she said. "I'd never guess it was you if I hadn't been told."

"I suppose that's a good thing," I said. "I understand you're coming with us to the Food Expo."

She nodded as we strode up the walk. "As are Agents Means and Quinn. You've met them?"

I hadn't. I also couldn't imagine how much difference our disguises would make if we were being tailed by agents wearing suits, sunglasses, and radios in their ears.

She must have read my mind because she quickly added, "I'll be wearing casual clothing, as will the other two. I'll change before we leave. We'll have several other agents with us. Don't worry, our little group is designed to blend in."

I had my doubts about our effectiveness on that score, but it didn't really matter. All that did was keeping Josh's presence there a secret. As long as that could be accomplished, we were fine. No matter that I was wearing a summer dress to an event where most everyone else would be in chef's whites or blue jeans.

Rosenow and I parted ways at the kitchen where she promised to be back in less than fifteen minutes. Bucky had his back to me, stirring a pot on the stovetop. "Good morning," I said to him.

"Ready for your Expo?" he asked without glancing up. When he did, the look on his face was hilarious. "Oh," he exclaimed, utterly discomposed. "I'm sorry. I thought you were . . ."

By that point, I was laughing.

He turned off the burner and stepped closer. "Ollie? Is that you?"

"What do you think?" I asked, pirouetting in front of him.

"I think you ought to buy every component of that outfit."

That wasn't at all what I'd expected. "Why? You like me better this way?"

He was shaking his head, but he was laughing. "No, but think of the advantages. With all the trouble you get into, you can slip into your disguise and get away with even more than you have already."

"Thanks, Bucky."

Josh showed up. He recognized me right away from our prep session the day before. "Hey, Ollie, are you ready?" he asked. "Look at the agents they assigned to me. Aren't they fun?"

Behind him were two tall men, the younger one dressed much like Josh was. With his baseball cap, blue jeans, and funky shoes, he was probably in his late twenties. He wore a white T-shirt with CHEF IN TRAINING across the front. Over this he wore chef whites, left open—to cover his gun, yet provide easy access, no doubt. "Nice shirt," I said. "Are you interested in cooking at all? Or is that just to fit in?"

"Disguise," he said. "I'm Agent Means. I want to be sure you know that our orders are to guard the boy. You understand."

"Of course I do." And I did. Even though Sargeant and I were to be watched, Means here wanted me to be aware that in an emergency situation, it was Josh's security they cared about. Not mine. Not Sargeant's. I got it.

"And you must be Agent Quinn," I said to the other man. A little older, closer to my age than the other agent, this fellow was wearing business casual: Dockers, button-down collared shirt, and a sport jacket. He maintained a relaxed expression that contrasted with the intelligence in his eyes, looking every inch the part of a handsome suburban dad.

"Yes, ma'am," he said. He held his hand out and we shook. "It's good to meet you."

"Are we traveling as a group?" I asked. "It doesn't seem as though we all work together as a unit, if you know what I mean."

Means took the lead. "Agent Quinn will be with the subject . . ." He caught himself as he looked down at the president's son who was staring up with big eyes. "That is, he will be with Josh the entire time. To casual observers, you, Josh, and Quinn will appear to be a family out for the day. As for Mr. Sargeant—"

"Yes, what about me?"

We all turned.

"Oh my—" I cut off my exclamation by clapping a hand to my mouth. As promised, he hadn't shaved that morning. The stubble actually looked good on him. Made him more human, I thought. He wore black jeans and dark gym shoes. He was almost able to carry off that casual look, but the black T-shirt featuring Pink Floyd's classic *Dark Side of the Moon* rainbow album cover was more than I could handle. He'd tucked the oversized shirt into his jeans and secured it with a silver chain belt. The best part, however, was the salt-and-pepper ponytail that hung out the back of his baseball cap. By adding that touch, Thora had made certain Sargeant couldn't remove his hat indoors without exposing his disguise.

Sargeant's glare was malevolent as he sidled over. "You will not snicker at my expense." His voice was a growl, meant just for me. He held his head up high as he addressed Means. "What were you about to say?"

Means nodded a greeting to the sensitivity director. "You four will be traveling together. Agent Rosenow will trail behind Mr. Sargeant, Ms. Paras, Agent Quinn, and of course, Josh. To the world, you'll look like a family unit: mother, father, son, and hip grandfather."

I said, "I see Mr. Sargeant as more as a favorite uncle."

A shadow passed his features as he and I made eye contact, but he nodded. "Yes. Uncle. Much better."

IT HAD BEEN SEVERAL YEARS SINCE I'D ATTENDED a Food Expo. In fact, the last time I had, I'd been one of the White House sous chefs, assistant to Henry. He and I hadn't spoken in a while. I wondered how my mentor was doing. I'd have to give him a call one of these days.

"Wow," Josh exclaimed when we handed in our tickets and stepped inside the great hall where the convention was being held. "This is huge."

It was. Highly illuminated, expansive, and offering far more chances to talk about food, trends, and techniques than we could possibly experience in one day, the Expo was a feast in more ways than one. The wide entrance area smelled of new carpet, but I detected delightful odors wafting our way from deeper within the convention center. Temporary cooking areas had been set up where chefs and their assistants prepared delectable samples for happy attendees. They shared their creations and distributed colorful brochures.

I smiled at the wonderment on Josh's face, remembering my first visit to an event like this. He was in for a treat.

Agent Quinn grabbed two complimentary plastic bags provided by the organizers to collect the freebies being handed out. I picked up two magazinelike brochures, handing one to Josh. I immediately opened the brochure to its center spread. "See this?" I pointed to the map. "Every presenter is assigned a booth number." I directed Josh's attention to the long banners strung overhead. "We can find anything you want to see as long as we know what aisle to look in." I flipped through the pages. "Take a look through and let me know if anything in particular interests you and we'll find it."

Captivated, he began to page through.

Sargeant was clearly a fish out of water. "What possible good can I do the boy here?" he whispered close to me. "Particularly when I'm dressed in this ridiculous getup. His mother is interested in teaching the boy diplomacy?" Sargeant harrumphed. "I do not understand at all."

I had no answer for him. While I would have much preferred to wander the spacious convention center on my own, I knew how important this trip was to Josh. Looking at the enormous effort put forth on his behalf to make today possible, I could tell his mother recognized its importance, too.

Josh seemed to be torn between perusing the book for ideas and wandering the great hall to see what might catch his eye. I put a hand on his shoulder. "Let's go this way." The big companies and TV networks tended to snag the plum central spots. We'd start there and see where it led. "Remember, we have to make time for Marcel's presentation."

Josh looked up, his eyes darting everywhere at once. "Yeah," he said distractedly. "I'm looking forward to that, too."

What surprised me more than the faux kitchen work areas and the giant Jumbotron displays that appeared to float in the tall, black ceiling overhead, was the fact that so many attendees were outfitted the way I was. Not pink dresses specifically, but nearly everyone—with the exception of the few children in attendance—was in business suits, or, at a minimum, smart casual. The last time I'd been here I'd worn blue jeans and had felt right at home.

Agent Quinn stayed next to Josh every minute, playing his role as doting father out with his son for the day. Sargeant, oddly, remained at my side. Agent Rosenow, wearing chef's whites, meandered behind us. I knew there were more agents in the crowd, too, but had no idea how many. The three agents accompanying us were keeping in contact with their colleagues, though I didn't know how. It had to be quite the challenge. With thousands of low conversations echoing in the wide space, there was no escaping its constant hum.

Quinn leaned over Josh's head, touching my bare forearm with his fingertips. Though we were supposed to represent a married couple, the familiar gesture felt weird all the same. "What time is Marcel's presentation?" he asked.

"One o'clock." I kept a protective hand on Josh's shoulder. He didn't seem to mind. "We should be able to take in a fair amount of the Expo before then."

Josh pointed past the busy booths to the main stage, far ahead. "Is that really Terry Lash?"

One of the event's many foodie superstars, Chef Lash was demonstrating his signature fried chicken and home-made sides. I'd met Lash on a couple of occasions when he'd visited the White House during the Campbell administration. He was pleasant enough, in small doses. Here, the ebullient and handsome chef stood behind a temporary counter on the main stage in front of about 200 folding chairs, most of which were occupied.

"Over there," I said, indicating the back row of seats. There were four together in one spot, and two more farther down the line. Quinn, Josh, and I sat together, Rosenow joining us next to Josh, while Sargeant sat alone. Means took up position behind us all.

Josh stared up, clearly overwhelmed but enjoying himself. The Jumbotrons above broadcast Terry Lash's every move, with a couple of milliseconds' delay.

"This is great," Josh said, almost to himself. He squirmed in his seat, trying his best to be taller. I was grateful for the huge screens that allowed him to view Lash as clearly as if we'd been in the front row.

We watched for a few minutes, and even though it was apparent Josh had a decent view of the presentation, he pulled himself onto my lap. "Is it okay if I sit here?" he asked after he'd gotten himself comfortable.

"It's fine," I said, smiling. Until I'd met Josh, I'd never felt entirely comfortable around kids, but this little boy was special. I hadn't realized that nine-year-olds could be so utterly disarming. With a pang, I also understood that it wouldn't be long before he stopped wanting to hang around with adults. Soon he'd want to spend all his time with friends instead. I placed my hands on his shoulders and whispered. "Watch how he chops that onion," I said. "It takes a lot of practice to be that quick and not slice your fingers to ribbons."

Josh nodded.

"Years of practice," I repeated. "Keep that in mind."

Quinn draped one arm over the back of my chair. What was meant to appear a husband's casual relaxation was probably a pre-planned move. If Quinn spotted anything amiss— and he would, with the way he never stopped watching the crowd—he could push us both down to the ground in one quick motion. It still felt odd, however, especially when his arm grazed my back. I sat up straighter.

After Lash's demonstration, we browsed stalls for about an hour, resisting hawkers' repeated requests for our contact information. Before we knew it, it was time for Marcel's show.

Back in the seating area, I spotted empty seats much nearer to the front than at Lash's. Marcel wouldn't recognize me in this getup, but I wanted to be able to tell him I'd been there, up close and personal. Quinn had other ideas, however. "The fewer people seated behind us, the better," he said, so we returned to the last row, where plenty of seats were still available. Josh scampered onto my lap again, Rosenow sat next to me, and Sargeant next to her. Means, again, stood nearby. As people filed in for the show, a woman tapped Sargeant on the shoulder.

"Is this seat taken?" she asked.

Sargeant said, "No, please, you're welcome to it."

Quinn assessed the intruder but didn't say a word. I supposed, to the Secret Service, everyone was a threat until proven otherwise. The woman next to Sargeant was younger than he was, closer to my age. Taller, too. What made me notice her, however, was the shock of hot pink in her chestnut-brown hair. The chunk of hyper-dyed hair stretched down from behind her right ear to her shoulder in a blast of brightness. I liked it. Not enough to have it done myself, mind you, but it looked good on her.

Sargeant leaned past Rosenow to whisper to me, "Getting in good with the First Family, I see," but there was no malice in the statement. He gestured toward Josh with his eyes. "You can't possibly be worried about job security anymore."

I smiled. "Not really," I replied just as quietly. Not that it mattered; Josh was busy talking with Agent Quinn next to me. "At first I was worried about Virgil, but things seem to be working out."

Sargeant leaned back. "He's a diva if I've ever met one."

I bit back a response. Good thing, because Marcel had just been introduced.

"Bonjour," the White House pastry chef said into his microphone. Despite the fact that his handsome, dark face and thick French accent were causing a great deal of swooning among audience members, I could tell by the quiver in his voice that he was nervous.

"I am 'ere today to 'elp you learn more about that most difficult of talents: preparing pastry to puff when it is baked. Before I begin, however," he turned to face each side of the stage, giving each a little bow, "I must not forget to thank the organizers of zees event. They have kindly invited me to be here for you this beautiful afternoon. I must also thank my dear friend and colleague, Olivia Paras, the executive chef of our nation's White House, who is in the audience today." He held a hand over his eyes as though looking for me in the crowd.

Josh twisted on my lap. "That's you, Ollie," he said, then clapped both hands over his mouth and turned an apologetic face toward Quinn.

The agent was not pleased. "Do not react," he said quietly.

Marcel kept looking and I hoped to heaven he wouldn't ask me to stand up and be recognized. "She is here," he said, stepping forward on the stage. "But perhaps she is not willing to make herself known." He gave a very French shrug and returned to his worktable.

I kept a hand on Josh's back. "No one heard," I said to Quinn. But a quick glance toward the woman with the pink shock of hair made me pause. She wasn't looking at us, not exactly, but something in her body language told me her interest in us had been piqued.

Quinn took another long look around. "All right," he said.

About halfway through Marcel's demonstration, the woman with the pink hair murmured to Sargeant, then got up and left.

"What did she say?" I asked when she was gone.

"That her break was up. I guess she works here," Sargeant said. "Why?"

"No reason."

"Ms. Paras," he said in a chiding tone. "You are without a doubt the nosiest person I have ever encountered."

Quinn had kept his arm around the back of my chair again for the entire show. I was relieved when Marcel finished, bowed to thunderous applause, and we could leave. I wouldn't rush Josh if he wasn't ready, but I got the impression he was bordering on information overload at this point. As for me, I'd seen all I needed to and looked forward to spending the rest of the afternoon with Gav.

"I think we've done a lot today, haven't we, Josh?" I asked. We talked for a few minutes about the presentations he most enjoyed and those he thought were a waste of time. I marveled at how quickly he'd caught on to what was substance, and what was mere fluff. "Is there anything we missed that you'd like to see before we take off?"

He took a look around the cavernous hall and shook his head. "No, but can we walk up one of the aisles we missed so we see new booths along the way? I don't want to repeat."

"That sounds fair," I said, thinking that I could be back home by three o'clock if I played my cards right. "Which aisle?"

He held a finger to his chin, surveying the area with great

concentration. At last he pointed to the second aisle from the end. "That one."

"You got it," I said, and we started off.

"I can't believe all the places I know," Josh said for the tenth time as we made our way to Aisle Two. "All the companies who make food and candy are here."

"This is how big businesses stay that way," I said. "The more familiar a brand name is, the more comfortable you feel with it. That means you're more likely to buy from them. Over and over. When I was here last time, the displays were much smaller and there were more startup companies. I'm really surprised at how much it's expanded."

I was losing his attention, so I tried again. "Last time I was here, it was mostly cookware and two or three big-name food companies. We've seen candy and chocolate companies; we've even seen vitamin manufacturers. That's different."

"I wish I could try some," he said, also for the tenth time.

Josh's bag was filled with samples of everything anyone handed him. Quinn had been adamant about Josh not consuming a single morsel until the bag could be checked out and cleared. The chances that anyone here knew that the president's son was in attendance were slim. But the Secret Service demanded absolutes.

"It's like trick-or-treating," I said. "I bet your mom doesn't let you have anything until she goes through it. Am I right?"

He nodded solemnly. "I bet we don't even get to go trick-or-treating this year."

I didn't know how to answer that, but Quinn leaned over. "I'll go over every single piece with you and your mom today, okay?" He straightened and gave me a rueful smile as if to say he felt sorry for Josh and his sister's fishbowl existence. "Ms. Paras is right: This is just like trick-or-treating, except for the fact that most of this is food instead of candy."

Pre-packaged, over-processed food for the most part, I

wanted to add. That's all Josh had been allowed to take. Our plastic collection bags weren't exactly conducive to amassing the fresh offerings. Still, I understood the boy's excitement and I hoped he would be able to enjoy most of his stash.

We wandered up Aisle Two, with Josh stopping at every booth along the way, maximizing our last few minutes. When I turned, I noticed a booth for a company I hadn't thought to look for here. My knees went a little weak.

I turned to Quinn. "Do you mind if I go talk to those people for a minute?"

His eyes narrowed. "What's up?"

I couldn't tell him the truth. "A company I'm interested in."

He glanced over at the giant logo. "Dietary supplements?" he asked. "You're into that stuff?"

"A friend of mine is," I said, fooling no one. Before he could give me the okay, I'd started toward Pluto's sage-green booth, intending to pick up any paperwork they might offer. There were no prospective customers in the made-to-look-like-a-doctor's-office scene, only a dark-haired woman with her back to me, adjusting the spotlights to best illuminate the sampling of Pluto's products on wide glass shelves.

I didn't need to bother her. At the mouth of the deep booth was a counter with a plastic display case offering all the paperwork about the company I could possibly want. I knew most of it would prove useless to me, but I gathered it up nonetheless.

The woman must have sensed me there because she turned.

I sucked in a breath of surprise.

It was the woman with the bright pink chunk of hair. "Hello," she said. "That was a great demonstration by the White House pastry chef, wasn't it?"

CHAPTER 14

"Y-YES," I STAMMERED, PANICKING AS THOUGH I'd been caught stealing. "Yes, it was."

She sauntered over and saw that I'd picked up every single one of the pamphlets they offered. "You're interested in dietary supplements, I take it?"

"I'm interested in your company," I said. That wasn't a lie though I was doing my best to come up with one. "I was . . . that is, I *am* interested in diet and foods and . . . uh . . . cooking. That's why I'm here." I punctuated that with a self-deprecating laugh, then chanced upon a genius idea. "I've heard great things about working at Pluto. You caught me doing homework."

"Oh," she said with a knowing look. "You'll want an employment application then, won't you?"

I didn't get the sense that this woman recognized me as a member of the White House staff but I couldn't be sure. She was either watching me oddly, or it was my guilty conscience chuckling on my shoulder. "I'd love one," I said. "I've been out of work for a while."

"What do you do?"

Time to stay with the truth. "I'm a chef," I said. "I've worked all over the world, as a matter of fact. But the job market is especially tough right now."

"It sure is," she said sympathetically. Pulling a folded sheet out from a stack beyond the sight of most visitors, she handed it to me. "You can fill it out here if you like, or if you prefer, mail it in. To be frank, that might be your best option. I have a lot to clean up here when the Expo is over and I wouldn't want it to get lost."

"Good point," I said. "That's what I'll do. Thank you."

I started to turn away, but she called me back. "What's your name?" she asked. "So I can keep an eye out for your application."

I hesitated. "Livvy," I said, keeping with a version of my real first name.

"What's your last name, Livvy?"

In my mind's eye I could see Bucky having a good laugh at my expense. "Livvy Reed," I said, borrowing his surname.

"I'm Sally Burns," she said. We shook hands. "Nice to meet you, Livvy."

"Nice to meet you, too." Out of the corner of my eye, I could see Quinn and Josh waiting for me. "Looks like the family's ready to go," I said. "Thank you again."

"Best of luck to you," she said.

"What was that all about?" Quinn asked when I returned to the group.

"Yes, Ms. Paras, you had me nervous for a moment there," Sargeant said. "That woman sat next to me at Marcel's event. Is she onto us?"

"I don't think so," I said.

"Then why on earth did you go talk with her? That wasn't part of the plan."

"Let's keep walking," Quinn said. He arranged it so that Josh walked between us again. Rosenow covered one flank, Means the other. Sargeant trailed. We made it back to our vehicle with no one giving us a second glance—or even a first one, for that matter.

Sargeant wasn't about to let the matter drop. As we settled ourselves and pulled out of the parking spot, the man was not exhibiting as much sensitivity as his title suggested. "Why did you engage that woman? What's going on?"

"And you tell me I'm nosy," I said in an attempt to derail the subject.

Unfortunately for me, Quinn picked up the thread. "I must admit, I'm curious as well. Was that a job application she handed you?" His eyes glittered in the sunlight that spilled in as we exited the dark lot.

"It's a long story," I said. "One that has nothing to do with today or any of you, so if you don't mind . . ."

Sargeant regarded me coolly. He folded his arms and stared out the window. "As you wish," he said.

Quinn asked, "You aren't looking for a new job, are you?"

Next to me, Josh spoke up. "You can't look for a new job, Ollie. You aren't, are you?"

His earnest face, the apprehension in his voice, and the way he scooched forward, though hampered by his seat belt, tugged at my heart. I put an arm around him. "No, Josh. I'm not. She misinterpreted my interest and I didn't want to be rude."

When we got back to the White House, but before we alighted, Josh reminded Quinn that he'd promised to go through all the freebies in his bag that same day. Quinn said he'd have it back to him within an hour.

The car stopped behind the south entrance and, as we disembarked, I grabbed my plastic bag of freebies. "Uh-uh," Quinn said, catching the edge of it and preventing my exit. "I have to go through that one, too."

I laughed. "It's for me. Not for anyone in the First Family," I said.

"Can't be too careful."

Sargeant scrambled out from behind me. "I cannot wait to change from this monstrous outfit," he said. With a shudder, he added, "Thank you for an illuminating adventure. I know my presence added a great deal to the boy's experience."

His sarcasm wasn't lost on anyone. There had been no chance for Sargeant to interact at all with Josh. I also knew that it didn't really matter. Mrs. Hyden had pressed the sensitivity director into this adventure in order to keep her husband happy. If the president believed that Josh was learning about diplomacy on the same trip he learned about food, everyone was happy. Except, perhaps, Sargeant.

He bustled off.

I turned to Quinn. "When do I get my goodies back?"

Quinn looked amused, so I pushed my luck. "All I really want is the paperwork I picked up. You can keep the munchies."

He adopted a curious expression. "I'll tell you what, Ms. Paras. I'll give you the entire bag back in one hour. Will that do? I'll bring it to you in the kitchen."

I needed to change clothes and freshen up anyway. "Sure, that sounds great."

HAPPY TO BE LOOKING LIKE MYSELF AGAIN after scrubbing my face and changing into jeans and a cotton top, I headed back into the kitchen. Thora wasn't around today and I didn't want to leave the wig and bright pink outfit lying around where it could get lost or misplaced. I had no idea when she and her team would return, so I packed the disguise into my gym bag and decided to take it home until I knew what to do with it.

While I waited for Quinn to return with my goodie bag and Pluto paperwork, Bucky and I discussed Marcel's presentation at the Food Expo and menu plans. The two SBA chefs we'd hired for the evening were hard at work preparing dinner. The president and Mrs. Hyden were entertaining a group of mayors and their wives tonight. Dinner for sixteen.

I'd offered to help while we waited, but Bucky tossed that suggestion aside. "You're supposed to be on vacation. Speaking of which . . ." He got a glint in his eyes. "Seems to me you've been in a really good mood lately."

Uh-oh. I pressed my hands to my chest. "What are you saying? That I'm usually grouchy?"

He wagged a finger at me. "Don't try to get around it; you know what I mean."

"I'm sure I have no idea."

"And I'm just as sure you do." He took a step closer. "There's someone special in your life, isn't there?"

"Psh," I said, giving him a dismissive hand motion. "You're seeing what you want to see."

"Curious," he said, close enough to me that the two worker-bee chefs wouldn't overhear, "you're trying to put me off the scent but you're not out and out denying it."

He was good. Still, I wasn't about to spill. "I see no reason to—"

"Ollie," he said very quietly, "keep in mind that I've worked next to you for quite a few years now." He winked. "I can tell."

To maintain the charade at this point felt wrong. But owning up didn't feel right, either. Fortunately for me, Bucky seemed to understand. "I don't know who it is," he said. "No idea at all. I thought I did, but . . ." He let the words hang before picking them up again. "It doesn't matter who. If you're happy, we're happy."

"We?"

"Cyan and I have talked."

"About my love life?"

He scratched the back of his bald head, but he was grinning. "We ran out of conversation while you were gone. Don't worry. We waited until Virgil was out of range."

"Thank goodness for small favors."

Bucky held up his hands. "So? Who is he?"

"I thought it didn't matter."

"Anyone we know?"

I shook my head. "Not telling."

"Come on. A hint?"

"Not yet."

"Ms. Paras," Quinn called from the doorway.

I turned to see the agent making his way past one of the SBA agents. He held the plastic goodie bag and as I approached, he handed it over to me. He was still dressed in his "suburban dad" getup, but he'd donned an identifying Secret Service pin and wore a cord in his ear. "Thank you very much, Agent Quinn," I said, digging into the bag to ensure all my Pluto paperwork was still there.

"My pleasure," he said.

"Did you find anything amiss?"

"No, ma'am," he said.

Bucky was watching our interchange closely. I wasn't surprised. After my near-admission about actually having a love life, my assistant would be looking to put a face to the mystery person's identity. I was certain he was assessing Quinn's potential.

For his part, the agent didn't seem eager to leave the busy kitchen. "Thank you again," I said, hoping he'd take the hint.

He didn't. With a consternated look, he tilted his head. "Would you have a moment for private conversation, Ms. Paras?"

Bucky must be having a field day now. "Sure," I said.

He led me out of the kitchen just around the corner. We stood beneath the stone archway that still bore the scars of fire from when the White House was attacked by the British in the War of 1812.

Quinn was taller than I was, but most people were. He wasn't quite Gav's height, but his light eyes pierced me much the way Gav's had when we'd first met. I had no doubt I was in for a lecture.

"Ms. Paras," he began, and I braced myself. "May I call you Olivia?"

I hadn't expected the question. Startled, I replied. "Sure, but I'd prefer Ollie."

"Thank you." He gave a brief nod. "Today when you left the group to talk to the representative at the Pluto booth, you took us by surprise. We would have been happy to make allowances for you to stop there, had we known your desire to do so."

As far as Secret Service admonishments went, this one registered as mild. "I didn't know the Pluto booth was going to be there," I said. "Otherwise, I would have mentioned it ahead of time. I apologize for any trouble I caused."

"No trouble," he said, making me wonder how this guy ever made it into the Secret Service. Most of the agents I'd encountered viewed deviations from "the plan" as sacrilege. Why was I getting off easy?

"If I may ask," he continued, "what it was about Pluto that aroused your interest? Not that I mean to pry, but . . ." He let the thought hang, one eye narrowed at me, scrutinizing.

"Nothing of national importance, trust me," I said. "My dad worked for that company a long time ago, a fact I was reminded of recently. I was curious."

That seemed to satisfy him. "Thank you. I appreciate your honesty."

He didn't say it with a sneer. Didn't seem suspicious, didn't appear to doubt my words. "Anytime," I said.

Quinn held his hand out back toward the way we'd come, as though opening a gate to allow me to pass. "I'm sure your kitchen awaits your experienced hand. I won't hold you any longer. If I have any further questions, Ollie," he said, hesitating ever so slightly before using my name for the first time, "may I assume I will find you down here?"

"Actually," I smiled, "I'm on vacation until Monday." I could tell I'd confused him. "I'm only in today because the First Lady asked me to take Josh along to the Food Expo, but now . . ." I glanced at my watch, "I'm out until first thing Monday morning."

"I see." His brows came together in an expression I couldn't read. "Enjoy your time off."

CHAPTER 15

"HERE WE GO AGAIN," GAV SAID.

I blew out a breath. "Let's hope we have better luck this time."

Dusk was beginning to fall; Gav and I picked our way along an uneven sidewalk to visit Michael Fitch. We'd been obliged to park halfway down a winding block, the only open spot between a dented pickup and a rusted blue sedan.

This neighborhood had seen better days, probably fifty years ago. Mostly small ranches and one-and-a-half-story cottages, the homes here were in need of a good spruce-up, but weren't decrepit. What the area lacked in pristine homes, however, it made up for in foliage. Trees were huge, swollen with trunks as wide as airplane tires.

Kicking up in advance of an approaching storm, wind gusts whisked through the shadowy leaves forming a rocking overhead canopy that shushed like shuffled steps, making me glance back behind us repeatedly.

Kids played in front yards, halting their jump ropes and holding onto plastic balls as they watched us make our way to Fitch's home.

"I guess they don't get a lot of visitors around here," I said.

"Why are you nervous?" Gav asked. "It's not like you."

I didn't answer.

"This area's safe," he went on. "A little worse for wear, but it's no mecca for crime."

"It's not that." I could barely see the sky through the heavy tree branches above us, but I looked anyway. "I just know that if Fitch doesn't help us, we're back to square one. That has me on edge."

He didn't say anything. A car squealed around the corner, windows open, its radio bass turned up so high it made my heart thrum as it roared past. "Such a difference from Linka's neighborhood, huh?" I said.

Gav's expression was thoughtful.

"What?" I asked.

"I have a good feeling about Mr. Fitch."

"You do?"

Gav gave me a wry smile. "Not about the man, but about him helping us. I'm not sure why, but I have a feeling he'll be more approachable."

"I hope so," I said as we stopped in front of Fitch's house. It was one of the few on the block without a huge tree in the parkway, a blue-frame one-story home with a peaked roof and open attic windows. Colorless curtains whipped outward like twisty arms reaching into the breeze.

The lawn here was overgrown with crabgrass and weeds. No evergreens, no shrubs of any kind broke up the stark foundation's gray drabness. We took the three concrete steps to the front door. I shot Gav a glance and a shrug that said,

"What do we have to lose?" and pressed a thumb against the cracked plastic doorbell.

No cheery chimes sounded from inside. "You think it's broken?"

Gav leaned over the wrought-iron handrail and knocked on one of the home's three front windows, making the sash wobble. "This place needs work." He glanced up at the cock-eyed aluminum awning over our heads. "One good wind-storm and that thing's history."

Noises from inside let us know the knock had been heard. Footsteps, the creak of rusty hinges, and then for the third time since I'd begun this quest, a woman answered the door with a quizzical look on her face. Dark eyes shifted back and forth and I could see that she was trying to figure out who we could be. I couldn't help but make comparisons between her and Linka's wife. Although she, too, was casu-ally dressed, this woman didn't sport yoga pants and tight tank top. She wore light-colored capris and a baggy gray T-shirt with an iron-on beer logo that had cracked and begun to peel.

"Mrs. Fitch?" I asked.

Three inches of outgrowth told me it had been months since she'd last colored her hair. She must have thought the same thing at that very instant because she ran a self-conscious hand through her shoulder-length tresses. She didn't wear makeup, but the bones in her slim face made me believe she'd been quite lovely in her younger days. Without opening the screen door between us, she said, "What do you want? I'm not buying anything."

I glanced up at Gav, who had taken a step back, no doubt to appear less threatening. He had his hands crossed in front of his waist, like a well-behaved schoolboy might. His air was mild, his gaze inquisitive.

"My name is Olivia Paras," I said. "I think your husband used to work with my dad."

She shook her head as she took a step back into the house.

"My husband hasn't worked in a very long time," she said. "Sorry."

One of her red, chapped hands grabbed at the door as she made ready to close it.

"At Pluto," I said quickly. "Pluto, Incorporated."

She stopped mid-motion, gaze darting back and forth between us again. My words had clearly hit their mark. Warily, she asked, "What did you say your name was?"

I told her. "My dad was Anthony Paras."

Something sparked behind her eyes. "I remember that name," she said, bringing her lips in. "Not sure how, though. Sounds familiar. How long ago did you say this was?"

"Long time," I said. "May we speak with your husband?" I asked, knowing I had to push now or this option would be lost to me forever.

She twisted her mouth, scanned my hands, then cocked her head toward Gav. "And who's he?"

"Boyfriend," I said. "May we come in?"

"I don't know that Mickey's going to want to talk to you," she gave a half-hearted shrug, "but no sense leaving you out here while he makes up his mind. Might as well bring you back so he can get a look at you first." She waved us in, saying, "Let me get this door closed. We got a window air conditioner in the kitchen and I don't want all the cold air escaping."

The first thing to hit me when the door shut behind us was the smell. Acrid and unpleasant, I remembered this odor from when I was a kid and we'd visited some friends. I'd been polite enough of a youngster not to ask what the stink was until I could catch my mom alone. She'd whispered that her friend had probably accidentally left one of her pot's handles over an open flame. "Burnt plastic," she'd said.

"We just finished dinner," Mrs. Fitch said as she made her way through the dimly lit living room. "I was cleaning up." A beige couch sagged along one end of the room while across from it, a brand-new big-screen television held a place

of honor. Two small paintings flanked a plastic orange sun
clock on the wall above the sofa. The unframed oils were
much too small for the wide space and looked to be amateur
attempts at capturing still life: a cluster of grapes draping a
misshapen apple. A bottle of wine next to a book.

We stepped along a thin gray rug that covered the
squeaky wood floor, past a well-worn easy chair that could
have rivaled Archie Bunker's. Everything in the room was
threadbare and worn. Old. I was touched by the many doilies
carefully arranged atop tables and across the back of the
couch cushions. A valiant attempt to make the place feel
lived-in rather than shabby.

The dining room, immediately behind the living room,
was dark. Even with the lights off, however, I made out what
looked like an antique mahogany table and matching cabinet. Amateur paintings were centered on every open wall
here, too.

"Who's the artist?" I asked.

"Mickey." She blinked and tried to smile. "He never gives
up." Mrs. Fitch took a right, opening an accordion plastic
door to reveal a well-lit kitchen. Small by any standard, it
had dull yellow tile walls trimmed in gray. The burnt-handle
odor was gaggable in here where it mingled with the smell
of cigarette smoke—stale from the ashtray full of used butts
on the table, and fresh from the one Michael Fitch lit as we
walked in. I blinked to keep my eyes from watering.

His wife whacked the plastic accordion door closed
behind us. "Keeps in the cool, you know?" she said. To her
husband: "Hey, Mickey, this girl wants to talk to you about
her dad. From your Pluto days."

Mickey Fitch stared up at us with eyes as yellow as the
kitchen walls and as saggy as his living room couch. His
sickly skin tone and skinny frame made me wonder if he
was battling more than nicotine addiction. "Yeah, I know.
Thought you'd show up yesterday." Coughing, he used one
foot to shove at the chair across the table from him. It

scraped backward across the dingy linoleum and threatened to topple over before it settled. "Take a seat." He took a deep drag of his cigarette as we sat at a vintage 1950s table that looked brand-new.

As I lowered myself onto the turquoise vinyl seat trimmed in silver brads, I ran my hands along the table's chrome edge. "This is great," I said. "It's in beautiful condition."

"It was mine growing up," his wife said, clearly pleased that I'd complimented her furniture. "My name's Ingrid, by the way."

She looked as far from an Ingrid as I'd ever imagined. For me, the name Ingrid conjured up elegance, wealth, soft violin strings, and pastel bucolic settings. But I could tell she'd been a beauty once. Maybe Ingrid fit her after all. She turned to her husband. "You didn't tell me you were expecting anybody."

He hadn't taken his eyes off me from the moment I'd walked in. Gav took the seat to my left, but Fitch didn't seem to notice.

"Can I get you something to drink?" Ingrid asked, bending down as though she wouldn't be able to catch our answers if she'd remained upright. "We have tea and water in the fridge."

"They aren't staying long enough," Fitch said. He worked the cigarette to the other side of his mouth. "I don't have anything you want."

"No, thank you," I said to Ingrid as though Fitch hadn't all but slammed the door on our conversation. Odd, I thought, inviting us to sit if he really had nothing to say.

Ingrid didn't sit down to join us. She made her way to the sink behind Gav and started washing the dinner dishes, keeping the water low enough to be able to hear our conversation.

"How did you know we were coming to see you?" I asked Fitch even though I was pretty sure I knew the answer.

"Harry Linka called," he answered, confirming my

suspicion. He leaned forward, both elbows on the table, arms crossed. "What're you doing, bringing up old stuff from so many years ago? What's it to you?"

Was he serious? "Anthony Paras was my dad," I said in a tone that implied that was explanation enough.

"I remember Tony." A shadow crossed his features. It could have been smoke, but I thought it was something more. "Your dad, God rest his soul, is at peace, right?" He didn't wait for me to respond. "Let the dead have their rest. You let this go, okay, little girl?" As if to emphasize that it didn't matter, he blew a smoke ring toward the ceiling.

I mirrored him, placing my elbows on the turquoise tabletop, crossing my arms and staring him straight in the eye. "I haven't been called 'little girl' in a long time," I said. "And I'm not so sure my dad is at peace. I don't think you believe he is, either, do you?"

Fitch glanced away.

Ingrid, who'd stopped washing dishes and was patently listening in on the conversation, asked, "Is that the man who was murdered all those years ago?" then answered her own question with a hand to her throat. "It is. I remember now. Oh, I'm so sorry, honey," she said to me. "That was your dad, huh?"

"Ingrid." Fitch's voice was sharp.

She ignored him. "You must have been just a little thing back then."

Ingrid wouldn't have answers for me, but I knew Fitch would. Still, it wouldn't hurt to be nice to the woman. She was one of the first people to show any sympathy about my dad's death. To everyone else, it had been so long ago that the story was better forgotten.

"I was," I said. "I barely remember him."

"Then why bother me?" Mickey asked.

I ignored the question, instead choosing to push my luck. I wasn't going to give up until he kicked me out. "Why did you leave Pluto?" I asked.

He slid another glance toward his wife. One corner of her mouth curled downward and she turned back to the dishes. To us, he said, "Disability."

Unlike Linka, Fitch here wasn't confined to a wheelchair. Disabilities came in many different forms, however. "I'm sorry to hear that," I said. Pushing again, I asked, "What happened?"

Mickey worked his tongue along his teeth, as though attempting to dislodge an errant morsel from dinner. "Ticker problems," he said, tapping his chest. "My doc told me I had to quit. If I didn't I'd be dead in a couple of months."

Behind Gav, Ingrid made a noise.

Fitch took another long drag of his cigarette, regarding me carefully.

"Was this before or after Harold Linka's accident?" I asked.

"After," he said. "Couple weeks later."

I sat back a little, putting the pieces together. "That's quite a coincidence," I said. "Three executives out of work from Pluto in a little over a month's time. My dad was murdered, Linka had his accident, and then you were released on disability."

His brows gave a disinterested jerk upward. "Like you said, coincidence."

I could feel tension emanate my way from Gav. "How's your heart these days?" I asked Fitch. "Have you had any surgery or do you go for therapy. . . ." I let the thought hang hoping he'd fill in the details.

"Nope. Nothing like that." He stubbed his cigarette into the pile of gray ash next to him. "I'm the picture of health." He gave a phlegmy cough. "'Course, my lungs would be better off if I gave these up." Out of the corner of my eye I saw Ingrid's head turn slightly. Fitch must have noticed the movement but he didn't acknowledge her. He stared at me with baleful eyes. "Quitting Pluto was the only medicine I needed. Kinda like a miracle, huh?"

"I guess it was," I said. "Where did you work after that?"

He lit up another cigarette and I could tell it was to slow the conversation. "Haven't held a job since. Ingrid's been a good wife all these years. Just like that old commercial, she not only brings home the bacon, she fries it up for me, too."

My heart went out to the woman studiously washing dishes, her back to us. Probably so we couldn't read the disappointment on her face. I thought about her husband's artwork proudly displayed on bare walls and the meticulously placed doilies. This wasn't a woman who sought pity.

"You don't want to hear my sob stories," Fitch said. "You came here to ask about your dad. You want to know who killed him."

My heart leapt. "I do."

"Sorry that you came all this way for nothing, then, because I can't tell you that."

"Can't or won't?"

He smirked. "Can't tell you what I don't know. He was where he shouldn't be, that's all anyone knows for sure."

"I don't believe he was selling Pluto's secrets to a rival corporation."

Fitch shrugged, but didn't respond.

"Do you?" I asked.

"I liked your dad," he said. "He was fair. A decent guy. You don't meet too many decent guys anymore."

Ingrid had turned fully now. Drying her hands on a dish-towel, she said, "I remember how upset you were when that happened." She gave me a sad look. "When your dad was killed, I mean." To Fitch, she continued, "You were so upset back then. I never saw you like that before." She narrowed her eyes at him. "You scared me, Mickey. You kept saying that things were wrong, really wrong—"

Fitch cut her off. "You think? Yeah, things were wrong. A guy I knew had been killed in cold blood. Was I supposed to be happy about it?"

"It was more than that," she said. "You know it was. Maybe if you talk about it—"

"There's nothing to talk about," he fairly shouted. "End of story." To me, he said, "Get out of here. I'm done reminiscing for the night."

This little interchange had been the biggest break I'd gotten yet. I wasn't about to leave. Not until I got answers. Gav didn't seem inclined to move, either. "Mr. Fitch, I'm not trying to get anyone into trouble."

"Sure you're not." He sent a scathing look at his wife. "She's talking out her backside. She doesn't know anything that went on at that place."

"But you do," I said simply. "What happened to my dad? I know you know."

He slammed both fists on the turquoise tabletop, making us all jump. "I do not know." His lip curled showing his teeth but I got the sense his anger was directed inward, not at me. "Get out of my house. I don't want to talk anymore."

"But . . ."

"You heard me. Ingrid, get these people out of here. Don't let them in again." He pushed himself up to a standing position and shuffled to the far side of the refrigerator, toward a door I hadn't previously noticed. He waved a hand up over the top of his head in a dismissive gesture. "You shouldn't have let them in."

The resigned look on her face let me know that not only was she used to him barking orders at her, she was used to complying. "I'm sorry," she said, opening the plastic accordion door again. "I think you better go now."

We filed out ahead of her, making our way quickly to the front door. She opened it for us as I fished in my purse. "Here," I said impulsively. "This is my business card. If, for any reason, your husband changes his mind . . ."

She gave me a skeptical stare. "I don't know that he will," she said. "He's pretty worked up."

"My cell phone number is on there, too," I said.

She looked down at the little card for the first time, her eyes jumping back to meet mine in sudden surprise. "You work at the White House?"

"I do."

Ingrid's demeanor had morphed from submissive to fearful. "Mickey's not in any trouble, is he?" She gave Gav a quick scrutiny. "Are you an FBI agent? You aren't planning to arrest him for anything, are you?"

Gav's voice was quiet but firm. "If he's not guilty of anything, he has nothing to worry about, does he?"

CHAPTER 16

"GUESS WHAT I PICKED UP FOR YOU," I SAID TO Gav Sunday morning as I dug through one of the many bags I'd lugged in and dropped onto his table.

He stood next to me, coffee cup in one hand, pawing through my grocery purchases with the other. "I thought I was making dinner tonight."

I grinned. "You left your shopping list on the side of the refrigerator. I figured I'd pick up what you needed since I was going out anyway."

"I would have gotten to it this afternoon," he said, "but that was nice of you. What did you go out for?"

I'd tucked it behind my back. "You really want to know?"

He gave me that narrow-eyed amused look I loved so much. "Please," he said, deadpan. "The suspense is killing me."

"Ta-da!"

He held his coffee mug in both hands and nodded, decidedly unimpressed. "A shower curtain."

"Told you that you needed a new one."

After I pulled the fabric out from its plastic packaging, he fingered it. "I'm seeing a new theme in my life here."

I gave him my best suspicious glare. "And that is?"

"Showers. They appear to play a major role in our relationship."

"How so?"

"Let's examine the evidence," he said. "You admit that you, your mom, and nana discussed me while I was in the shower." He pointed. "Your mom, nana, and I talked about you while you were in the shower. We all talked about your mom while she was in there." He tapped his lips. "How did your nana escape this fate?"

"She sneaks away when no one is paying attention," I said.

"Smart lady. All this and now you bring me a brand-new curtain for my apartment." He held it up one-handed, allowing the red plaid fabric to tumble to his feet. "No balloons. Very masculine. But I can't help thinking all this talk of showers is the universe's way of telling me that I need to clean up my act."

"You?" I asked with a laugh. "You're the straightest arrow I've ever met."

He put the coffee mug down on the table with a solid *clunk*. "You haven't seen my dark side."

I stepped closer, pressing the shower curtain between us as I tilted my face to look up at him. "Will I?"

A noise rumbled in his chest. "Let's hope not."

THAT EVENING, WE CLEARED OUR DINNER plates away. "This was wonderful," I said for the third time.

Gav shook his head. "I'm but a lowly peon in the world of haute cuisine." He pointed toward the countertop. "Take away my reliable *America's Test Kitchen Cookbook* and I'm hopeless."

"That's an excellent book. I've used it plenty of times myself."

"No way."

"Way," I said.

"I'm sure my technique could use some improvement."

I gave him a look.

He turned red. "That came out wrong."

"Everything was wonderful," I said, now for the fourth time. Gav had made pan-seared chicken with basil and tomato relish, along with mashed potatoes, fresh green beans, salad, and mint ice cream for dessert. "Food doesn't have to be haute cuisine to be delicious."

"Tell me you weren't critiquing every bite."

I stopped in the middle of wiping down the table. "I wasn't," I said. "I don't. You cooked for me. It doesn't get any better than that."

I could tell my words cheered him. "The green beans were a little too crunchy," he said.

"The green beans were fine."

I rinsed dishes then loaded them into the dishwasher while he put the dining room table back in order. "How's Mrs. Wentworth doing these days?" Gav asked.

"I saw her a couple of days ago. We had less than five minutes to talk, but she asked about you right off." I laughed, remembering the encounter. "She told me to make sure you knew she said hello and wanted to know when—" I caught myself.

He pushed the second chair in and came up behind me. "Wanted to know when . . . what?"

I kept loading, pretending I hadn't noticed any blip in the conversation. "When she was going to see you again."

Gav didn't say anything, but I could feel his eyes on me. We both knew I was lying. "Ollie."

I looked up.

"That wasn't what she was asking, was it?"

I talked fast. "You know Mrs. Wentworth, she's so nosy. I mean, back when you and I weren't even seeing each other yet she kept asking when you were going to make your move."

Mrs. Wentworth and her longtime beau, Stan, had recently gotten engaged and all she wanted to talk about were her impending nuptials and my chances for getting engaged, too. Flaming heat engulfed my face and it wasn't from the steam rising up as hot water poured from the spigot. "She's just being Mrs. Wentworth."

"I understand," he said. Thankfully, he let the matter drop.

Later on, we were seated on his sofa, TV off, watching the stars come out in the summer sky. We were both at the couch's far end, turned to face the windows. I leaned back against him, my legs stretched out, ankles crossed at the sofa's other end.

"Back to work tomorrow for both of us," I said.

He murmured what sounded like agreement.

"You've been quiet since dinner," I pressed. Actually, he'd been quiet since our Mrs. Wentworth conversation, but I decided to dance around that. "What's up?"

"Not much, just thinking," he said. As he spoke, I could feel the words reverberate against my back. He had one arm slung up against the top of the sofa cushion, his hand on my shoulder. I liked being here. I liked being with him. I could be myself, always.

"About what?" I asked.

He hesitated long enough for me to know that he wouldn't be completely forthcoming. I knew better than to expect a lie, but I was fairly sure whatever his answer, it wouldn't be 100 percent truthful. "About our meeting with Michael Fitch yesterday. I'm sorry we didn't get further on this before going back to work," he said.

"We got a lot further than I expected."

He made a noncommittal noise. "We *are* a lot further," he said, "than I ever expected to be at this point."

I turned. From the look in his eyes, he wasn't talking about our investigation into my dad's death. For once in my life, however, I chose not to pry. "Hey," I said, dropping my feet to the floor. "I have an idea."

I was eager to add lightness to what could become a heavy subject. Gav seemed to need that right now.

"Tell me."

"Let's go hang that new shower curtain."

He gave me a look that said, "Really?" but heaved an amenable sigh. "Okay."

Taking the bathroom's tension rod down wasn't a problem. I slid the hooks off one side and allowed the plastic balloon–decorated monstrosity to tumble to the floor. "I should have gotten new hooks," I said when I looked more closely at the clear C-shaped gadgets. "Chrome would look good in here."

Gav leaned against the edge of the cabinet vanity and pointed. "But mine won't rust."

"You're right about that."

He studied me with a look that made me curious. I wanted to ask what was on his mind because he was clearly troubled. Rather than force the issue, however, I started working, inserting the plastic Cs into the buttonholes sewn into the red curtain, then sliding them into the holes of the shower liner, and finally onto the tension rod. I'd gotten about halfway through the process, working silently, ever aware of Gav's brooding presence.

I chanced a look up. He'd crossed his arms, still watching me.

"Ollie," he said, his voice gravelly, low.

I stopped what I was doing. "What's up?"

A stranger just happening by wouldn't have been able to

read the myriad of emotions that worked themselves across his features the way I could. My stomach clenched in response.

"We need to talk," he said. "About us."

I wasn't a teenager, or even a chipper twenty-year-old, so I wasn't completely blindsided. I'd felt the weight of an impending "talk" all evening. My heart raced. I resumed popping hooks on the tension rod, adopting a cheerful tone. "Okay," I said, "let's talk."

With my attention suddenly diverted from what my hands were doing, the hooks I'd been stringing began to slide off. I tipped the tension rod to keep the rest from toppling off the far end, losing my grip on the ones I hadn't hooked up yet. Three clattered to the tile floor.

Gav didn't seem to care about the mess I was making. "You have a career here in D.C.," he said. "An important one."

I picked up the hooks. "I do."

The apartment fell silent. Bathroom walls closed in around us. He swallowed, looked away, then back at me. "I have a career that's important to me, too. One that could take me away at any time. Far away."

"I know that."

"I told you I was passed over for an overseas assignment."

"I'm really sorry about that."

"Don't be." He waved that away. "No permanent damage. They think all I need is time. That I just need to get you out of my system."

"And?" I asked, steeling myself. "Do you?"

"No."

We stared at each other, he with his arms across his chest, me with the tension rod in my hands. "Is there something you're not telling me?" I asked.

He squinted at me, an expression I recognized. Whatever he was about to say would hurt.

Going for the preemptive strike, I guessed, "You're leaving, aren't you?"

He opened his mouth to answer but I cut him off.

"There's a position that's opened up, right? You're taking it."

Once I'd opened the floodgates, I couldn't stop my babbling.

"Soon. It's soon, isn't it? You've gotten word that something is coming down. Tomorrow?" I glanced down at the half-put-together project in my hands. It seemed such a useless, petty endeavor. I glared up at him. "You don't even want this new shower curtain, do you?"

I swore I heard him chuckle.

"The shower curtain is great," he said. "The best shower curtain in the world. I love the shower curtain. And I'm not going anywhere. Not yet."

"Then . . . what is it?"

He kept his arms crossed and the pain in his eyes was back. "I'm damaged goods. You know that."

I started to disagree, but he shook his head, silencing me.

"Let me say this my way, okay?" Even though he was across the room with his back to the wall, he drew into himself, farther away from me. Whatever it was he needed to say, he clearly needed space.

I wished we weren't having this conversation across a bathroom.

He stared at me, looking determined, hurt, and vulnerable all at the same time.

Sorely tempted to throw the blasted shower curtain to the ground and shout, "Just get it over with!" I fought the instinct and held my tongue, waiting.

He didn't move, but every inch of him tightened. Another agonizing minute went by and Gav looked around the little room as though suddenly realizing where we were. "Maybe we should talk about this another time."

Exasperation made me blurt, "No. Now."

He gave the briefest of nods. "Okay." He knew me well enough to know that I wouldn't let this drop.

"I can't . . ." he began. "That is, *we* can't . . ." He pulled in a deep breath and let it out slowly. "I can't . . . be engaged."

My tight grip on the tension rod loosened. "Come again?"

"I can't be engaged," he said again, enunciating clearly as though that would make him easier to understand.

"Engaged? As in, to be married?"

He nodded.

"I don't understand why you're bringing this up—"

"My track record speaks volumes. I can't do it again."

"I've told you before: You're not a jinx."

"I can't endanger you."

"You won't." The little C-hooks teetered precariously near the edge of the tension rod. I tilted it to keep them from falling, buying time. "But," I began carefully, "I didn't think we were at that point yet."

"I worry about you," he said. "I worry for your safety."

"Are you kidding? I worry more for yours," I said. "I have a safe job as a chef."

"Where you get into more than your share of trouble."

"I'm not in any trouble now," I said. "Or hadn't you noticed?"

"That doesn't mean—"

"Gav," I said gently, "life is dangerous. You and I both know that. Something could happen to me, but it wouldn't be your fault. Something could happen to you—" I stopped when I heard the words I was saying. I shuddered, then said, "I don't ever want anything to happen to you."

"I'm making you uncomfortable and that wasn't my intent," he said. "It's just that you and I are so right together."

"We are," I agreed. "Believe me, I'm sensitive to your history. I do understand. I've never expected you to . . . that is, I never expected us to . . ." Now I was the one having trouble coming up with words.

"Ever?"

I smiled. "If and when the time is right, we'll both know."

"That's the thing," he said, pushing off from the wall, "when the time is right, I'll want to act. Immediately. We can't have an engagement. We can't plan. We have to just do." He pierced me with his gaze. "That's not fair to you. You're not the one who the engagement gods seem to hate."

"I wouldn't know," I said, trying to lighten the moment, "I haven't ever tempted them."

He closed the distance between us, grasping both my arms and pulling me closer. C-hooks spilled to the floor, taking the new curtain with them. I let the tension rod drop.

"Someday, I don't know when," he said, "the time will be right. And when it is, the only delay will be what's required by law. Three days, I think."

"Three days."

"Unless we fly out to Las Vegas."

"No way."

He stared down at me. "That's assuming you're willing."

I knew better than to answer, but he put a finger across my lips just the same.

"No words now," he said softly. "All I ask is that you think about it."

CHAPTER 17

WHILE CYAN PREPPED INGREDIENTS FOR A ragout, and Bucky and I cleaned a variety of mushrooms Monday morning, Virgil put the finishing touches on breakfast for Mrs. Hyden and the kids. The president had taken his morning meal in the West Wing several hours earlier. During the school year, the president tried his best to share as many meals as possible with his family. With the kids on summer break and sleeping a little later in the morning, however, schedules had changed. Two breakfasts, two lunches, and occasionally two dinners, depending on how late the president stayed at his desk, had become the new norm. Virgil grumbled about it incessantly.

"I'm telling you," I said in a low voice to Bucky and Cyan when Virgil stepped out of the kitchen to grab an item from the refrigeration area, "as much as I miss working on the family's daily meals, having Virgil around has turned out to be a godsend."

Cyan's brow puckered. "That's a stretch, don't you think? He's helpful, yeah, but on his own terms."

"You have to admit, we have a lot more time these days. I've been able to work with Josh. We've all benefited from having more freedom to experiment than we have in the past. Our last state dinner was astounding. Thanks to you, Bucky. You've been coming up with adventurous new combinations."

Bucky's expression took on an air of studied nonchalance. "Thank you," he said, but I knew him well enough to recognize that my praise had hit home. "You're right about us having more time, but I can't say I care very much for our little diva."

"Personalities aside, he's become an integral part of this kitchen," I said.

"I wish they'd settle on a permanent chief usher," Bucky said. "Then maybe we could discuss the pecking order in this kitchen. Right now, Virgil thinks he's your next-in-command. That was my position. I'm not thrilled with the idea of coming in second to him."

I wanted Bucky to be my first assistant, too, but I wasn't sure how much sway I'd have with Doug. "It'll be best to wait until we have a firmer hand at the chief usher helm," I agreed.

"Until then, it's for better or for worse, I suppose," Bucky said.

His phrasing warped me back to my conversation with Gav the night before. It had played in my head repeatedly, to the point that I'd had difficulty falling asleep. I didn't believe for a moment that Gav was a jinx or that the dubious gods of engagement, or whatever he called them, had targeted him for tragedy. That wasn't what had kept me staring unblinkingly at the dark ceiling so late into the night. What had bounced in my brain were little pings of fear and guilt, combined with out-and-out longing.

I didn't know. Not yet. He and I had been together for a

relatively short time but we'd known each other for several years. The truth was, I'd never felt so comfortable, so at ease with being myself, with anyone else in my life. Gav saw me for who I was, as I saw him for who he was. We were good together. Better than good.

And his eyes twinkled when they looked at me.

I couldn't ask for more. Nor did I want to. At this point in my life, I knew that if I were ever to be married, it would be to Gav.

The question was, Could I be married when I had such a strong solo streak in me? He was right. His career was as important to him as mine was to me. Neither of us would be willing to give up all we'd worked for just because the other one—Gav, most likely—had been transferred.

I'd been on my own for so long, depended on myself so completely, that it was hard for me to imagine giving up that part of my life for anyone.

But Gav wasn't just anyone.

"You still with us, Ollie?" Cyan asked, waving thyme-covered fingers in front of my face. "You zoned out there for a minute."

"Sorry," I said, shocked that I'd stepped out of the conversation so completely. "Lots on my mind, I guess."

"Are you in some kind of trouble again?" Cyan asked.

"Where did that come from?"

Cyan and Bucky exchanged a look.

"*Am* I in trouble?" I asked. "That's news to me. I've been incredibly well behaved lately."

"You aren't investigating anything?" Bucky asked.

I couldn't share anything about my dad without explaining Gav's involvement, so I countered with another question. "What is going on here? You two seem to be much better informed than I am."

Again, the shared look.

"Quit it," I said. "What's going on?"

Virgil took that moment to reenter the kitchen, arms

laden with ingredients for whatever he had planned for lunch. He scooted behind Bucky without a word and went to work at the far countertop.

"You know that Agent Quinn," Bucky said. "He was in here early this morning, asking where you were."

Cyan added, "Secret Service agents don't usually come calling for you, Ollie. Not unless you're in hot water."

Virgil snorted. Measuring out butter, he turned to join the conversation. "Yeah, and then they swarm the place."

I pooh-poohed their comments. "I never turned in my disguise from Saturday. I didn't know who to give it to, so I took it home. I figured it would be nice if I at least cleaned the dress before I returned it. I'm sure that's why he's looking for me."

Cyan's and Bucky's exaggerated agreement and wide-eyed gestures told me they thought I was covering because Virgil was in the room.

"Really," I said, "if it's something else, I'm sure I'll find out. But I bet that's it."

"Or . . ." Virgil chunked a hand on his hip and turned to face us, "Quinn is sweet on you."

That made me laugh out loud.

Virgil waved his knife in the air, cutting through my mirth. "No, seriously. Think about it. When you're in trouble—which I've had the pleasure to experience more than once—this place is crawling with agents. Now it's just one: Quinn."

Bucky narrowed his eyes. "That's true."

"It's the costume, I'm telling you," I said.

Even Cyan looked skeptical. I was sorely tempted to call Quinn up on the phone just to put the matter to rest, but that may have been construed as protesting too much. "Fine," I said, "believe what you choose. When he shows up here, you'll understand."

About an hour later, Josh tumbled in, his mother following a moment later at a much more sedate pace. The boy

held one of the freebies we'd picked up Saturday. I recognized the DVD's cover immediately as one from a major
brand that had presented there. "Did you watch this, Ollie?"
he asked, eyes bright as he held it out for me to inspect.

From behind, the First Lady placed her hand atop her
son's head. "It would be nice if you said hello to everyone
first, don't you think?"

He looked around the room as though noticing everyone
else for the first time. "Oh, hi," he said. "I mean, good morning." To Virgil, he said, "Thank you for breakfast; it was
great." He twisted to shoot a grin up at his mom then turned
to face me again.

"This shows how to make a cheese fondue, step-by-step,
including stuff to dip. Can we do that today?" He looked
around the room again as though expecting any of the other
adults to shut him down. "My mom says if I make it, we can
all have it as part of dinner tonight when Dad's back
upstairs."

At this, Virgil sniffed, reaching for the DVD. Josh, who
had once held Virgil in high regard, eyed him suspiciously
before handing it over. Virgil examined the case, front and
back. "This was created by LaPlace Cheeses," he said, his
face scrunching with exaggerated pain. "I'm sure they made
certain to highlight all their own products in making this.
And two million people have this exact same recipe." Handling the DVD case with only the tips of his fingers, he
returned it to Josh. "I wouldn't ever make such a generic
item."

Downcast, Josh turned to me. "I guess this isn't all that
great then, is it?"

My earlier kind words for my colleague suddenly tasted
sour in my mouth. At that moment, if I could have banished
Virgil permanently in order to save Josh from the man's
careless insensitivity, I would have—in a D.C. heartbeat.

"Let me see it, Josh," I said, taking it from him. "There
is nothing wrong with LaPlace Cheeses," I said. "Not a

darned thing, and I would be happy to work on it with you. The one thing Virgil might be forgetting," I added, shooting a tight smile at my colleague, "is that every single recipe we prepare for our families is wonderful in its own way. We might follow this exactly; we might make a few adjustments along the way. Would that be all right with you?"

Josh's mood rose as I talked. "If we make adjustments then it becomes our recipe, doesn't it?"

"It can," I said, carefully. "We'll see what we do with it. It will be a learning experience for both of us."

"When can we start?"

I was about to answer when Agent Quinn came into the kitchen, stopping short when he spotted the First Lady and Josh there. "Ma'am," he said to her. He gestured the way he'd come. "I didn't realize we had members of the First Family down here. I'll come back another time."

"Hang on, Agent Quinn," I said. This was perfect. I could wipe out Cyan's and Bucky's romantic intimations right now. "You were looking for me earlier?" I asked. Without giving him a chance to respond, I continued, "Is it about returning my disguise?"

Agent Quinn seemed struck dumb by my question. "No, Ms. Paras. I'll be back later." He did a quick turn and was out of the kitchen before I could say another word.

"That was odd," Cyan said. She grinned at Bucky, who sent me a meaningful smirk.

"I'm sure he'll be back," he said.

I was a little rattled. I had no doubt my staff's matchmaking radar was way off, but having a Secret Service agent coming to talk was disconcerting nonetheless. I'd had enough experience to know that they rarely came bearing happy news.

Forcing my mind back to the present, I turned back to Josh. "Let's do this right after lunch, shall we? If that's okay with your mom." I glanced up.

Mrs. Hyden raised a finger over Josh's head. "That's fine

with me," she said, "but I would like a moment of your time," she used the same finger to point the way Quinn had departed, "if you wouldn't mind."

I followed her out, wondering what was up. She took a quick left and walked briskly to stand outside the kitchen service elevator. "What can I do for you?" I asked.

She smiled, but her eyes were sad. "Josh is having a tough summer," she said. "Abby has made new friends out here and, being thirteen, she's begun to view Josh as more of a nuisance than an endearing little brother."

Exactly as Doug had described, I thought.

The look on the First Lady's face was resigned. "I knew this day would come, and I don't blame Abby. She spends time with him, but most days she'd rather be giggling with her friends. I get it. I was her age once." Her bottom lip twisted with wry humor. "Too long ago to mention." She shook off the thought, continuing, "The worst part of it is, Josh hasn't had the same kind of social success Abby has. He's made a couple of friends, but . . ." She sighed. "This hasn't been an easy adjustment for him."

"I'm sorry to hear that," I said. "Can I help in some way?"

"You already have. Whenever Josh comes back upstairs after working with you, he's full of energy and back to his normal, cheerful self. You've been a great role model for him. Last week, the days you were off were tough for him. Because we have to be so careful all the time, he's become a lonely little boy."

My heart broke. I instinctively glanced back toward the kitchen, wanting to rush in there right now and tell Josh he was the greatest kid I'd ever met. "I'm so sorry," I said.

"I know it isn't part of your job description to keep Josh busy . . ."

"I'm happy to have him down here," I said sincerely.

Her frown lines softened. "Thank you, Ollie," she said. "Even if Josh changes his mind and decides to be a firefighter or a baseball player when he grows up, I know he's benefiting from being around you."

That had to be one of the most gratifying things anyone had ever said to me. My mouth went dry with surprise. "Thank you," I said. "But it really is my pleasure. He's a great kid."

"I think so, too," she said with a smile.

It probably wasn't my place, nor any of my business, but the moment was right. "Has . . ." I faltered, but pushed through anyway, "has his dad had any change of heart about Josh's interests?"

Mrs. Hyden wrinkled her nose and in that unguarded instant I saw her more as a contemporary—a friend sharing a disappointment—than as First Lady. "Not really, but I have hope. He's been busy lately and isn't able to see what Josh is working through. I believe, in time, however . . ."

She let the thought hang. I nodded my understanding.

She slid a hand down the side of my arm. "Thank you, again. For everything." She and I walked back to the kitchen, where she collected Josh. He promised to return immediately after lunch for our cooking lesson. When they left, I realized she hadn't asked me to keep our conversation confidential, hadn't asked for my word that I wouldn't talk about the president or his son to others. She trusted me.

I turned to my team. "Okay, what's next?" I asked with a particularly full heart.

CHAPTER 18

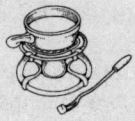

JOSH AND I HAD SPENT THE BETTER PART OF an hour slicing cheeses to sample before we settled on a combination. While we waited for a batch of Gruyère to soften, I'd had fun explaining a few tricks of the trade to my star pupil. Little things, like how to clean up as you go, how to turn vegetables into fun garnishes, and why we always rinse dishes in hot water. Bucky and Cyan had gotten into the spirit and by the time Fondue Combo Number Seven, as we so cleverly named it, was ready, the four of us were laughing and sharing war stories with an enraptured Josh.

After Virgil had served lunch, he'd disappeared from the kitchen. I was thrilled to have him gone while Josh was here. While the moody chef must have engendered some good will with the family that had prompted them to bring him to the White House, he clearly chafed under my authority.

"Look at this," Josh said, dipping a palm-tree carrot into the creamy cheese.

I wagged a finger at him. "What have I told you about playing with your food?"

"That's how you learn what works and what doesn't," he answered with no small degree of pride.

"Exactly."

From the doorway behind me, a very familiar voice. "Ms. Paras, a moment of your time?"

I turned to see Gav there. "Special Agent Gavin," I said, feeling my cheeks go pink. I hoped to heaven that Cyan and Bucky were paying more attention to Josh than they were to me. I'd have a hard time explaining my schoolgirl blush.

"A situation has developed," he said. "Can I pull you away from your duties for a few moments?"

"Of course."

He pivoted and strode out of the room. I wiped my hands on a nearby towel, then pulled my apron off.

"What's up?" Bucky asked under his breath. "You really are in trouble again, aren't you?"

I gave a helpless shrug and told the truth. "I have no idea what's going on."

He stared at the doorway then back at me. "Whenever that guy shows up, I know you're in deep. Be careful."

I could detect no underlying subtext leading me to believe he thought anything about Gav other than his being an agent who occasionally brought chaos into our lives. "I always am," I said.

When I made it out into the hall that surrounded the kitchen, Gav gestured to follow him across the center hall into the Map Room. "Sorry to pull you away," he said, after closing the door behind us.

"This is unusual," I said. "What's happened?"

"I have a meeting across town this afternoon," he said. "I won't be reachable for most of the evening."

He could have told me that over the phone. "Okay," I said.

His voice dropped and he spoke so softly I could barely

hear him, even in this quiet room. "My friend Joe wants to see us tonight."

I stopped myself before asking, "Yablonski?" because I knew Gav wanted to keep this collaboration as private as possible. While staffers weren't prone to eavesdropping, it never hurt to be careful. "But you just said you're busy tonight."

"Which is why you'll have to go on your own."

"I have no idea how to get out there again," I said. "Remember, last time I was paying more attention to the files than I was to the directions."

He shook his head. "New rendezvous point."

"Where do I go?"

"You'll be contacted."

I gave him my best "Are you kidding me?" look. "What, is this some kind of thriller movie now? Do I have to worry about being tailed?"

He gave me a lopsided grin. "There's always the risk of people following Joe. Some good guys, some not. Fortunately, no one will be watching your movements—at least, none that we know of."

"That's a nice way of saying I'm not all that important, isn't it?" I asked, a little chagrined.

"I would never say that."

"Thanks," I said, still in a complete state of disbelief. "Who will contact me, or is that a state secret?" My voice had risen, and I strove to quiet it. "Sorry. It's just that I don't fancy having some breathy stranger jump out of the shadows because he's been sent to talk to me."

Gav's grin widened. "That's exactly why he will have a code word."

This was almost too much, even for me. It was hard not to laugh. "Which is . . . ?"

"Balloons."

I must have reacted because he quickly added, "I came

up with it. I kept thinking about that old shower curtain . . ."

"Maybe we should have left it where it was," I said uneasily.

"No, I want the new one. It's a good change."

Wow, weren't we the demonstrative couple?

"When will I be contacted?"

"I don't know yet," he said. "It's still being arranged."

I resigned myself to tonight's covert meeting, wishing Gav would be able to be there, too, but knowing I was perfectly capable of handling it on my own. Joe Yablonski might be a tough old bird, but if Gav had that much respect for him, he had to be okay.

"You'll call me when you get in tonight?" I asked.

We both jumped as the Map Room door opened.

"Thank you, Ms. Paras," Gav said, brusquely. "I will let you get back to your duties." Smoothly, Gav greeted our guest. "Agent Quinn," he said without inflection. "We were just finished here."

Quinn seemed as uncomfortable stumbling upon us as I felt being caught. "Nice to see you again, Agent Quinn," I said, still very curious about what he'd wanted to talk about earlier. "I know our conversation got cut short this morning." I waved into the open room as we moved to depart. "Whenever you're done with your business in here, feel free to stop by the kitchen again."

He wore a disconcerted look. What was up with that? Could Bucky be right? Had I inadvertently gotten into trouble again? It wouldn't be the first time I was the last to find out. Was Virgil right? Was Quinn interested in me? "My apologies, again," he said. "I didn't mean to interrupt."

He left the room, his business there forgotten. "Good luck tonight," Gav said. "Let me know how it goes when you can."

"I will."

* * *

BUCKY AND CYAN LEFT AT FIVE. I STAYED TO
assist Virgil plating the Hydens' six o'clock dinner, which
went off without a hitch. I had to give my colleague credit.
Everything he'd prepared looked great and smelled even
better. Once we'd cleaned up after ourselves, Virgil packed
himself up and thanked me for staying to help.

Maybe there was hope for him yet.

I tugged off my apron, changed out of my work attire,
and dillydallied a bit, double-disinfecting the countertops
and making sure the place was pristine before shutting off
the lights. I leaned in the doorway for a moment, looking
around. Mornings and evenings were the best times; everything was quiet. Days like this one were rare. There were
no political upheavals or major catastrophes in progress and
everything in the world felt right.

How long would that last?

I pushed off the wall, ready to depart for the night. As I
turned to leave, I jumped. "Agent Quinn," I said when the
man appeared in front of me.

"I didn't mean to startle you," he said. "Do you have a
few minutes?"

I remembered Gav's instructions about being contacted
later tonight, but I didn't believe another five minutes would
make much of a difference. "Sure," I said, "what's up?"

One of the maintenance staffers zoomed by, rolling an
empty laundry bin. "Excuse me," he called, causing me to
step out of the hallway that rimmed the kitchen and back
into the dim room.

Quinn scratched his head. For a Secret Service agent, he
was a lot less sure of himself than most.

I noticed for the first time that he was carrying a diplomatic pouch and a file folder. "It's a good thing I caught
you," he said. "This came for you this afternoon and it's
marked 'Urgent.'" He handed the pouch to me.

"Thanks," I said, hefting it. "Doesn't feel as though there's anything in there." I studied the outside. "Who is it from?"

"Beats me."

"I appreciate you walking this over, but I'm sure you could have left it when you stopped by earlier."

"It only arrived an hour ago. That's not why I stopped by before." He blinked and held up the file folder. "I have this for you. I thought it best to discuss this when no one else was around."

He had my interest now. Tucking the diplomatic pouch between my elbow and ribs, I took the file folder, opening it as I asked, "What is this?"

"You seemed interested in Pluto," Quinn said, "and you mentioned your dad worked there a while back. I thought I'd dig up whatever I could from our files," he added.

"That was nice of you," I said sincerely. What I held in my hands looked to be almost identical to what Gav had come up with. I wasn't about to tell him that, and I took my time paging through the copies he'd made, trying to buy myself time. If I was reading signals correctly, this was a twist I hadn't expected, though Virgil and Bucky had. Not only that, I didn't want Quinn "helping" me overmuch with this project. At this point I didn't know what I might find.

"I can't thank you enough," I said. Before he could provide ideas on how I might be able to thank him, I held up the diplomatic pouch. "I guess I'd better see what's in here before I leave, don't you think?"

I turned the kitchen lights back on and placed the pouch on the nearest horizontal surface, opening it and wishing Quinn would leave. To his credit, he didn't crowd, remaining a respectful distance away while I retrieved and opened the single sheet of folded paper within. The note instructed me to visit a franchise restaurant on G Street. Once there, I was to walk in and order a small coffee and a bagel. "Okay," I muttered to myself. More cloak-and-dagger.

"Bad news?" Quinn asked. "Anything I can help you with?"

"I'm fine," I said with a glance at my watch.

"You're leaving, obviously. Can I give you a ride somewhere?"

That was about the last thing my mysterious colleague would want to see, being escorted to the rendezvous point by a Secret Service agent. "Thanks, but that might be awkward."

Quinn confused my meaning, but for once I was grateful to be misunderstood. "Oh, sure. See you later."

I breathed a sigh of relief when he was gone.

TRAFFIC BEING AS BAD AS IT WAS, I DECIDED to walk to the coffee shop rather than flag a cab. It was still warm, and would be for a few more hours, but I kept up a brisk pace, needing to stretch my legs, to move. I enjoyed being outside in the fresh air.

I scurried across G Street and spotted the coffee shop immediately, set back from the road in a sea of concrete. The neon OPEN light hanging in the window was unlit and as I drew closer I realized that all the inside lights were off. A sheet of paper had been taped inside the glass door with hand-lettered words: SORRY. CLOSED DUE TO ELECTRICAL PROBLEM. SEE YOU TOMORROW, WE HOPE!

I fisted my hips. "What now?" I asked rhetorically. Not expecting an answer, I leaned forward, cupping my hands against the glass to peer into the darkened coffee shop. No one inside. At least, no one in the public part. I detected shadows moving in back.

I turned around, scanning the area for anyone who looked as though he or she might be looking for me. No one jumped up and waved hello or took any notice of me. Commuters rushed by: men in suits and business casual and women in skirts and gym shoes, purses pulled tight to their sides. All of them walking with purpose. Tourists maintained a more leisurely pace as families consulted colorful maps and pointed south and southwest.

The note instructing me to show up here didn't specify a time. I wondered if my late departure from the White House had caused problems after all. If it had, Yablonski would no doubt give Gav an earful about me.

There wasn't much for me to do but go home to my apartment and await further instructions, if any. I was disappointed in one sense, relieved in another. Although Yablonski may very well be a valuable ally, and despite Gav's insistence otherwise, I got the distinct impression he hadn't liked me very much. Even more, I think he didn't like the fact that I'd become important to Gav.

I waited another moment, giving my fellow commuters one last look. A bum on a bench stared at the sky with one hand pillowing his head. He mumbled to himself, didn't even turn my way. Ten steps away, a young guy in a black suit paced while talking on his cell. He stared right through me. Clearly, he was seeing whoever was on the other end of his invective-littered rant.

I turned away from the coffee shop, bumping into a blonde man. Twenty-five, tall, wearing a gray suit and a loosened blue tie, he was out of breath. "They're closed?" he asked, looking over my shoulder at the taped sign.

Was this my contact? "Apparently."

"Hi," he said. "Are you meeting someone?"

A-ha. This had to be him. "I think so."

"Who are you here to meet?" he asked.

He hadn't given the code word. "Why don't you tell me first who you're meeting?"

Momentarily disconcerted, he straightened his tie. "I'm sorry it's closed. Maybe there's another place to have coffee nearby?"

"I think you and I are meeting two other people," I said. "I'm not your blind date."

"Oh. I'm sorry. I guess I'm mistaken," he said, stumbling over the words.

"Got it," I said, taking my leave. "I hope you find her."

I was about to leave the general area—to grab the Metro and head home—when my stomach reminded me it had been quite a while since I'd eaten. I remembered that I didn't have much in my house to choose from, either. Although I'd helped myself to a few tidbits during the afternoon, I needed a more substantial meal. Less than a block away was a fun new create-your-own-salad place. I headed for it.

Within minutes, I took a seat at a counter facing the window and watched the passersby as I dug into my arugula salad with fresh tomatoes and shaved Parmesan. I'd have to tell Gav about the glitch with the closed coffee shop. Maybe he'd be able to get in touch with Yablonski and make things right.

I wondered what Yablonski had wanted to tell us.

I finished my salad, took a last sip of water, and tossed my trash, wishing I could talk to Gav right now. I knew he'd be tied up late into the evening, so there was no hope of that. I'd stuffed the information Quinn had provided about Pluto into my cavernous purse. Maybe when I got home I'd go through it. The chances of Quinn uncovering an important tidbit we'd missed were slim, but I preferred to be thorough. Plus it would give me something to do tonight all by my lonesome.

I'd just stepped onto the sidewalk in front of the salad shop when a car pulled up into the no-parking zone in front of me. The dark sedan had tinted windows, a dented passenger side door, and a crooked bumper. The driver got out, stood in his open door, and waved to me. "Ms. Paras?" he asked.

"And you are?"

"Come with me," he said.

I wagged a finger at him, taking note of the busy sidewalk

around me. "I'm not about to get into a car with a person I don't know."

The guy was mid-forties, maybe older. Paunchy, with a ring of brown hair around his sweating head, he wore a plaid short-sleeved shirt and a glare of impatience. "Ms. Paras, how do you think I know your name if you're not supposed to come with me?"

Too many people—some with diabolical plans in mind—had attempted to get me to go with them. "Sorry," I said, hands up in the air. "Not going to happen."

We were starting to cause a scene. People were giving us odd looks as they swerved around me on the sidewalk.

I gave the guy one more moment to provide the code word, then decided to walk away.

He grunted loud enough for me to glance back. He'd leaned toward the open door, keeping both hands on the roof, looking like Kilroy but without the overhanging nose. He held up an index finger, which I assumed was a signal for me to wait. I didn't.

I heard the door slam, and Mr. Plaid Shirt jogged toward me, sweat stains darkening his shirt deeply below both arms. "Wait," he called, without shouting.

I let him catch up. Nothing at all like the young man purportedly waiting for his blind date, this guy's breathless speech came out with chunks of spittle. "What the heck is wrong with you?" he asked by way of greeting.

"I don't know you," I said. "Unless you can prove who you are, I'm not going anywhere with you."

He rubbed the side of his face, glancing back at the idling sedan. "Oh yeah, right. Hang on. I remember. Balloons. Happy now?"

I gave him the evil eye. I didn't want him to be right, but he was. "What's your name?"

"You don't need to know." He pinched my elbow between his thumb and forefinger. "Can we get going now?"

I yanked my arm free. "I am perfectly capable of walking on my own. I am not getting into that car until you tell me where we're going."

"He said you were difficult," the guy mumbled.

"Who said that?"

This sweaty guy had big eyes, the kind that look like giant white cue balls with itty-bitty dark marbles in their centers. "You got any idea how much trouble you're making for my boss?"

"No, I don't."

By this time, we'd reached the car. He didn't answer, simply opened the back door on the passenger side and ordered me in.

I wasn't happy to be herded like a reluctant sheep, but I obliged.

"Good evening, Ollie," Quinn said from the other end of the backseat.

CHAPTER 19

"WHAT ARE YOU DOING HERE?" I ASKED.

"I was supposed to meet you at the coffee shop," he said, with an amused shrug. "We didn't anticipate an emergency closure."

The bald fellow had closed my door and come around to the driver's seat. He pulled into traffic, muttering up a blue streak.

"Wait, I don't get this. Why didn't you say something back at the White House?" I asked. "And . . . wait." It dawned on me that I hadn't ever met Quinn until our stealth operation at the Food Expo on Saturday. "Hey . . . are you really a member of the Presidential Protective Division or are you just a plant?"

Quinn leaned back against the door, watching me. "Good job. You put that together fairly quickly."

My brain was on overload. "But why?"

Quinn seemed far more at ease here than he ever had at

the White House. "A gentleman you and I both know . . . the gentleman you will meet with this evening . . ." He waited for me to acknowledge that I knew he was talking about Yablonski. I nodded. "That man put me on special assignment to keep an eye on you at the White House."

"Why?"

"I didn't ask. I do what I'm told."

"But today in the kitchen, we were alone," I reminded him. "Why didn't you say something there?"

"We can't take chances of anything we say being overheard."

This was too much intrigue for my tastes. I rubbed my forehead, vaguely aware that we'd turned and were heading west. Trying again, I asked, "You don't know why I'm meeting with . . . this gentleman, do you?"

"Not yet," he said.

"So where are we going?"

"Let me ask you something," Quinn said as the bald guy took a right turn. A break in traffic allowed him to speed up, which he did with gusto. "What business do you have with our mutual friend? And what does any of that have to do with the information in that file I gave you?"

"Who says they're related?" I shot back. "Why did you make those copies for me, anyway?"

"There's nothing in there you couldn't have found on your own," he said.

"You didn't answer the question."

"No," he said, "I didn't."

We were silent for about a mile or so. "Massachusetts Avenue?" I asked when we made another left. "Are you taking me to one of the embassies?"

Again not answering me, Quinn asked, "What is your real interest in Pluto?"

"Why do you care?"

He leaned forward, speaking softly, but there was an edge to his voice I didn't understand. "I don't believe for a moment that it's because your father used to work there. Everyone in the Service knows about your tendencies to get into trouble—"

"Why?" I asked before I could stop myself. "What's going on with Pluto?"

I should have let him finish. From the way his face closed up it was clear he'd believed I knew more than I did. I felt more in the dark than ever. "I've got nothing against the company," I began carefully. The last thing I wanted to do was say anything that brought my father's service record into question. That was another matter, one completely separate from his Pluto days. I didn't want anyone looking into that until I had gotten the information, myself. "I was interested in the company because my dad died when I was really little. Anything I can learn about him is like gold to me."

His scornful gaze didn't soften. "I'm not sure I buy it. Not that it matters. Our mutual friend will deal with this."

The "mutual friend" euphemism again. "Does *he* know who I'm meeting?" I pointed to the driver, who seemed to be constantly checking his mirrors and blind spots. Suddenly it dawned on me why. "Does he think we're being followed?"

The driver met my eyes in the rearview mirror. "We aren't being followed," he said with disdain, "but it never hurts to be too careful. You could learn a lesson about that."

"What is this, pick on Ollie day?"

Quinn seemed to find that funny. "Our driver is fully apprised. If you sense his ambivalence," he leaned forward to pat the guy on the shoulder, "it's because driving subjects around is way below his pay grade."

I didn't know why I was instantly irritated, but my suddenly caustic tone couldn't be helped. "So then why aren't we referring to our *mutual friend* by name?"

"One never knows who's listening."

"I can't believe this is all because I'm bad for agents' careers. Give me a break," I said, feeling the ire rise, "I'm a chef, for crying out loud. Don't you think this is overkill?"

"Let's hope so," Quinn said.

We were silent for the remainder of the ride.

OUR BALD CHAUFFEUR PULLED UP AT A BUS stop just outside the National Cathedral. "We're here," Quinn said. "Let's go."

We left the car and driver, taking a short winding walk up to the giant church. "Isn't it closed?" I asked, with a look at my watch.

Quinn never broke his stride. "This way," he said.

A guard at the door was waiting for us. He let us in and told Quinn where to find him when we wanted to leave.

Once inside, we made our way down the center nave. I looked up at the stained glass windows that lined either side, high up, about thirty feet from the floor. A large black net had been stretched along the length of the center aisle to catch pieces of stone that might fall on unsuspecting visitors.

The earthquake that had hit D.C. had caused damage to several of our cherished monuments, the National Cathedral included. The church had been closed to visitors for months after the quake, and had only recently reopened. In a city that boasted countless structures of beauty, the cathedral was a standout. I hoped for all our sakes that repairs moved quickly.

Of all the stained glass windows I'd seen in my life, those here were among the most vibrant in color and unique in subject matter. Although the sun was waning and the bright windows weren't quite as spectacular as I knew they would be on a sunny afternoon, they were beautiful just the same.

A violet-and-indigo-hued window high to my right captured the beauty of stars and planets on a clear evening. I'd never been able to find the carving that purportedly was designed after Darth Vader, and didn't expect I'd have time to look for it tonight.

I followed Quinn to a set of stairs, which I knew led down to the crypt. I wasn't faint of heart, but I did have to ask, "You're kidding, right?"

"Ladies first," he said.

Quinn had become brusque, uncommunicative, and all business. Earlier this afternoon, I'd been convinced he was nervous because he wanted to ask me out. Was I delusional, or what?

Quinn led me through several awe-inspiring passages and finally stopped in a small nook with a kneeler, a set of vigil candles, and a narrow stone stairway curving up to a dark unknown. Quinn handed me a dollar. "Here," he said, "when you're ready."

I was about to ask ready for what, when I understood. I knew the vigil candle routine. Put a donation in the little metal box and you earned the right to light a candle for a deceased loved one.

"I'll be upstairs," he said.

I peered around the corner to watch him walk back the way we'd come. I didn't turn back to the vigil lights until I saw him make a left far down the corridor. The silence in the little area was deafening. I'd heard that phrase before, but understood it now. I was underground, surrounded completely by thick stone and the honored dead.

I folded the dollar, worked it into the metal donation box and lit a candle. Maybe it was supposed to be a signal, maybe it was nothing at all, but I couldn't help but think about my dad and whisper, "I'm going to find out what happened to you if it kills me."

"Let's hope it doesn't," Yablonski said.

I heard him before I saw him marching down the curved stone stairs with his back as straight and tall as if he was trying to touch his head to ceiling.

"Where does that lead?" I asked when he made it down to my level. I started to peer up the stairs, but he waved me away.

"There's no one up there," he said. "You can be certain of that."

"I wasn't—" I started to say then thought better of it. "Gav said you had information of interest. I understand that you don't want to be seen with me. Why can't you be seen with Gav? If you met with him, he'd be happy to tell me whatever you shared with him."

"Young lady—"

"My name is Olivia." I reminded him with a little clip to my voice. "I'm Ollie to my friends, but Ms. Paras works, too."

He cleared his throat. "Yes, of course. Before we get to the substance of this conversation, I will answer your question with one of my own. You are here by yourself because I need to know something for my own erudition."

"And that is?"

"What are your intentions with regard to my friend Leonard?"

"Gav?"

He flinched. "I understand that I am considerably older than you both, but I don't understand how it is you refer to him by his surname rather than his given one. If you truly cared about him, that is."

"I do," I said levelly. "Make no mistake about that."

"*If* you do," he repeated, stressing the word, "how can you not use his first name? That seems disrespectful at a minimum, and cruel."

I took a step back, as though slapped. "He prefers I call him Gav," I said, angry now. "That's what you wanted to talk about?"

"I also have information for you, so don't go running off yet. You'll be disappointed if you do."

"What kind of information?"

"Answer my question first. I haven't seen my friend this deep in a relationship in a very long time. And you and I both know how things turned out for him."

"You believe that nonsense about him being a jinx?"

"I believe he will not survive another loss. You and I both know how reckless you've been in the past."

"Reckless?" I nearly squeaked. "That's condescending. If you knew exactly how each of those situations really went down, you would understand."

"Ms. Paras," he said in a more gentle tone than I could have expected given my raised voice, "please understand, I do know. Everything. About every situation you've been involved in."

That rendered me speechless.

"I am not here to criticize you."

"Then why was that the first thing out of your mouth?"

He closed his eyes for a moment and I guessed he was counting to five. "Let me begin again. You have helped the White House." He waited for me to acknowledge that he'd used the word *helped*.

"Go on," I said.

"The truth is, you've kept the Secret Service informed as much as you possibly could have. That doesn't excuse your involvement, but it does mitigate fault."

"Gee, thanks." I tried to tamp down my anger. "I'm sorry," I said. "That was uncalled for."

His expression shifted, enough to let me know he appreciated my apology. "I am here for two reasons: one business, one personal. Before we get to the business, I wanted to talk about you and Leonard. My fear," he said, "is that he will go to any length to protect you. As I said, he can't withstand another loss like the tragedies he's already endured. He will see to it that nothing like that ever happens again."

I began to see Yablonski in a new light. "And you're afraid that my tendency to get into trouble could ultimately hurt Gav?"

"Yes. He will put himself at risk. His life at risk. Anything to avoid losing you."

"Because I'm looking into my dad's history?" I asked. "How's that going to get me into trouble?"

"As far as I can tell at this point, it won't," he said. "I'm not worried about that. What I'm worried about is that Leonard sees a future with you. A future that could be cut short because of your reckless behavior."

I was about to protest but he stopped me with a look. "Consider my words. That's all I ask. Now, for the other matter."

I bit back the anger streaming up the back of my throat. "Go ahead."

He shook his head as he began. "I haven't been able to get to your father's military history yet. Not without raising suspicions. What I have been able to do, however, is look into Pluto, Incorporated."

Was he about to provide the same basic information that Quinn had this afternoon? This would have been a complete waste of time. "Anything of interest?"

"Quite," he said, surprising me. "I would not ordinarily share the following information with you, but it may be in all our best interests to do so."

"It's not classified, is it?"

He gave me a look that screamed "stupid question," and began again. "I wouldn't share anything classified with you. I will tell you, however, that what I'm about to impart is not the kind of information a civilian might be able to dig up on his or her own. It's confidential in that regard."

"Yet you're willing to share it with me. Even though you don't like me very much."

"Whether I like you is immaterial. What matters is that you trust me. Leonard assures me that if you do, you'll be more likely to heed my instructions."

"There's truth in that."

"You will keep whatever I share with you confidential?"

"I'll tell no one except Gav."

"Fair enough. Here's as much as I know at the moment: Pluto, Incorporated is currently under investigation."

"By whom?"

He didn't like being interrupted. I could tell by the quick flash of teeth before he spoke again. "Authorities I do not care to name are looking at the company right now. That's as much as I can tell you."

It became obvious to me that this meeting was more to talk about Gav than about my concerns. But finding out that the company was under investigation was something.

He wasn't finished. "Agent Quinn tells me you engaged in conversation with a Pluto representative."

"I did," I said. "I didn't give her my real name. And I was disguised at the time."

"I am aware of the circumstances. What I do not understand is how you think any information you glean about the company from their ads could have any bearing on your father's murder."

I shrugged. "You never know what you'll find until you look."

"Indeed."

"Has Gav told you about our conversations with my dad's former colleagues?"

"We haven't had the opportunity. Why don't you fill me in?"

I did. I told him about our visit to Harold Linka's home and our more recent talk with Michael Fitch. "He knows something he isn't telling us," I said. "I hope to find out."

"How do you intend to continue?"

"I plan to talk with him again. A little pressure could do the trick. He seemed fidgety."

"Do not visit either individual again without informing me first."

"Why not?"

"I can't tell you that. And please keep me updated."

"Via Gav?"

He gave a curt nod.

"And you'll keep me updated as well?" I asked.

That quick flash of teeth again. "To the extent I can." He

waved toward the stairway. "Go on. Quinn will be waiting for you upstairs. He'll see you to the car and home safely."

"Thanks," I said. "One more question."

He not only didn't like being interrupted, he got annoyed when people didn't jump when he issued an order. "Does anyone else know that Gav and I are involved?" I asked, adding quickly, "Have you told anyone? Quinn, for instance?"

"I see no reason for him to know your business."

"Good." I started away then stopped. "I appreciate your help, you know. Even if I seem ungrateful, I'm not. But I am protective of Gav."

"As am I." He gave me another tight grimace. "Leonard is the son I never had. Any assistance I render you is done only as a favor to him."

You didn't get much clearer than that. "Understood," I said.

CHAPTER 20

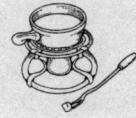

WE WERE AT FULL STAFF TUESDAY MORNING, with Virgil preparing the family's breakfasts and Cyan, Bucky, and I discussing the four official dinners the Hydens had planned for the next couple of weeks. Cyan had her elbows on the countertop, palms supporting her chin as we studied the data we'd been given. "Half the guest list is attending all four dinners," she said. "I guess that means no repeat items for these events."

"I guess not," I said. "Looks like we'll have to come up with four amazing, original dinners. But that's what we do best. I'm not worried."

"Neither am I," Cyan said. "Coming up with menus is fun. Preparing them even better. It's keeping it all straight in my head that I'm concerned about."

"That's why we keep such scrupulous notes," I said. "In fact, I wanted to ask you about what you meant by scribbling—"

"Olivia, there you are." Thora, the woman who'd outfitted me in my disguise, swooped into the kitchen, taking in the area all at once. "Is this where you work your magic, dear?" she asked. Without waiting for me to reply, she reached out to Bucky, grasping his hand in both of hers. "So wonderful to meet all of you talented chefs. I am so in awe of the work you do for the president and his family each and every day."

Virgil turned. "I prepare the family's daily meals," he said. "They only work on the social events."

"My mistake," Thora said without missing a beat. "You must be Virgil. So wonderful to finally make your acquaintance." When he looked down to wipe his hands on his apron, Thora gave me a conspiratorial wink. "I've heard *quite* a bit about you."

He perked up at what he assumed she'd meant as a compliment. "Have you?" he asked. "Let me show you around then." Virgil took a few moments to explain his creations, over which Thora oohed and aahed at appropriate intervals. When she thanked him and insisted she leave him to his work, she returned to our little circle and I made quick introductions with the rest of my staff.

"What brings you to the kitchen?" I asked. "If it's about the wig and dress, I have them at home, but I'll be happy to bring them back whenever you want."

"No rush, dear. I have quite a stash of supplies. That's not what I came to see you about." She sent a wide smile to Bucky and Cyan before fixing glittering eyes on me. "You wouldn't have a moment for some girl talk, would you?"

Me? Girl talk? This woman clearly did not know me well. "Sure," I said because I was curious, but mostly because I was polite. "Follow me."

We stole into the China Room, a room I generally associated with bad news—a trend I was eager to reverse—and closed the door behind us. "What's on your mind?"

For the first time since we'd met, Thora was flustered. Her smile was still brilliant, but she patted the side of her hair, fluffed her neck scarf, and twisted her multi-ringed hands as she chattered inanely about nothing in particular.

"Thora," I said in a quiet voice, "what is this all about?"

"Your friend," she said finally, in a quiet, confessional tone. "I find myself utterly smitten with your friend and I wondered if, perhaps, you would do me a stunningly huge favor and talk with him to see if, perhaps, the feeling is mutual?"

"My friend," I repeated, thinking back to the last few moments in the kitchen. "Virgil?"

Her hands fluttered skyward. "Oh heavens, no." She gave an affected shudder. "I'm talking about your friend Peter."

It took me a long moment of feeling stupid before I made sense of her words. I barely got the question out. "Sargeant?" I knew my voice betrayed my incredulity.

"He's such a doll." Thora was beside herself trying to stifle giggles. "Do you believe there's any chance he might be interested in me?"

This was almost too much for my little brain to handle. "I don't know," I said honestly, "but he'd be a fool not to."

"Oh, thank you, you are so sweet," she said. "Ever since our meeting the other day, I haven't been able to get him out of my mind."

"Peter Everett Sargeant," I said to be clear. "That's who we're talking about."

"Yes, indeedy." She covered her mouth with both hands as though reluctant to share a secret, but continued talking with barely a pause, "This all sounds so junior high, doesn't it? At my age, though, I neither want to waste time nor embarrass myself." She made a happy so-so motion with her head. "Embarrass myself *unduly*, that is. We should all feel free to let our authentic selves out for the world to see." In a whisper, she added, "But with matters of the heart, I am a bit more cautious. You understand."

"I'll talk with him," I said. "How may I get in touch with you?"

"Of course, silly me," she said, digging a business card from a tiny beaded purse hanging from her elbow. "Here you are." She tapped it with a long red fingernail. "Let him know he can call anytime. And thank you."

"WHAT WAS THAT ALL ABOUT?" BUCKY ASKED on my return. Cyan looked interested as well.

"Long story," I said, rubbing my eyes. "Did I just get back from vacation?"

"You did," Cyan said.

"Then why do I feel as though I need another one?"

"It gets worse," Bucky said.

I looked up. "What?"

"Doug wants to see you upstairs."

I couldn't help it; I groaned aloud.

"Too much work for our fearless leader?" Virgil asked in a mocking voice. "Maybe it's time we got a chef who knew how to take charge."

I didn't have the energy for a comeback, but Bucky and Cyan rose to my defense, chiming in together to tell Virgil how wrong he was. "Stop," I said, putting my hands up. "You're not going to change his mind about me, so don't waste your breath."

Virgil smirked, as though he'd won this round.

"I'll see you guys in a bit. Let's hope whatever Doug wants to see me about is low priority."

I took the steps two at a time, wanting to stretch myself, wondering what in the world Thora saw in Sargeant and why she'd enlisted my help to make a love match. On my way up, I ran in to the object of my contemplation on his way down. "Peter," I said, not knowing exactly what to say next, but wanting this particular task scratched off my to-do list as soon as possible, "will you have some time this afternoon?"

I noticed that he seemed startled, as though I'd pulled

him from deep thought. "Today?" He looked up and down as though a copy of his schedule was printed on the steps. "I'm not certain. A situation has come up."

He, like Thora, was flustered.

"Everything okay?" I asked.

A frown creased his brow. The tight persnickety personality he was so fond of was nowhere to be seen. "I don't know."

He started to descend the steps again, forgetting me immediately. I watched until he turned the corner. I'd have to try again another time.

Doug was in his office on the phone, as usual. He waved me in and wiggled his fingers to indicate I should shut the door.

When he hung up, he folded his hands on his desk, looking like a little boy in a desk that was too big for him. "I have good news," he said.

"I love good news," I replied, gauging his mood at this pronouncement. "What is it?"

"The president and First Lady are close to a decision about naming a permanent chief usher."

My heart sank. Not because we didn't need a chief usher at the helm, but because of Doug's obvious glee. "That's great," I lied. "Who's in the running? Beside you, that is?"

"That I don't know," he admitted. "They've interviewed at least a dozen potential candidates, but I know for a fact that most of them washed out. As far as I know, it's between me and one other man."

"How do you know? You met the candidates when they came for their interviews?"

He shook his head. "The Hydens are keeping the list of interviewees quiet. I happen to have a few connections." He winked. "They're getting close to a decision, and a good friend of mine overheard them saying that they're impressed with my work."

"You mean Virgil overheard," I said.

Doug could barely sit still. "Virgil wouldn't be able to sway them. He hasn't been here long enough. But you could. Sway them, I mean."

"What are you talking about?"

"Write a recommendation for me. You've got capital with them. They'll listen to what you have to say."

"Whoa." I waved my hands. "Hold on. First of all, if they're ready to name you to the position, you don't need me."

He scratched the back of his neck and for the first time looked unsure of himself. "They didn't exactly say me, not precisely. Virgil said they don't use names in front of him. They talk about the 'Ivy League' candidate, the 'California' candidate, like that. I'm apparently the 'in-house' candidate."

"Virgil shouldn't be repeating their conversations, you know."

"There's nothing of national security in . . ." he began.

"You think that makes it okay?" I couldn't even begin to describe how wrong it was for Virgil to toddle back with business the Hydens believed was being conducted in private. Something needed to be done about that. At the moment I didn't know what it was. In the meantime, I decided to probe a bit deeper. "Listen, Doug, I know how much you want to be named to the permanent position, but I think it would be a mistake for me to get involved."

"We've both worked at the White House longer than the Hydens have."

"So?"

He looked at me with irritation, as though I was stupid to not comprehend. "You and I know what's best for them."

I wanted to tell him he was being ridiculous now, but he was so focused on himself he wouldn't recognize good sense if it slapped him across the face. "I've got people waiting for me," I said.

"Hold on a minute, please," he said. "It's probably only a matter of days before they make an announcement."

"The anticipation builds."

He didn't even notice my sarcasm. "It would mean a lot to me if you'd write that recommendation. I know the Hydens have been looking at people from the outside. If you could tell them how much better it would be for all of us to promote from within . . ." He stared up at me with imploring eyes. "Please, Ollie. This is really important to me."

Doug wasn't cut out for this job and I couldn't say that he was, no matter how hard he tried to convince me otherwise. I didn't want to hurt his feelings, but I didn't know how to extricate myself without crushing him with the truth.

"Don't ask me for that, Doug," I said, in a last-ditch attempt to let him down gently. "I can't."

"Can't? Or won't?" His gaze turned hard. "What happens when the new guy is some ex-military who runs the staff like a drill sergeant? Or some twenty-five-year-old smart aleck? You'll be sorry then."

I started for the door. "You may be right."

"Just wait," he said to my back. "They'll name me, even without your recommendation. I'll remember this. We'll see how different life is around here for you then."

Angry at him for putting me in this position, angry at myself for trying to spare his feelings when he clearly held mine in contempt, I opened the door and turned. "Threatening me because I won't comply is beneath the position of chief usher." I smiled, showing teeth. "Unfortunately, however, you just proved it isn't beneath you."

His mouth gaped.

"Think about that," I said and walked out.

VIRGIL WATCHED ME CLOSELY FOR THE REST OF the afternoon. Or was it my imagination? Bucky, Cyan, and

I worked through all our plans, both of them pulling me aside on separate occasions to ask if I was all right. "A lot on my mind," was all I could say. If Doug was right about his having the inside track on the permanent position, I might eventually regret my actions upstairs.

Nah.

Whether he got the nod or not, worrying about it wasn't going to help. I tried to bury myself in work, belatedly remembering my promise to Thora. "Has anyone seen Sargeant recently?" I asked.

No one had. I went to the computer and sent a note asking him if he might have a few minutes to talk. I didn't give any indication of the subject matter. How would one phrase it, anyway? "The woman who'd dressed you in a Pink Floyd T-shirt and ponytail wants to know if you'd like to date her?" Hardly the stuff of interoffice correspondence.

I signed off and thought about calling Gav. I hadn't heard from him the evening before, but he'd left me a text this morning to let me know he was up and out again. There were long spans where we didn't see each other at all. I hoped we weren't in for one of those now. Of course, I always hoped that.

I needed to talk with him about my meeting with Yablonski. I decided that my interactions with the caustic fellow were coloring my mood and I didn't like it one bit. I looked around the kitchen. They would be fine for a few minutes without me. I decided to give Gav a call. "I'll be right back," I said, pulling my cell phone out of my pocket as I made my way out toward the pantry. "I'll be upstairs if you need me."

I made my way to the Butler's Pantry on the main level. With no official meals going on right now, I knew it would be quiet there. As soon as I reached the narrow room, I made my way to the window and dialed. "Hey," I said when he answered. "You have a few minutes?"

I heard the smile in his voice. "I'd love to say anytime for you, but we both know how that works. Yeah, what's up?"

Now that I could talk, I found I had too much to say for a phone conversation. "Last evening was interesting, to say the least," I said. "I'm itching to talk with you about that. And about . . . politics going on here."

"Politics? In the White House? Surely you're mistaken."

"Ha-ha," I said. "Not those kind of politics. I mean the really annoying kind."

"What's wrong?"

"I have another call coming in. Hang on."

I pulled the little device away from my ear and debated answering. I didn't recognize the number, but curiosity won out. "Hello," I said.

A woman's voice. "Is this Olivia Paras?"

"Yes, how may I help you?"

I had my back to the rest of the pantry, but noises made it clear that another person had come in. I turned to see Quinn there. I raised a hand in greeting.

"This is Ingrid," she said, "Mickey Fitch's wife?"

"Oh, hi," I said, dumbfounded. "How are you?"

Quinn crossed his arms and leaned against the far wall, mouthing, "I'll wait."

I shook my head, but he either didn't notice or pretended not to.

"Not good," Ingrid was saying. "Mickey's been acting strange since you were here to visit."

"How do you mean?" I asked, giving Quinn a hand-brushing signal to please leave.

"He's been different," she said. "He doesn't talk and he snaps at me when I ask him what's wrong."

That didn't seem much different from the attitude I'd observed.

Quinn had pushed off the wall as though to heed my request. He looked at his watch, then up at me.

"What do you need from me?" I asked Ingrid, but Quinn seemed to think I was talking to him. He tapped his watch, then pointed out the door that led to the State Dining Room. I nodded, eager to see him gone.

"Mickey gave me a box yesterday," she said. "He told me not to open it. Said I wouldn't like what was inside."

Quinn closed the door behind himself and I breathed a sigh of relief.

"Did you?" I asked. "Open it, that is?"

I could almost hear her shake her head. "He taped it shut."

So much for trust. "Where is he now?"

"That's the thing. I don't know. He took off as soon as he gave this to me. Didn't say when he'd be back."

"What do you want from me, Ingrid?"

"Mickey told me to give the box to you."

That shut me up. "Me?"

She sounded near tears. "I'm worried about him. He isn't so good in the world by himself, you know? He has problems."

"I understand."

"Can you meet me?" she asked. "He told me to give this to you, but he also said not to let anyone know I was doing it. That scares me. Like he thinks people are watching. He's so paranoid, and most the time I think he's just off his nut, you know? But it's different this time."

"Where are you?"

"I'm out by where my sister lives. I took the train. Mickey said to stay away from home until it was safe. I could meet you somewhere close to you," she said. "I know my way around the city."

As oddball as I'd found Mickey Fitch, I couldn't dismiss how much her words chilled me. "What time?" I looked at my watch.

"I don't know, maybe about eight o' clock? Eight-thirty?"

"At night?"

"It'll take me a while to get out there from here. And I kinda want to keep moving, if you know what I mean."

I thought of asking Gav if he—

Oh geez! Gav was still on the other line.

"Sure," I said talking fast now. "How about we meet at one of the monuments or memorials," I said. "You pick."

"Oh . . . I don't know."

"How about the FDR one?" I suggested. "It's not out in the open. We'll be able to find a quiet place to talk."

"I guess."

"Which era?" I asked.

When she didn't answer immediately, I realized I'd confused her.

"It's in four sections," I said, "like giant outdoor rooms, one for each of his presidencies. We can meet in any of them."

"Oh, I don't know . . ."

I wracked my brain for a part of the exhibit she wouldn't be able to miss. "The breadline," I said, wanting to get back to Gav before I had to face Quinn. "There's a life-sized sculpture of men standing in a breadline. I'll meet you there."

"Breadline?" she asked, unsure. "You mean . . ."

I was probably short with her. "You know, back during the Depression when people stood in line for bread. There are statues there. You can't miss them."

She didn't sound terribly convinced when she said, "Okay, I'll see you there around 8:30."

"Looking forward to it," I said automatically, making a face to myself as I heard the happy phrase I usually reserved for friends. She hung up and I clicked over to Gav. "Argh," I said again.

"I thought you forgot about me."

"Never. Hey, listen, all of a sudden I can't talk, but I need to know what you're doing tonight."

"I'm free in about an hour. What's up?"

"Tell you later. Can we meet out here? Say around six?" I named a local restaurant.

"This sounds like it's going to be good. Catch you then."

I hung up in time to see Quinn return. "Off the phone now?"

"What's up, Agent?"

"Yesterday," he said, lowering his voice and stepping closer. "Outside the coffee shop, you had a conversation with someone. Who was it?"

I pointed to myself. "I had a conversation? I don't remember that."

He stared at me with dead eyes. "You don't remember talking with a young man?"

"I didn't—Oh!"

"You remember now?"

"That wasn't much of a conversation. When I found the shop closed, I looked around for likely suspects. He seemed to be looking for someone, too. I thought he was my contact. I was wrong. He was looking for a girl."

Quinn raised an eyebrow.

"I got the impression it was a blind date."

"That's all it was?"

I put my hands up, feeling cranky because of Doug's bombshell and subsequent request, the pressure while I'd been on the phone, not knowing what I might be walking into this evening with Ingrid, and because I didn't like being interrogated as though I'd done something wrong when all I'd done was follow the rules. "Yeah, that's all it was. Are we done here?"

Quinn's teeth nipped his lower lip on one side. "Yes, ma'am," he said. "All done."

Agitated and frustrated with myself for losing my temper, I excused myself as I passed Quinn and took the circular staircase down to the ground floor.

"You missed Sargeant by about thirty seconds," Cyan said when I returned.

Oh yeah, the Thora situation. "Which way did he go?"

She pointed out the other doorway. I was torn. We were cleaning up for the evening and I hated to leave my staff with all the last-minute business.

"I thought he said something about the curator's office," Cyan said, "but I can't be sure. We're just about done here. If you need him, go on."

"I hate to leave all the work to you guys."

Virgil gave a hearty snort.

Bucky rolled his head toward the other man, shooting him a derisive look that Virgil missed, completely. "You get stuck here late more than anyone," Bucky said to me. "If it makes you feel better, come back here after you talk with Sargeant. You can double-check our cleanup."

"Thanks," I said, heading out again.

Sargeant was just exiting the curator's office when I caught up with him. "Peter," I said, heartened to notice he was looking less dazed than he had last time I'd seen him. "You have a moment?"

He went tense immediately. Would we always have this effect on one another? I thought about his assurances that his observations of me and Gav would be kept confidential and I decided to press forward. "This won't take long," I said.

"Certainly." He waited, clearly expecting me to start talking here in the center hall.

That would not do. I peeked into the nearby library. The last time I'd been in here it had been with Sargeant, going over mug shots. "There's no one in here."

He didn't remark, simply followed me in. I could tell curiosity was getting the best of him, but he wore an air of calm I hadn't seen on him for a very long time.

"What's so pressing, Ms. Paras?" he asked when I closed the door.

Now that I had him here I barely knew where to begin. "It's a matter of some delicacy."

"Oh?"

I gave a self-conscious chuckle. "This may seem very odd. I feel strange in this situation . . ."

"Ms. Paras," he said sharply, "I have never known you to mince words around me. Please get to the point."

"You're right. Here it is as plainly as I can give it to you: Thora, the woman who set up our disguises for the Food Expo, is interested in you." I waited for that to sink in before adding, "Romantically."

If I'd have taken one of the heavy tomes from the shelves and smacked him across the face with it, he couldn't have looked more surprised. "You know this?" he asked. "Or do you simply suspect?"

"She asked me to act as intermediary."

"Oh," he said again, but this time with that dazed look on his face again. He massaged the small area between his brows and closed his eyes for a moment. "Today is certainly a day fraught with surprise."

"What else has happened?" I asked.

He shot me a quizzical glance, then his gaze relaxed. "It may shock you to hear this, but I'm sorely tempted to tell you. Unfortunately, I'm not at liberty to discuss it. Not yet."

"Sounds serious."

He took a sharp breath. "Yes."

"When you can discuss it, if ever, I'll be happy to do what I can to help."

His mouth twisted, half up, half down. I couldn't tell if he was trying to smile and his muscles simply couldn't remember how, or if he was about to chastise me again. "That time may come. In the meantime, this situation with Thora . . ." He didn't look displeased. "Quite unexpected."

"If you're concerned about letting her down I can tell her—"

"No, no, that's not it."

My turn to be taken aback. "All right then, whatever you want." I suddenly remembered the card and dug it out of my pocket. "Here, she gave me this. It's all yours."

"Thora," he said to himself as he studied it. "She's tall."

"She is."

Making eye contact once again, he smiled. It was a sight I hadn't often had the opportunity to experience. "Is she here today?"

"I saw her this morning. I'm sure if she's still around, Doug will be able to find her for you."

His eyes clouded. "Doug does not care for me overmuch."

"That makes two of us."

He made a noise that could have been a chuckle.

"Have you heard that the Hydens are thinking of naming him to the position of chief usher, permanently?" I asked.

He frowned. "That would be a travesty."

"I agree."

CHAPTER 21

GAV AND I LEFT THE RESTAURANT A LITTLE before eight, giving us plenty of time to walk to the FDR Memorial and get there well before our appointed time with Ingrid. I'd brought him up to date on my clandestine trip to the National Cathedral and subsequent discussion with Yablonski. I left out Yablonski's review of our love life.

I finished by saying, "He didn't have a lot to share beyond the fact that Pluto's being investigated. He wouldn't even tell me for what. He doesn't want me to visit Fitch or Linka without letting him know, so I suppose we ought to tell him about this visit with Ingrid tonight."

Gav listened, taking several moments to reply. "He won't be reachable this evening. I know that much. I'll contact him first thing tomorrow. We'll know more by then."

"Another thing," I said. "Why didn't you tell me that Quinn was one of Yablonski's go-to guys?"

Gav expelled a breath that could have been a laugh. "It

never occurred to me to mention it. Yablonski has connections in every possible corner. There are plenty of people around us every day with ties to him. From here on, it will be better if you assume he has eyes and ears everywhere."

I gave him a sidelong appraisal. "Et tu, Brutus?"

He laughed for real this time. "You know better than that."

As we strode west along the National Mall, Gav looked up at the dimming sky. "I'm very glad I'm able to come along on this excursion," he said. "Mickey's wife calling you out of the blue raises flags."

"For me, too," I said. "I don't know what to expect."

The first time I'd visited the FDR Memorial, I'd come at it from the back and walked through in reverse chronological order. That hadn't made the experience less enjoyable. In fact, I liked being able to take in each presidential term before moving backward through time. I had, however, returned on multiple occasions to go through from beginning to end. That's where we started today.

We passed the statue of Franklin Delano Roosevelt in his wheelchair on our way to the breadline sculpture. Ingrid wasn't there yet. "It's still a few minutes early," I said. "Let's walk around."

Tourists took pictures of each other, posing with the statues of men in the Depression-era breadline, as well as with the one of a seated man, leaning forward in eager attention, listening to one of FDR's Fireside Chats.

Gav and I meandered, looking like tourists ourselves. We headed deeper into the presidency, admiring the many waterfalls and stonework. "This place is magnificent," I said. "It's one of my favorite memorials."

Gav gave a low chuckle. "You say that about all of them."

"I suppose I do," I said. "Whenever I visit, I'm overwhelmed by their beauty."

He grabbed my arm, silencing me as Ingrid came into view. She walked quickly, gripping a small box tight in her hands, looking this way and that, like a shoplifter making a furtive getaway. And not a particularly adept one, seeing as how she missed us watching her. As she hurried past, a flurry of birds rushed out from one of the nearby trees with a wild rustle of wings and flutters. Ingrid gave a tiny yelp, clasping the box closer and ducking away.

We started after her, catching up as she reached the breadline exhibit. Her head twisted right and left; she was clearly looking for us.

"Go on," Gav said. "I'll keep an eye on you from here."

I approached the woman. "Ingrid?"

She yelped again, spinning to face me, one hand flying free from the side of the box to clutch at her throat. "Oh, it's you," she said. "You scared me."

The way she studied the people near us, a family with kids in strollers, an elderly couple, a group of twenty-somethings placing baseball caps atop the breadline heads for photos, made me believe she was losing her grip. Her eyes were wide and it looked as though she hadn't slept in days. "I came from my sister's," she whispered. "Going right back there after this. Mickey said that if this got into the wrong hands, it could be bad."

Ingrid thrust the box at me as though eager to be rid of the vile thing. "Here, it's yours now."

I hefted it. Lightweight and no bigger than a paperback, it didn't resemble the shoe box my mom had saved my dad's letter in, but it reminded me of it just the same. I didn't want to examine it too closely in front of Ingrid. "And you have no idea what's in here?"

"None," she said. "Scout's honor. I never seen Mickey as worked up as he was when he gave it to me. I'm afraid for him."

"Why didn't Mickey come with you?" I asked.

Ingrid looked ready to cry. "I told you, I haven't heard from him. Not since yesterday. I left a note at home telling him I'd be by my sister's and I thought he'd call or something."

"You haven't been back home yourself?"

"Too scared."

She backed away from me, eyes darting from side to side so quickly I didn't think she was giving herself time to digest what she was seeing. She gasped.

"What?" I asked.

Stepping closer once again, she lowered her voice. "That boy was on my train," she said. "I noticed him at my station. He got on the same time I did. He followed me here."

I glanced at the object of her scrutiny. An average height, average build young man wandered about twenty feet away. He wore a baseball cap with the brim pulled low over his eyes, plaid shorts, and running shoes. I couldn't get a look at his face, but he didn't seem to pay us any attention. I was about to say as much when he shuffled away into the next outdoor room. "He's gone," I said unnecessarily.

"I think he was following me. Now he knows I met you and gave you the box."

Gav couldn't have been close enough to hear our conversation, but he must have read our body language. The boy had about a ten-second head start before Gav followed him away. Despite the fact that it was getting dark now, I wasn't worried. There were plenty of tourists around.

"Ingrid," I said, placing a hand on her forearm. "You should be okay now. Why don't you call your husband and let him know you gave me the box. Maybe he's home, waiting for you."

"Maybe," she said, unconvinced. "He told me to tell you something else—something I knew, but we promised never to breathe a word of it to anybody."

"What is it?" I asked.

She swept the area with cautious reserve before inching still closer. "I don't know why he wants me to tell you," she said, her voice wavering. "I don't know what good it's going to do anybody. It could only get us into trouble, I think."

If ever a person needed to be coaxed, it was Ingrid. "He must have had a good reason," I said, "and I'll bet it will be good for me to know once I open the box."

Rocking back and forth on her heels, she gave the object a biting look of scorn, as though it held all the power in the world and was responsible for the plight of her life. Maybe it was. I'd find out soon enough. In the meantime, I couldn't allow her to leave without delivering the entire message. "What did he tell you to tell me, Ingrid?"

Maybe it was hearing her name, but she seemed to snap out of her reverie. She took a breath, visibly steeling herself. Whatever she was about to impart wouldn't be easy for her to do.

"He wasn't sick when he left Pluto," she said at last. "Not even a little. Healthy as a horse and just as stupid."

"Wait," I said. "I don't understand."

"Listen," she said, "all's I know is that when Mickey was working there at Pluto, he was scared about something but he wouldn't ever tell me what it was."

"Before or after my dad was killed?"

She pointed at me. "Right after. I'd gone and forgotten about it—it's been so long, you know—but ever since you showed up, he's been nervous again." Panic turned her mouth downward and I was afraid she might break into tears.

"Right after your father was killed, Mickey came home all shook about things at work. At first he told me he was upset about losing a friend, but he got worse over the next few days instead of better. I'll never be able to forget how your dad's murder changed our lives. And not for the better."

Anger sparked from her dull eyes, though I could tell it wasn't directed at me. She was seeing a story play out before her, her stinging criticism directed at events that had happened many years ago.

"About a week after the murder," she continued, "Mickey wanted to quit his job. Told me he planned to give his notice even though he didn't have anything else lined up yet. I thought that was a bad idea and said so. We were thinking about starting a family right then." She gave a sad laugh but didn't elaborate. "Mickey insisted that he had to quit, so I told him go ahead if it was so important."

"Did he?"

Ingrid shook her head. "Came home that night shook up worse than ever before. Another guy at work had a bad accident." *Harold Linka.* "They thought he wasn't going to make it through the night. Mickey said that he couldn't quit now. I asked was it because they'd be shorthanded with the other guy gone, but he said no."

I had a feeling I knew the answer to the question I was about to ask. "Then why couldn't he quit?"

"Mickey said what happened to the other guy was a warning. He said if he quit, they'd come after him."

"But he did quit," I reminded her.

"He went on disability," she corrected. "He got my doctor brother-in-law to make a diagnosis that wasn't true. Said that he was so sick he couldn't work or he'd die."

This sounded hokey. "You're trying to tell me that Pluto—"

"*Shh!*"

"You're trying to tell me that your husband believes that the company injured Harold Linka on purpose?"

She nodded. "That other guy knew everything that was going on. More than Mickey did, and as soon that guy opened his mouth, they tried to kill him."

"He still works for them," I said, poking a hole in her story. "He works from home."

"I'm telling you what happened," she said. "Doesn't

matter what's going on now. You weren't there when it was going on twenty-five years ago. Mickey knew that if he tried to quit, it would look suspicious. So he figured another way out."

"By claiming a disability."

She made a noise of disgust. "Barely enough to live on, so I took a second job." The look in her eyes was weary—not just physically, either. "It's been tough for both of us." She took a step sideways. "Now you know it all."

I didn't. I fought the urge to rip the box open right then and there, to see what was inside before Ingrid hurried off, in case I had questions about any of it. But Ingrid was liable to turn into a puddle of panic right in front of me.

She sent worried looks all around. "I stayed here too long. That guy may come back."

With Gav trailing him, I doubted it. "Do you need help getting home?"

She shook her head, waves of fear emanating from her as she started away. Now that her mission was accomplished, it was clear she couldn't wait to be gone.

"Ingrid . . ."

"I don't want what happened to your dad to happen to Mickey."

"You think it could?"

"I don't know what to think." She eyed the box in my hands. "It's your problem now," she said. "I don't want nothing to do with it. All's I want is for me and Mickey to have things back the way they were." She started off again, turned and said, "Don't you be calling or showing up anymore."

She didn't wait for me to respond before she was gone, in the opposite direction the young man had disappeared.

Gav came back around the breadline a moment later. "Think about the devil," I said. "Where did you go?"

"I followed that kid."

"Ingrid said she thought he was following her."

"I'm not surprised."

"Why?"

"Got a weird vibe from him. He seemed to be paying attention to your conversation before Ingrid pointed him out to you. I wanted to know why."

"What did you find out?"

"Not a thing. He couldn't have been more than fifty steps ahead of me, yet I couldn't find him."

"Gone?"

"In a flash. You noticed how he was strolling when he was here?"

"I did," I said.

"Seems to me he took the rest of the exhibit in a flat-out run. No other way he could have been gone without me seeing."

"That's not good."

"Did he seem at all familiar?" Gav asked.

"I couldn't get a good look at him. Too dark, and with that hat . . ."

Gav and I stood there, he watching one direction, me the other. "I guess we got what we came for," I finally said, showing him the box. "Let's find out what's inside."

CHAPTER 22

WE WAITED UNTIL WE WERE BACK AT MY apartment to open the mysterious package. In the kitchen, I used scissors to cut through the shiny brown packing tape Fitch had used to secure the small container. "You ready?" I asked as the lid came free.

"The bigger question is, are you?" Gav said.

We both stood next to the kitchen table, breathless. I lifted the lid, eager to see what was so damaging that Mickey had ordered Ingrid to make sure she hadn't been followed. Inside were several sheets of paper, folded in half. I lifted the pages out, disappointed there was nothing more beneath.

"Fitch has a flair for the dramatic," I said. "Three sheets of paper could have easily fit in a standard envelope mailed from his local post office."

"Let's see what he has to say."

We sat at the table, Gav pulling up a chair so we could sit next to each other. I unfolded the papers and scanned the first, Gav reading over my shoulder. Although I was a quicker reader, he was always more thorough. As I finished each page, I handed it to him.

The room was quiet, with only the hum of the refrigerator and the occasional car horn outside to keep us company.

When we got to the end of the missive, I turned the final sheet around, hoping for more, then waited for Gav to finish reading. When he did, he met my gaze. "There's no doubt Fitch is a lunatic," he said, "but if any of what he's alleging here is true, the repercussions could be explosive."

"I started this to find out the truth about my dad, not to bring down a corporation. All I want is to know that my dad wasn't the villain in this story."

Gav's mouth was set, grim and tight. "Then you'd better hope everything Fitch claims is true."

I laid the three sheets side to side on the table between us. What we'd read was nothing short of a manifesto. Fitch's tiny, cramped handwriting, interspersed with underscores and exclamation points scratched in so violently they occasionally ripped the page, was a real eye-opener.

Like Gav said: If any of it was true.

"Look at this," I said, my eyes roving, finding the passages I most wanted to discuss. I pointed to one of Fitch's first assertions. "Here. Remember when we visited Craig Benson? The Cabrigan flag he had in the corner? That fits. Sylonica is the sworn enemy of Cabriga. It's been that way for as long as I can remember."

Fitch told a story that was high on emotion and short on detail, but what he claimed to know, while damaging to Pluto Incorporated, would be personally ruinous to Craig Benson. Back when my dad worked for the company, Fitch wrote, Craig Benson had arranged to have "special shipments" of supplements sent to Sylonica under the guise of humanitarian aid. The supplements, however, were anything but. Benson directed that Ingredient X, a deadly toxin, be included in all products sent to Sylonica. While levels of

Ingredient X wouldn't immediately kill those who ingested it, it would most certainly hasten their demise.

"If this is true," I continued, "Craig Benson was attempting to kill people halfway across the world, in the name of loyalty to his family's country."

Gav pursed his lips, letting air escape in a thoughtful whistle. "The problem I see is that this is all very self-serving," he said. "Fitch is making some outrageous assertions here without offering a shred of proof."

"My dad found out," I said, "according to Fitch. That's why they killed him."

"That's quite a claim." Gav tapped the pages in front of us. "Notice how nothing he states here can be confirmed unless we find this so-called proof." Gav shook his head as he read aloud. " 'Craig Benson is a creature of habit. He always kept everything under lock and key in his antique desk. I wouldn't be surprised to find out all the proof is still there.' "

"I wonder what kind of evidence he's talking about."

Gav chewed on his lower lip. "There's nothing in this that's actionable. We can't get any kind of warrant or move forward. Not without more."

"Do you think this is what Yablonski was talking about when he told me that Pluto was being investigated?"

Gav considered this. "According to Fitch, all this happened twenty-five years ago. Why would Pluto be under investigation now? Fitch can't be suggesting that this has been going on all these years without anyone noticing."

"I think that's exactly what he's suggesting."

"Why not take this to the authorities then? Why all the drama sending his wife with a secure package, claiming she might have been followed," Gav pressed, "unless Fitch is working hard to manufacture mystique?" He sat back and stared at the ceiling. "I'm not saying this can't be true. I'm saying that we need to proceed with caution."

I'd been thinking along similar lines. "I hate to say it,

but because my face has been in the paper enough times, Fitch may be counting on me to run with this. But to what end? Unless he holds a deep grudge against my dad that we're unaware of—and he wants to take me down because of it—I can't imagine why he'd make all this up."

Gav steepled his fingers in front of his face. "I can't either. We're missing a piece of this puzzle."

"I want to go back."

"Where? Pluto?"

"Yes," I said, gritting my teeth as I stood to pace. "I want to watch Craig Benson's face as he reads the letter. Then I'll know."

"That won't be good enough for you. Admit it." He waited for me to look at him. "And if any of this is true, can you imagine the kind of danger you'd be walking into?"

"Let's think about this." He listened while I strode back and forth in the small room, explaining how I could bring Benson to justice. And once my father's name was cleared of wrongdoing—the way I always knew it would be—I would take on the government and prove that any charges the military had brought against him were just as false.

"I could arrange to meet him," I said, in a moment of brilliance. "Hang on." I tore out of the room and returned a moment later with the disguise from Thora. Waving it in front of me, I said, "I can wear this and meet him at a public place. I could confront him with what Fitch wrote and see where it leads."

Even as I spoke aloud and tried to make reason fit my wishes, even as I heard the words pour out of my mouth, I recognized the impossibility of what I was proposing. Gav remained silent, his attention on me, the look in his eyes changing from skepticism to sorrow.

At last I couldn't take it anymore. I sat, spent, dropping the blonde wig and pink dress into my lap. "It won't work, will it?"

He shook his head. "All you would do would be to let

him know you're on to him. That will probably only make things more difficult. For everyone."

He was talking about the alleged investigation into Pluto that Yablonski warned about.

"I know. I don't want to mess things up if Yablonski is already on to them." I raised my eyes to the ceiling and covered them with my hands. "My dad is innocent," I said.

"I know."

"It's not good enough. Not until I can prove it."

"I know that, too."

"Maybe," I said, doubting the words even as they tumbled out of me, "your friend Yablonski will have an idea about what we can do next with this letter."

Gav hesitated and in that instant I could read that he didn't want to disappoint me by throwing obstacles in my path or by pointing out the obvious. "Maybe," he agreed, but I knew he wasn't confident his friend would let us in on an active investigation. "It's worth a try."

"Tomorrow, then?" I asked. "I could probably ask Quinn to make contact for me, but I bet this would be better coming from you."

Gav folded the pages and tucked them into his wallet. "First thing tomorrow, I'll give him a call."

I placed a hand over one of Gav's. "Thank you," I said, "for listening."

"I wish I could do more."

THE NEXT MORNING, I THREW MYSELF INTO preparations for our next big event, ticking items off my list and arranging for a tasting with Mrs. Hyden. With Virgil upstairs and Cyan lending a hand in the Navy Mess, it was just me and Bucky in the kitchen. I cruised on autopilot, waiting to hear from Gav, or even from Quinn, that perhaps Yablonski wanted to speak with me again.

Nothing.

Hours went by without a word. I checked my phone every three minutes, until Bucky called me out on it. "What is up with you today?" he asked. "You haven't been this jittery in weeks. What kind of trouble are you in this time?"

"None," I said. "I'm waiting for a call."

"Anyone special?"

I forced out a laugh as though that was the silliest of questions. "Yeah, I'm waiting for word from my boyfriend. We plan to elope tonight."

He gave me a critical glare. "I wouldn't doubt that."

"Yep," I said, pulling my phone up out of my pocket. "As soon as he calls—"

At that, the phone came alive, bringing with it my boring, yet serviceable ringtone.

Bucky smirked. "Should I summon the limo?"

I glanced at the display. Gav.

Starting for the door to give myself privacy, I answered.

"Turn on the TV," he said without preamble.

I stopped in my tracks. "What?"

"Turn on the television," he said in a voice that didn't invite argument. "Now."

I pivoted and returned to the kitchen, clicking the mouse to take the computer out of standby mode. "What channel?"

"Doesn't matter."

This couldn't be good. As I loaded the page we usually used to track news, I said, "Is it about the White House?"

Bucky came over to watch.

"No," Gav said. "I'll call you back in a minute."

He hung up.

"What is this?" Bucky asked.

My jaw dropped as the story unfolded before me. A dark-haired woman with a handheld microphone narrated the scene behind her. "Repeating our breaking news: We are here in Fairfax, Virginia, in front of Pluto, Incorporated, waiting on word from authorities."

I wanted to shake the computer to make her words come faster. "What happened?" I asked aloud.

"What's going on?" Bucky asked. "Why is this important to you?"

"I don't know yet," I said, trying to block him out. The woman was speaking again.

"Police are not releasing details," she said, "but those employees we've been able to talk with claimed they heard gunfire." The reporter stood back, gesturing toward a young woman who was talking to another reporter. Even though I could only see her profile, I recognized her as Erica, the receptionist. "This woman told us that a man stormed in earlier, brandishing a gun. Before she could call for help, he'd raced into owner Craig Benson's office. The woman heard shots fired. At this point, we do not know what state Mr. Benson is in, or what injuries, if any, he may have sustained. Stay tuned."

"Mickey Fitch," I said under my breath.

In my peripheral vision, I watched Bucky's attention bounce back and forth between the screen and my face. "What now, Ollie? Talk to me. What's going on? Why do you know about this?"

I held up a finger, waiting to see if they had any more specifics to share, but the reporter began rehashing everything she'd already said. I turned to him. "It's a long story," I said.

My phone rang. Gav. "I saw it," I said when I answered.

"It had to be Fitch."

"What do we do now?" I asked.

Bucky didn't even try to conceal his eavesdropping. He watched me as I gripped the phone tightly, and I realized I didn't care if he listened in. I'd known Bucky for years now, and he'd never broken a confidence.

"I'd gotten in touch with my friend earlier," Gav said.

"You know . . ." Frustration and the feeling of being useless made me interrupt. "I'm getting tired of being so careful with 'our friend' and 'your friend.' " I tried to lower my voice, but anger had mounted itself in my chest and needed to vent before it exploded all over everyone. "What good is all this subterfuge when we can't prevent situations like this?"

Gav didn't answer. I knew he was waiting for me to calm myself. I knew he felt as helpless as I did. He was just handling it better.

"I got in touch with him," Gav said again, this time avoiding the "my friend" euphemism. "He wants to meet this afternoon. At his office."

My sarcasm reared its head one more time, though there was significantly less bite to my words when I asked, "Not some clandestine, out-of-the-way secret meeting place?"

"Apparently not."

"What's changed?"

"I don't know," he said. "I'm sure we'll find out. I'll pick you up in twenty minutes."

"I'm at work."

"Quinn will handle your absence. See you in twenty."

When we hung up, Bucky gave me a sad, knowing look. "I thought you might stay out of trouble for a while this time," he said. "It's starting again, isn't it?"

I heaved an uneasy sigh. "To be honest, Bucky, this one started a very long time ago."

CHAPTER 23

GAV PICKED ME UP IN A GOVERNMENT-ISSUE vehicle, and insisted on silence until we parked and made our way into a nondescript office building. He allowed me to pass first through the revolving doors. Together, he and I crossed the two-story glass-walled lobby to the elevator banks.

"I'd called Joe first thing this morning, as promised. I told him about the letter," Gav said while we waited for an elevator to arrive. "As soon as the news broke about Fitch, he called me back and insisted we come in immediately."

"We don't actually know it was Fitch who invaded Pluto," I reminded him. "The news hasn't released—"

"It was Fitch."

He was making an effort to avoid eye contact. "What else do we know?" I asked.

"I'm sorry," he said, "but Joe told me to let you know that Fitch was killed."

"How?"

"The details are sketchy but apparently security took him down."

Gav held his arm against the elevator's door to allow us to board. We remained silent again on the ride up until we arrived at our floor, where we found ourselves in a narrow hallway.

I was processing all he'd told me when a woman in combat fatigues stepped out from one of the doors that lined the corridor. Clear skin, brown hair pulled back into a low bun, she instructed us to follow her.

At the far end of the corridor, she opened a white door and allowed us in. "I will be outside if you need anything," she said and shut the door behind us.

Yablonski stood as we entered. "And what have we gotten ourselves into now?" he asked rhetorically.

Positioned behind a massive metal desk with his back to a wall of windows overlooking the city, he gave off an air of smoldering fury. The office itself was no more than a large storage room, with two eight-foot tables along the walls, both of them piled high with bankers' boxes. A discreet knock at the door and the uniformed young woman entered, carrying three metal folding chairs, which she set up in front of the desk before ducking out of the room once more. I wanted to ask who the third one was for, but the scowl on Yablonski's face kept me mum.

"Sit," he said, as he resumed his own seat. "A man burst into Pluto today, threatening to shoot people. A man you"— here he lasered his gaze on me—"recently interviewed. A man whose wife dropped a bombshell of information in your lap last night, which I only learned about this morning. Have I left anything out?"

"Not that I can tell," I said, keeping my chin up even as we sat down.

"When I agreed to help my friend Leonard find out about your father, I wasn't aware of the current investigations into

Pluto. Nor"—here he took a deep breath—"was I aware that my inquiries on your behalf would pull me into these investigations. And now with this Fitch business . . ."

"I had no idea he was planning to go to Pluto," I said.

He glared at me.

"What happened there today?" I asked.

Clearly exasperated, Yablonski looked to Gav, who maintained a stoic expression.

"Mr. Benson is being very tight-lipped at the moment," Yablonski said, "but we've talked with several witnesses. They report Fitch being agitated. He was shouting."

"About what?"

Yablonski sent me a withering glare. "What do you think?"

I needed to hear it.

"Fitch demanded that Benson 'come clean' about murder and about mass killings." He stretched his lips, then continued. "The witnesses had no idea what he meant by that, of course. But we do, don't we? He was talking about your father's murder and about the shipments to Sylonica, as described in the letter Leonard told me about today. To us, these are disturbing allegations. To the rest of the world, Fitch is a garden-variety lunatic who cracked under stress, determined to kill the hand that fed him."

"What does that do for the investigation?"

"Your investigation is over. The only man who may have been able to assist you, Mickey Fitch, is no longer able to help."

"Harold Linka may have known what was going on, too."

"The man won't talk."

"How do you know that?" I asked. "Have you even tried?"

When he smiled, it was ugly and frightening. "We are not so inept as you would like to believe," he said.

I rubbed my temples. There was too much to take in at once. Too many fronts to manage. "So why bring me here today?" I pointed to Gav. "Why summon us both here? Why not just reprimand me long-distance?"

"Because," he said with a sidelong glance at Gav, "I may have more success corralling your efforts if I share what information I can."

I was stunned. "There's more?"

He shouted at the door. "Come, Ms. Byrne."

When she walked in, I nearly jumped out of my chair. The shock of pink hair on one side rendered her instantly recognizable. This was the woman I'd met at the Food Expo, the one who'd asked my name and with whom I'd discussed job openings. I remembered immediately. "Sally Burns," I said.

She was dressed much more flamboyantly this time in cerulean-blue pants, a stylish long yellow jacket, and flowery blouse. "It's Sarah Byrne, actually," she said in a light Australian accent. "I've adopted the name Sally Burns while undercover."

"Undercover?" I turned to Yablonski. "She's one of yours?"

He nodded as Sarah took the empty chair. "Sarah's been enormously effective in her role. With her . . ." he coughed, ". . . unconventional appearance . . ."

"And the fact that I'm a jazz singer in my spare time . . ."

Yablonski interrupted, "Yes, that. I can't deny that the combination has been effective. No one ever suspects Sarah as being one of ours."

She held her hands out, grinning. "Don't mess with success."

Yablonski turned to me. "Let's talk about your visits to Harold Linka and Michael Fitch again."

"I told you about those already," I said.

"Yes, you did. And we will go over them again. And again, if necessary. Sarah and I need you and Leonard to remember every detail, every nuance, whether you believe it important or not."

I glanced over at Gav. He looked as unsure as I did. "What are you looking for?" I asked Yablonski.

"If I told you, that would influence your responses, wouldn't it?" he said. "Now, let's start at the beginning, shall we?"

Three hours later, I was spent from talking, from answering the same questions more times than I could count. Gav seemed to be holding up much better than I was and I realized he'd probably been trained in handling interrogations, which is what this had turned out to be. Sarah and Yablonski came at us with questions about Fitch's and Linka's homes, their wives, their demeanors, and their reactions to my showing up on their doorsteps. Twice during the interrogation Yablonski called the fatigue-clad woman in to refresh our water when we ran dry.

By the time we called it quits, my throat was parched, my tongue was numb, and I urgently needed to use the washroom. I couldn't leave yet, though. I needed an answer to a question of my own. "What about my dad?" I asked when Yablonski dismissed us.

His lids were heavy over bloodshot eyes, making me realize our grilling had taken a lot out of him, too. "Ms. Paras, when you and I first met, you agreed to cease your investigation on my command."

"If you had good reason," I reminded him.

"Bringing you in this way, introducing you to Agent Byrne, and providing you with the knowledge that we are in the middle of a difficult investigation isn't enough for you?" The words were sharp, but his attitude had changed. He was weary.

"I can't give up on my dad. Not yet."

"I can't stop you from looking into your father's life, but only where it does not overlap with Pluto, Harold Linka, or Michael Fitch. I'm sorry, but I have to order you to let this matter drop."

I hesitated.

"Ms. Paras, this is a matter of national security. Your cooperation is essential."

I sucked in a deep breath. "Then you have it," I said.

THURSDAY MORNING, I WAS BACK IN THE White House kitchen, bright and early. I'd scrubbed potatoes, chopped onions, and started a chicken marinade before anyone else made it in. It was busywork, but keeping my hands occupied while my heart was in turmoil was the only way I could work through this.

Much as I wanted to, I couldn't hate Yablonski. He was doing his job. He'd promised that he wouldn't ask me to back off my investigation unless it was necessary. I believed him. I had no choice. The fact that Gav trusted him went a long way to mitigate my vengeful feelings toward the man. Yesterday I'd sensed, however briefly, that he sympathized with my plight and that he wouldn't have asked me to sacrifice my quest if it wasn't absolutely necessary.

I dug handfuls of asparagus out from our chilled storage and set to work trimming the stalks for later use. The mound of fresh greenery would keep me engaged for an hour, at least.

Virgil, the first to arrive after me, was immediately suspicious. "What are you doing in so early?"

"Keeping busy," I said.

Perhaps it was the tone of my voice that quelled his curiosity. He left me alone after that. When Bucky and Cyan arrived and greeted me a few minutes later, I smiled, said hello, and went back to work. Preparing meals in the White House kitchen was one of the true joys of my life, but today I had to force myself to push through tasks that normally had me humming.

"Everything okay?" Bucky asked quietly when Virgil stepped out. "You get things sorted out yesterday?"

How to answer? "It's not that," I said. "It's personal."

"I'm sorry, kid," he said with kindness in his eyes. "You let me know if there's anything we can do for you."

"Thanks, Buckster," I said with forced cheer. "I'll survive."

"Whoever he is," he continued, "he doesn't deserve you."

I decided to let Bucky believe my sadness had to do with a broken heart. In a way, it was true, except that the "he" in question was my dad, and Bucky was wrong. My dad deserved far better than I'd been able to give him.

A few hours later, I was pulled from my musings by the sound of Josh calling my name. "Ollie!"

He stood in the doorway. "Hey, Josh," I said as he made his way in accompanied by his sister, Abby. A contingent of Secret Service escorts accompanied the duo. "What's up?"

"I told Abby about how much I've been working down here with you."

His sister had lingered in the doorway a moment, finishing a conversation with one of the other staffers.

"Hi, Abby," I said as she stepped in. "How's your summer going?"

"Really well, thanks." She then greeted everyone else in the room. "My mom asked me to bring Josh down this morning. He wants to ask a favor."

"Could we throw a party?" he asked. "A small one, I mean? Abby says we could invite her friend Jillian and Jillian's little brothers. They're twins," he added with delighted emphasis. "Almost my age, she says. Mom says we can invite them over, but if I want to have a party, I have to check with you first."

"Of course," I said, feeling a buoyancy in my heart that had been missing all day. "When do you want to do this?"

Josh had already given this serious thought. "I wanted to have it on Saturday, but some diplomat who's too important to change is coming, so I think Sunday. Would that be okay?"

"Absolutely," I said. "This will give me a fun thing to look forward to."

"Really?" he asked so earnestly I wanted to hug him close and kiss him on the top of the head.

"Yeah, really. What sort of party did you have in mind?"

"A cooking one," he said without hesitation. He tried to tamp it down but I could see the puff of pride in his chest. "We could all work together on making snacks and then play games while we eat them. Is that okay?"

"Fine with me," I said, catching Abby's tight smile over Josh's head. In that instant, I read that she was going along for her little brother's sake. "We'll see what sorts of ideas we can come up with. I'd like to work with you on this beforehand." I shot another glance up at Abby. "Both of you. Do you have time now?"

"Yeah!" Josh said.

Abby shook her head. "We have to go with Mom to that library opening in an hour, remember?"

He sighed his disappointment. "Can we plan it together tomorrow?"

"I'm looking forward to it," I said, consulting the calendar. "Wait, it looks like you two are out all day tomorrow."

"That's right," Abby said. "We're helping clean up at a children's rehabilitation center. Sorry, Josh, but we won't be back until late."

His face fell.

Tomorrow was a scheduled day off for me, but I wouldn't have any hesitation coming in for these kids. Desperate for positive goals right now, I said, "I can be here tomorrow anytime you want. Do you know what time you'll be back?" I took a look at the calendar again. "It seems as though you'll be here for dinner."

"I think Mom said we'd be back by three o'clock."

"Three o'clock it is then," I said. "I'll be here, Josh. You feel free to join in the planning, too, Abby."

"No," Josh said, "I want to plan for some surprises."

Abby looked relieved.

I laughed. "I'll call upstairs for you tomorrow at three and we'll get started on our plans."

"You sure this is okay?" he asked.

"I wouldn't miss it for the world."

When he and his sister left, good cheer went with them. I took a breath and started back to work, hoping the overwhelming feeling of loss would soon pass, knowing deep down it would haunt me forever.

CHAPTER 24

I FINALLY MADE IT THROUGH THE DAY, SELFISHLY pushing my staff out the door early so that I could keep some of the evening quiet to myself. There were people who found peace in meditation. I found it in working alone.

Snapping off the kitchen lights after an hour of cleaning and busywork, I headed to the MacPherson Square Metro station to go home. Gav had been in training all day today and would return for another full day tomorrow. We'd known about these two days of intense physical and mental stress for a while now and we'd agreed to limit our contact to a phone conversation or two until the weekend hit and he could relax again.

"I'll be in no shape for decent conversation after training," he'd told me. "Plus, I imagine I won't smell so great, either."

At the time, I'd laughed. Now, I wished I was seeing him tonight, no matter what. I needed him.

The thought stopped me short.

I needed him.

I hadn't ever felt as though I'd needed anyone before. Not since I was a kid at least and required my mom to guide me through life. This was different, though. I didn't need Gav because I couldn't make it in the world alone. That, I could do. We both knew it.

I needed Gav—my heart ached when I thought about it—because I could no longer imagine life without him.

I swallowed the emotion that threatened to overpower me as I continued on my way. I made it through the ticket turnstile and to the loading platform that would whisk me home to Crystal City. I didn't know what the evening would hold for me, but I couldn't wait to get there.

I meandered through the crowd of commuters to take a spot near where the train's midsection would hit. I stared at the concrete walls as I waited.

I zoned out apparently, because when a male voice next to me whispered, "Take this train often?" I gave a little yelp of surprise. A moment later, I reached out to him. "Gav," I said, feeling emotion bubble up again. "You're here."

He'd followed me from the White House and chastised me all the way home about how I needed to be better aware of my surroundings. "You should have caught me, Ollie," he said.

I didn't argue, both because he was right and because this very normal conversation would help us find a way back to our safe haven where there were no clandestine meetings, suspicious supplement companies, or shadowy corners where people handed us mysterious boxes.

"Aren't you supposed to be too tired to be out and about tonight?" I asked.

He kept an arm around me the entire ride. "Being with you today is more important than sleep." He tugged me a little closer and added, "I even showered first."

* * *

THE NEXT MORNING, I ROLLED OUT OF BED AT
nine in the morning, late for me. Gav's training had started
at five A.M. and he'd left my apartment late last night, still
needing to pack a fresh duffel before he reported in. I knew
he was in for a grueling day. After rigorous exercises and
hours of emergency drills, he'd then be required to face an
evening of review with his superiors and peers. I didn't
expect to hear from him until at least nine o'clock tonight.

I puttered around my kitchen for about an hour, drinking
coffee as I attempted to read the newspaper. Nothing stuck
with me from any of the headline stories, and after blindly
turning yet another page, I gave up.

Coffee cup in hand, I wandered out onto my apartment's
terrace. Though small, it afforded me a birds-eye view of
the neighborhood below. Nothing out of order, nothing
wrong. I sipped and stared, replaying every word of our
conversation with Yablonski in my head.

Meeting undercover agent Sarah Byrne proved to me,
once again, that there were forces at work of which I was
unaware. Situations I didn't understand. I might not particularly care for Yablonski, but I respected him and his
authority.

I kept coming back to one statement, however. He'd said
that he wasn't asking me to stop looking into my dad's history; he was ordering me to steer clear of Pluto and all its
employees, present and past. I'd agreed and I wouldn't go
back on my word.

A little voice in my head piped up to remind me, "You
could talk with Eugene Vaughn again."

"What good would that do?" I asked aloud.

The only answer was the rush of the wind in the trees
below and the soft sounds of traffic nearby.

Gav and I had discussed this option last night. He'd

offered to go with me if I decided to make the trip, but I'd told him, truthfully, that if I did go back, I preferred to do it alone. Eugene Vaughn had made it clear he wouldn't talk in front of others, even people like his nurse, a person he obviously trusted. I'd gone back and forth on the idea. Gav thought it could be worth a shot. I did, too, but I worried about getting my hopes up once more only to see them dashed again.

I reminded myself that Vaughn had been a dead end. He'd been either reluctant or unable to share information. Part of me believed that the aged man really was losing touch with reality; part of me wondered how much of his forgetfulness was an act.

I took another sip of coffee, which had cooled. I stuck out my tongue at the stale bitterness, then considered my options: get fresh coffee, sit at my kitchen table all day feeling sorry for myself, or find a more productive endeavor.

Vaughn had nothing to do with Pluto, so Yablonski couldn't begrudge me another visit to the old man. Even Gav concurred on that score.

"Watch out 'Uncle Eugene,'" I said to the clouds, "I'm coming back."

AN HOUR AND A HALF LATER, I WAS SHOWERED, dressed, and driving to Eugene Vaughn's home. I had plenty of time to get back to the White House by three to work with Josh.

I pulled up just past noon, took a deep breath to calm myself, and prepared to do my best to politely pry. Roberta was on duty again, answering the door with a smile of recognition. "Olivia," she said, "how nice."

"I don't mean to bother Eugene," I began, "but—"

"Don't worry." She opened the door wide to allow me in. "He's been expecting you."

"He has?" I asked as she led me back into the living room.

"Uh-huh," she said.

If it weren't for the fact that he wore a different color shirt, I would have believed he hadn't moved since I'd been here. He assessed me sharply with those elfin eyes. "Don't stand there staring, young lady, come over here and talk to me."

When I moved closer, he asked Roberta to bring us sweet tea again. She returned a moment later with our teas and a tray on which she'd prepared his lunch. "I made enough for both of you. It's important Eugene eats on schedule."

I desperately wanted Roberta to leave us alone, but she was required to hold Eugene's plate for him in easy reach, so he could choose items, one at a time. Thus trapped until lunch was over, Eugene, Roberta, and I made small talk over tea, red grapes, a sliced apple, chicken noodle soup, and a small supply of crackers spread with peanut butter.

The entire respite couldn't have lasted more than twenty minutes but I was itching to ask my questions.

When Roberta finally cleared everything away, she winked and said, "You two will want privacy." She pointed over her shoulder. "I'll be in the kitchen if you need anything."

Eugene watched her go. "Don't be listening at doorways, now."

She was out of sight but her voice rang through the small house. "I'll put on some music if that makes you feel better."

"It does."

Turning his attention to me, he asked, "What have you started?"

My spirits took a decided turn upward. "You *know* what's going on?"

"I know that you came here asking about your father's

troubles at Pluto. A week later, one of his former co-workers storms the place with a loaded gun. That's more than coincidence. How did that happen?"

I shook my head. "I'd prefer you tell me."

Keeping silent, he stared.

"I've got all day," I said. Not true, but he didn't need to know that.

"I don't know what you're talking about."

"Uh-uh. You know more than you're letting on. Don't try fooling me again with your feigned forgetfulness. You know precisely what went on at that company, and you probably even know what's going on there now." As I spouted off, he watched me, too patiently for my tastes. I wanted to get a rise out of him. Maybe then I'd learn something.

"You are your father's daughter. No doubt about that," he said at last.

I was through with the wistful reminiscing. "Don't start," I warned him. "I've talked to everyone I could think of. I've asked questions and now a man has been killed. Don't you think I feel responsible for that?"

"Don't feel guilty about Fitch's death."

"Why shouldn't I?"

"You prefer being called Ollie, don't you?"

I sucked back my impatience. "Yes."

He glanced past me as though to ensure Roberta wasn't about to come creeping around the corner. "Ollie," he said softly, "I can't tell you anything you don't already know."

"Why not?"

He watched me, shrewdly. "It isn't for me to tell."

"Listen," I said, trying a different approach, "I understand that you don't want to get anyone into trouble. I'm guessing there are still loose ends and people who could lose their jobs if your interference in the Arlington matter was discovered. I understand why you can't—"

In a flash, his bony hand had closed the space between

us. He gripped my arm hard enough to hurt. "You do *not* understand."

I didn't wince, even though I wanted to. "Then explain it to me."

Speaking slowly, he said, "You must let this matter drop."

When I opened my mouth to protest, he cut me off. "No argument. Not anymore. You are playing a game you don't understand in a field laden with land mines."

I tugged my arm away. "Fine," I said. "I know I can't have all the answers. That's been made abundantly clear to me of late."

At that, Eugene raised his eyebrows.

I ignored that. "Tell me one thing, then. Just one."

He shook his head.

"You don't even know what I'm going to ask."

"Yes, I do. When all is said and done, all you really want to know is how your father came to be buried at Arlington. I gave you the best answer I could when you were here last time: He deserved to be there and I made sure he was. Child, you need to stop. Right here, right now."

I sat back, frustrated with him as well as with myself. This had been a waste of time. I shouldn't have bothered. Too late, I realized that no matter how much I'd believed I'd convinced myself otherwise, I'd gotten my hopes up after all. "So that's it?"

"I'm sorry."

"Are you?" I asked.

His hand reached out again, but this time he clasped my fingers. "Very sorry."

After a moment, I stood. "Thank you for your time."

He looked up at me, from beneath his wiry eyebrows. "You're not coming back, are you?"

I didn't understand. "Coming back?" I repeated.

"You've asked me for answers I couldn't give you. Am I so useless to you now? You're walking out of here, convinced

I'm the bad guy. It doesn't matter to you that your father and I were good friends. It doesn't matter that I've followed your life since you were a little child." He pointed to his front door. "Because I can't give you the answers you want, you're going to walk out that door and I'll never see you again."

I didn't know what to say.

His hand dropped back into his lap. "I'm right, aren't I?"

"I hadn't thought about it," I said honestly. "Why would you want me to come back? I obviously bring trouble wherever I go."

"Come back and visit me, Olivia. To talk. About you, about your life. I want to know you. For your father's sake. Please?"

Had I been so focused that I'd lost sight of others' feelings along the way? Apparently I had.

"I'm sorry." If it were possible, I felt even worse than I had when I'd first arrived. I glanced at my watch. "If it weren't so late, I'd stay a bit now. But I promised someone I'd be back at three."

He nodded. "Go on, then. Don't forget me."

I was about to answer when the doorbell rang. "Who are you expecting?" I asked. Not that it was any of my business.

"No one," he said, then shouted, "Roberta, someone at the door."

"I can get it while I'm here," I said.

He waved as if to say "whatever."

I started for the door, but Roberta hurried in, iPod in hand, earbuds pulled down around her neck, wires running along her chest. "Sorry, I'll get it."

"I'm leaving anyway," I said.

"Ollie," Eugene called to me, curling a finger, "one more thing."

I returned to stand next to his chair as Roberta swung open the front door. "Hello," she said. "May I help you?"

"What is it?" I asked Eugene.

In the background, a male voice said hello. I could make out very little else.

"Friends of Mr. Vaughn's?" Roberta asked, sounding perplexed.

"What did you forget to tell me?" I prompted.

With his eyes on the door and a solid grip on my wrist, Eugene said, "You must remember to be careful. Very careful. You understand?"

"I do," I said.

The voice outside was answering Roberta. "Here to see Mr. Vaughn."

"He wasn't expecting—"

She barely got the words out when her face flipped upward, backhanded by an unknown assailant. I didn't have time to react before a man rushed through the door, then another. Seconds later, a third. The first two trampled past Roberta. The third picked her up, dumping her onto the floor in the center of the living room. Curled into the fetal position, she held both hands to her face and sobbed.

It all happened so fast, I couldn't do anything. All three men were young, tall, and powerful looking. I was shocked into paralysis even as they ordered us not to move.

Finding my voice, I shouted, "What are you doing? Who are you?"

I didn't have to wait long for my answer.

Another man, blonde and instantly recognizable as the guy I'd run into outside the coffee shop—the fellow looking for his blind date—entered the home, pushing a wheelchair ahead of him.

"Olivia, my dear." From the chair, Harold Linka raised his hand in greeting. "You're just like your father," he said. "You don't know when to quit, do you?"

CHAPTER 25

ROBERTA'S SOFT CRIES WERE THE ONLY sounds following Linka's pronouncement. "What's going on?" I asked.

His men swarmed the room, brandishing switchblades as long and deadly as my chef's knives. As if we needed additional proof that we were in trouble.

The way they surrounded us, efficiently and without exchanging so much as a word, led me to believe we were in the presence of professional bad guys. As much as I tried to fight it, my voice quavered when I asked, "What's going on?" again.

Eugene Vaughn had become visibly agitated. He shook a fist at the men and bellowed, "Get out of my home."

Linka rolled deeper in to the room, regarding Eugene with curiosity. "Who is this, Olivia?"

My knee-jerk response would have been to snarl a sarcastic, "Like you don't know," but the genuinely inquisitive expression on Linka's face stopped me in time. Better to keep the truth to myself until I could figure out what was going on here. "A former professor of mine," I lied. My voice rose, still shaky. "Why? What are you doing here?"

"We were waiting for a moment to catch you alone. Away from the White House. Away from home." He glanced around the room approvingly. "You provided a lovely site for our conversation."

The blonde guy had left his charge to return to the front door. He gave a quick look up and down the street outside and shut the door with a sinking finality. "We're clear," he said as he trotted back toward the group. The four men watched our every move, looking ready and eager to slice us down at the slightest provocation.

Linka waited for the room to settle again. He watched me with eyes that fairly glowed with triumph. "Now, my dear," he said, making my skin crawl. "Tell me exactly what Michael Fitch told you."

I barely processed the question. Not that I had any intention of answering. My mind was far too busy attempting to make sense of this. I did my best to race through all the possibilities that Linka's appearance here could signify but nothing fit.

Only one truth became suddenly clear. "It was you who killed my father." I waited for him to reply. When he didn't, I asked, "Why?"

"He didn't know when to give up," he said. "Like father, like daughter, eh?"

I pointed to the nearest brute wielding a knife. "You've changed your M.O. No execution-style murder for me?"

"That's the secret to my resilience all these years," he said, clearly amused. "I know how to change with the times. No sense disturbing this quiet residential neighborhood. You understand."

Roberta sat up, and I could see that her bottom lip was bleeding; she seemed unhurt otherwise. "What's happening? Who are these people?" she asked between gasps of air.

Linka shushed her with a flick of his hand. "I am in charge here. I ask the questions. You will remain silent." To me, he said, "Let's try this again: I warned Michael Fitch not to talk with you. Did he listen? No. And now he's dead. Before you join him, maybe you'd care to tell me what it was he told you."

Unsure of where to take this, I deflected. "What do you think he told me?"

"You aren't making this easy."

"Why should I?" I looked around the room. "It's obvious you plan to kill us all."

I immediately regretted my outburst because Roberta's cries escalated into shrieking breathless sobs. "My kids," she cried. "My kids . . ."

Oblivious to her terror, Linka pointed to me. "Get her purse."

Immediately, the man behind me stepped forward and yanked the bag from my shoulder. He lumbered over to present it to his boss, then returned to his station behind me and Eugene.

"There's nothing in there you could possibly want," I said.

Linka ignored me, pawing through until he came up with my cell phone. He handed it up to the blonde man behind him. "Here, you work this thing. Find a listing for Gavin, or 'Gav,' as she calls him."

My heart leapt into my throat. "He's not going to answer," I said.

Linka's lips spread in an obnoxious impression of a smile, mocking me. He then directed blondie to text Gav with a message that begged him to meet me at this address because I needed help.

"Why?" I asked, still unable to comprehend. "Why?"

"Are you so dense? You and your Agent Gavin have gotten in too deep. I risk losing everything if you two continue on this little quest of yours. I need to stop you now before you dig any further." He regarded me coolly. "I suspect, however, you haven't yet brought your suspicions to anyone else. That's not part of *your* M.O., is it Olivia?"

I didn't answer.

"We'll wait for your knight in shining armor to pull up on his mighty steed."

Gav wouldn't get any text until very late tonight. I thanked heaven for that, but didn't feel compelled to share the information. "You should let us go now while you have the chance," I said. "He will take you down."

Linka said, "Sit. I have more questions for you."

I remained standing. "You have me. Let these two go. They don't know anything about you. Nothing about . . ." I stopped myself. ". . . The past. Let them go."

"Too late." He waved a casual hand toward Roberta and Eugene. "Innocent bystanders. Happens all the time. Of course, once we leave here everyone will believe *you* were the innocent bystander. To the authorities this will be a break-in gone wrong. Another unsolved crime. *Tsk*."

I forced myself to tune out Roberta's whimpers.

Linka consulted his watch. "I estimate that your agent boyfriend will be here in less than an hour."

"Then do yourself a favor and run while you can."

"Sit down, Olivia, and tell me what you know about me. What you learned from Fitch."

I knew nothing about Linka other than what he'd told us himself. But I wasn't about to tell him that. I shook my head. "I refuse."

"Fine. I have all day. We'll wait. I suspect you'll be more willing once your beloved is at risk."

One of the giant men grabbed my shoulders, forcibly sitting me down. Another man pulled Roberta up from the floor and threw her onto the couch next to me. We were more than a foot apart, but I could feel her body trembling. In the chair next to us, Eugene blinked a couple of times, glancing about the room, looking addled. "Who did you say you were again?" he asked Linka.

Linka, talking quietly to the blonde man, didn't answer.

"Roberta," Eugene tried again, speaking briskly, "why haven't we offered our guests any sweet tea? Where are your manners, girl?"

Linka finally paid attention. "Is he out of his head?" he asked me.

Why he expected me to tell the truth, I didn't know.

"He goes in and out," I lied. "Stress isn't good for him."

"Roberta," Eugene repeated, his voice rising. "Don't just sit there, go get us all some tea." He glanced down at the two glasses he and I had used, still on a low table. Feigning confusion, he pointed. "Whose are these?"

"Some professor," the blonde guy said. "What did he teach, anyway?"

I didn't answer.

Not knowing what to do and with her hands shaking, Roberta got to her feet. Linka snapped, "Do *not* make a move."

The guy behind her pushed her back down.

I had no idea what to do. Gav wasn't coming to save me. He was in training, blissfully unaware of the drama taking place and Linka's expectations of his arrival. I'd have to save myself—all of us. But how?

I looked around the room, into the dead eyes of the angry men. They didn't budge, didn't waver. Knives in fat fists were ready to slash the life out of us without a moment's hesitation.

It wasn't my nature to give up, but I felt smaller and more helpless than I ever had in my life. I didn't know what to do.

As though reading my mind, Linka rolled his wheelchair forward. To my frustration, he remained just out of reach.

The blonde man remained by his side, ready to beat me back if I clawed at him the way I wanted to.

With his unhurried manner, his commanding presence among these automatons, and his ease of control, Linka had clearly been a man in power for a very long time.

In control of what, though?

My father had found out, but the secret had died with him.

I turned to Eugene. The elfin eyes sparkled with intelligence. Perhaps the secret hadn't died. Not yet at least.

"Why isn't Roberta getting us all tea?" Eugene asked innocently.

"Listen," I said to Linka, trying again, "let my old teacher go and I'll tell you everything. He's not going to be able to identify you. There's got to be some kindness in you. I mean, you have a dog. You must have some compassion."

He laughed.

Laughed.

Undaunted, I pointed to Roberta. "She doesn't have any idea who you are or why you're here. Take me away and leave them here. They'll have no idea where we went."

Linka folded his hands across his stomach, the picture of patience. "I don't leave loose ends," he said. "Now, back to you. Was it Michael Fitch you intended to meet at the coffee shop? What happened when he didn't show up?"

I was dumbfounded by his repeated queries about Fitch and knew instinctively not to tell him that the sorrowful little man had pointed a finger at Pluto, not at Linka. "How long have you been following me?" I asked.

Linka disregarded the question. "Is that why you met with his wife? What was in the package she gave you?"

I craved, desperately, to come up with a lie that made sense, but I was at a deep disadvantage. Eugene's warning about a field littered with land mines echoed in my brain. I knew enough to get us killed, but not enough to save us.

"I refuse to cooperate," I said, "until these two others are released."

"Impossible."

I sat up a little straighter. "Then kill me now and cut the drama."

Roberta's eyes went wide with terror. "No!"

Linka leaned forward in his wheelchair. "I am a patient man. Why? Because being patient ensures I always get what I want. Too bad you never learned that lesson." Resettling himself in his chair, he checked his watch. "Your young man will show up soon enough. Once he's here, I guarantee you'll find yourself in a cooperative state of mind."

I glanced at the clock on Eugene's mantel. Although it seemed silly to even think about anything but survival at this time, knowing that I wouldn't make my meeting with Josh made me breathtakingly sad about letting him down.

The men made small talk among themselves and with their boss. I pretended not to care, but strained to hear every word, hoping for some clue as to why Linka had been threatened by my inquiries into Pluto and why he needed to know what Fitch had told me. No matter how I turned it, I came up empty. If Pluto was indeed selling tainted supplies to other countries, how could Linka, and not the Bensons, be blamed?

Unless the Bensons were behind today's coup, which seemed less likely with every passing moment, I couldn't see how Fitch's assertions affected Linka in the least.

"Where is he?" Linka asked me, not for the first time.

"Who?"

"Don't get smart with me, child. You won't like it when I retaliate."

I waited.

"Where is he?"

"I told you: He's too smart to fall for this. He'll figure it out and bring the cavalry with him." My words were brave, my insides panicked. I knew Gav wasn't coming. By the time he discovered what happened, it would be too late. For all of us.

Roberta had curled up on one end of the couch, looking as though she were trying to make herself small. Eugene sat in his chair, straight-backed as ever, occasionally coming up with random comments or queries that no one answered.

At one point, Eugene attempted to stand. Three men jumped into action, as though the frail elderly man posed any actual threat. "Get away from me," he said, thrusting his hands at them. "I need to use the washroom, let me through."

The men looked to Linka for direction and my heart sparked with excitement.

"Go with him," Linka said. "Scour the room for anything that could be used as a weapon. Check for phones. And do not leave him unsupervised. Not for a moment."

My elation fell, but rose again, slightly, when two men followed Eugene down a corridor. That left only one thug, the blonde guy, and Linka. If Roberta and I could . . .

It was now or never. I had to make my move.

I leapt to my feet, hoping to close the distance between us, hoping to tear at Linka's face. Anything to cause trouble.

I hadn't gotten three steps when my head was whacked from behind. The world went kaleidoscope bright, breaking into a dizzying, spectacular display of fireworks. Then, my lights went out.

CHAPTER 26

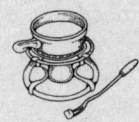

I CAME TO, VAGUELY AWARE OF BEING TUGGED by the arm.

"She's awake," I heard. Then, "Come on, get up."

I ached, but had a hard time localizing the pain. My vision was clear enough to know it was Roberta pulling at me, and to recognize that the lighting in the room had changed since I'd last been conscious. That meant time had elapsed. Linka watched with furious intent, as though I'd passed out on purpose. I raised a hand to the back of my head, where a lump formed. Touching it made me wince. "What . . . ?" I began.

"I'm tired of your antics," Linka said as I pulled myself into a sitting position on the floor. "Why isn't he here yet?"

Eugene was back in his seat, eyeing me critically. I looked up at Roberta, blinking my surprise. "How long have I been out?"

She started to answer, but Linka shut her up. "Why isn't he here yet?" he asked again.

Rage, despair, and pain built into a crescendo of fury. I refused to play his games any longer. Struggling to my feet, I shouted, "He's not coming, you idiot. When are you going to understand that?"

I managed to lower myself onto the couch without assistance. I wasn't woozy, but for a fleeting moment, I wished I were. Maybe then my head wouldn't pound. Sounds in the room faded in and out, crashing a rhythmic beat inside my brain. My pulse, I realized. I was hearing my pulse, magnified about a thousand times.

Linka grew more agitated by the moment. I wondered what I'd missed. "We can't wait any longer," Linka said to his men. "Let's get out of here. Get rid of these two, take the chef with us."

One of the big guys who had been silent until now, said, "That wasn't the plan."

"You think I don't know that?" Linka snapped. "We need her boyfriend. If we don't get him, we're no better off than we are now. Take care of the other two. Make it quick."

Roberta screamed, pulling herself into a ball on the couch. "No," she cried, "please, please. I won't tell anyone, I swear. I swear."

Linka was unmoved by her pleas. He rolled across the room, nearer to the front door. "Do it," he called over his shoulder.

The man behind Roberta pulled his knife up and started to make a move.

That's when the doorbell rang.

Everyone froze. Everyone except Roberta, who rocked back and forth on the sofa, eyes clenched, arms wrapped around her knees, low moans coming from deep within.

"It's him," Linka said with certainty. "Men, get out of the room. Make it look non-threatening."

"It's not him," I said. "It can't be."

The blonde man started for the door. "Not you," Linka said. "He's seen you. Go hide." He cast a disgusted glance at Roberta, then gestured to another of his men. "Get the door. Get him in here."

Although the pounding in my head remained a dull ache, I stood.

When the front door opened and Gav rushed in, I nearly wept, crying out, "No! Run." I shouted, pointing to the door. "Run!"

He took another step forward, but his stance had shifted. He whipped around, taking down the guy who'd opened the door with a punch to the man's gut. In the breathless seconds that followed, I saw him reach for his gun.

Too late. One guy grabbed Gav from behind, capturing him in a choke hold. Instinctively, I started to run to him, but the giant behind me had me in his grip. I shouted in a futile attempt to control events that were spiraling out of control. Another brute raced up and began bashing Gav in the face and stomach, grabbing his weapon and forcing him into a corner. I could hear heavy breathing, grunts of exertion, and I saw Gav's arms, straining for purchase.

Gav managed to wrest himself out of their grasp. He turned, pummeling one man in the face, landing blows right and left, while the other man sank to the floor, catching his breath. The fevered look in Gav's eyes was one I'd never seen before. It spoke of rage, fury, and the willingness to kill, right here, right now. His dark side.

He was winning the battle until the blonde guy jumped in. He and the first guy pulled Gav off of their cohort, hitting him with meaty fists that made chunking sounds. Gav doubled over in pain. When the blonde guy pulled a knife, a deep, wailing scream exploded from the depths of my soul. "No!"

Gav hit the ground with the thud of bone meeting hardwood. The blonde guy yanked his knife back and I crumbled to the floor when I saw the blood. Gav's blood. "No, no, no." My entire being ached with sorrow. Why was Gav here? He shouldn't have come.

A crimson puddle began to grow beneath his midsection. I screamed, "Gav!"

He didn't answer.

"Gav!"

Linka turned to me. "Now tell me what Michael Fitch told you."

I didn't look at him. I couldn't wrench my eyes away. Still pinned by two men, Gav wasn't moving. Not even a little. The pool of blood on the floor was growing wider by the moment.

"No," I said, as though hearing my cries from outside myself.

"Suit yourself," he said. "Your boyfriend is bleeding out. I give him twenty minutes, tops."

I had no breath. I had nothing left.

To the men holding Gav, he ordered, "Finish him."

They stopped at my scream. Linka turned to me. "Change of heart?"

I knew there was no hope anymore, but a spark inside me refused to let go. Not while we were still alive. Not if there was still a slim chance that I could help Gav.

I didn't know what kind of information Linka was looking for, nor how telling him any of it could save us, except to buy time. For a miracle? There were no other options. "Get Gav medical help and I'll tell you everything."

"You are joking," Linka said with a calm that made me want to rip his heart out. "He can't survive a wound like that. Tell me what Fitch told you or you'll be next."

"No," I said.

"This is your last chance."

"For what? To live for an extra fifteen minutes? Get him help." I folded my arms to show him I was determined, but in truth my whole body was shaking so badly I needed to hold myself tight. "Or not another word."

He smiled again, an ugly showing of teeth. "You're just like your father. So noble. So strong. So dead."

I tried to rush him, but the guy behind me was too fast, snagging me by the waist so that I dangled like a rag doll. I shouted, "You can't do this."

I knew I was grasping for final moments, but what else could I do?

"You're just making it harder on yourself."

Linka chuckled. His mirthless laugh echoed in the otherwise still room, mocking our futile efforts, stealing every last hope from my heart.

And then, the room exploded.

Glass crashed amid shouts and popping blasts that could have been gunshots. I was aware of heavy treads, loud voices, and being thrown to the ground. Roberta landed next to me, screaming and covering her head. A man in black shielded Vaughn. My mind registered each sound, each movement slowly, reasoning that knives shouldn't make that much noise, and wondering why I could still feel the wood against my knees. And where did that smell of gunpowder come from?

I couldn't make sense of it, but the man who'd been holding me had let go. I crawled on all fours toward Gav, keeping my head down, not knowing how I'd fight off the two men surrounding him, but knowing I had to try. I ducked past running legs, around furniture, and had just made it to Gav's side when I was lifted to my feet by a pair of meaty hands. "Out of the way, Ms. Paras," Yablonski said. He shouted to someone else, "Get the paramedics in here. Now!"

CHAPTER 27

"PLEASE, STOP THE BLEEDING," I BEGGED THE paramedics who worked on Gav. "Please." They were too busy to answer.

Kneeling behind the professionals' efficient circle of care, I tried talking to him directly, "Gav, it's okay." No response. The paramedics' expressions were grim as they exchanged looks that ripped hope from my heart. "It's okay," I said again, praying it would be so. "You're going to be okay."

I was aware of activity behind me. Other medics were taking care of Eugene and Roberta. Agents were making arrests. Sarah Byrne was handcuffing Linka. In the center of it all, Yablonski stood, issuing orders about evidence and protocols and other things I couldn't care less about right now.

"Gav, please," I said, watching as they started an IV line,

hating that the crimson pool beneath him seemed wider than ever. "Don't give up. You can't give up."

I stayed out of the experts' way, slowly becoming aware that commotion had settled down and that I had company. From my perch on the floor, Yablonski looked bigger than ever. "Will he live?" I asked.

The gurney arrived as Gav was being prepped for transport. Yablonski offered me his hand and helped me to my feet. His voice was rough. "Let's get you out of here."

"I want to ride with Gav."

"You can't. You're with me."

That was it. No argument. Gav was rolled out one door as Yablonski nudged me the opposite direction.

Sarah Byrne sent me a sad smile. "Stay strong," she said as we passed.

I swallowed, unable to answer.

Yablonski turned to her. "You have this, Agent Byrne?"

"Yes, sir."

Yablonski took my arm. "This way."

I was ushered into the backseat of a car, next to Yablonski. Quinn was at the wheel. I didn't even acknowledge him. I held my hands to my face, head down, not speaking until Quinn had us back on a main road. "Are we going to the hospital?"

"We are," Yablonski said. "You need to be looked at."

I picked my head up. "I mean Gav's hospital."

I didn't miss the two men's exchange in Quinn's rearview mirror.

"He is still alive, isn't he?"

Again, the look.

Yablonski stared out the window. "We don't expect him to make it."

I pulled myself into a ball against the door.

WE ARRIVED AT A HOSPITAL I DIDN'T KNOW existed. Small and secured by armed guards, we were required to stop at the gate before being allowed access. A black-and-white striped mechanical arm, like those in front of railroad tracks, rose after Yablonski barked orders, and I was rushed into a tiny yet extremely well-outfitted emergency room where a doctor examined the bump on my head.

Yablonski didn't leave my side. "Go to Gav," I said. "Please, he can't be alone."

My entreaties fell on deaf ears. "He's being prepped for surgery," he said.

"Surgery?"

"Don't get your hopes up."

Too late. "I need to see him."

"Not possible. Not now. Cooperate, Ms. Paras."

The doc diagnosed a concussion. No surprise there. I was given strict orders to take it easy and to report any nausea, blurred vision, or any of fifty other problems they tried to explain to me. I wasn't hearing any of it. I turned to Yablonski. "Get me out of here," I said. "Please."

For once, he seemed to take pity on me. "Let's go." He gripped my arm and led me down a vibrant blue hallway to a quiet waiting room far from where we'd first come in. "Leonard is in surgery in there," he said, indicating a set of double doors. "We will wait."

My stomach jiggled, having nothing to do with the concussion and everything to do with imagining doctors stepping through those doors with sad expressions on their faces and "I'm sorry," on their lips. I lowered myself onto one of the hard plastic chairs and sat, elbows on my knees and hands folded, tight with worry and prayer.

"Can I get you anything?" Yablonski asked.

I shook my head.

I DON'T KNOW HOW LONG WE WERE THERE. It could have been minutes, it could have been hours. We were the only two people in a waiting room that had no attendant, no television, no families wandering in and out. I eventually found my voice. "Is this some secret military hospital?" I asked.

"Something like that."

I had to ask. "How did you know? How did Gav know to come?"

"Leonard called me. He told us you were in trouble. He asked me for backup."

"But . . ." That made no sense. "If you were his backup, why did he come in by himself?"

"I couldn't assemble a team as fast as he could get to you. He knew he was walking into an ambush. He did it to buy time for us to get there." Yablonski's eyes were glassy. "I warned you," he said. "I told you he would give his life for you."

"He can't," I said, my voice cracking. "He's going to be okay."

Yablonski said nothing.

A few minutes passed. "They followed me," I said, not as an excuse, but simply to share what I'd learned. "They'd been following me ever since we visited Linka the first time. After Michael Fitch imploded at Pluto, they decided to grab me to find out what we knew." I cleared my throat. "They think we have some information, but . . ." I held out my hands, "I don't know what it is."

"No," he said, "you don't."

"But *you* do." I wasn't asking a question.

He didn't answer.

Hours later, I heard the sound of the doors *whoosh*ing open before I caught sight of the doctor coming toward us, pulling his surgical mask from his face. I jumped to my feet, head and heart pounding fear. "How is he?" I asked, unable to deduce anything from the medic's expression. "How is he?"

Yablonski steadied me with an arm around my shoulders.

The doctor must have been instructed to answer to him only because he didn't say a word until Yablonski said, "Tell us."

"We've repaired what we can, but he lost a lot of blood. If he makes it through the night, he might have a chance."

CHAPTER 28

I SLEPT FITFULLY IN A CHAIR NEXT TO GAV'S BED in the intensive care unit all night. Yablonski stayed with me, occasionally nodding off in the other chair across the glass-walled room. I took great comfort in the monitors' regular beeps and sighs. I watched fluids drip, drip, drip, into Gav's veins and tried not to cry when I looked at his poor, battered face. He didn't move, didn't react to noises in the room, not even Yablonski's random snores. Gav's right hand lay open on the sheet next to him. I held his fingers, softly, reveling in their warmth, desperately wanting to let him know that I was there.

At about six the next morning, I came awake with my head next to Gav's arm, my fingers still entwined with his. I lifted my head, not knowing what had roused me, except possibly the crick in the back of my neck. "Olivia," Yablonski was saying. He shook my shoulder, very gently. "Wake up."

I blinked, then rubbed my eyes with my free hand.

"Look," Yablonski said.

I did. Gav's lids were struggling to open and he seemed to be attempting to mouth words.

"I'll get the nurse," he said.

Gav settled down again, almost as though relaxing back into slumber. I squeezed his fingers, very gently. "Gav," I whispered, "I'm here."

Yablonski returned with the nurse and a doctor just as Gav's eyes fluttered open. "Ollie?" he rasped. "You're okay?"

My throat went white-hot, but I managed to answer. "I'm okay."

His fingers tried to squeeze back. "Good," he said, then fell unconscious once again.

Yablonski managed to talk me into taking a break. I needed to use the washroom anyway, and to splash water on my face. When I emerged, he pressed a hot cup of coffee in my shaking hands as he sat me at a utilitarian table in the middle of a staff break room.

"I don't know how much I'm going to be able to tell you," he began gruffly, "if I'm able to ever tell you anything at all. You understand?"

I nodded. "How is Eugene? And Roberta?"

"They're both doing well. Roberta is being debriefed and admonished to keep quiet about what went on in that house. From what Sarah has been able to tell me, she has absolutely no idea of Linka's identity. That's good."

"What about Eugene?"

I thought Yablonski might have almost smiled. "He's fully informed. Always has been. Eugene Vaughn is not a security risk. By the way, he sends his kudos to you for coming up with that 'He's a former professor' lie. That was good thinking on your feet."

I didn't really care about compliments right now. "Has your team told you how Gav knew to come out to Eugene's? He was supposed to be in training all day."

"I believe Leonard would prefer to tell you that story himself." Yablonski took a sip of coffee, then gave me a genuine smile this time. "When he's feeling up to it."

GAV HAD SUFFERED A LACERATED LIVER AND spleen, which had resulted in his emergency splenectomy, but with plenty of blood transfusions, he was upgraded to a normal room within a couple of days. Faster than anyone expected, he was up and on his feet, walking around his floor with minimal help. I stayed with him as much as I could, Yablonski arranging for me to come and go as I pleased via his personal car and credentials that allowed me through the guard gate. I worried about taking time away from my duties at the White House, but Yablonski assured me that Quinn had everything handled. I believed him.

Eight days after surgery, Gav was released. Yablonski accompanied us to Gav's apartment, where he helped me get him settled. Taking a long look around the space, Yablonski said, "Big enough for one, Leonard. Not two." He surprised me by adding, "You're going to need a bigger place if you and Olivia intend to do this right."

I looked up at the big man. He'd been there when we'd needed him. Through his efforts, Gav had been saved. I owed that man everything. He could be as cranky with me as he wanted for the rest of his life, and I'd still respect him until the day I died.

After we'd gotten Gav seated at his table, Yablonski added, "Will you be all right here without supervision? Seems like whenever the two of you are left alone for more than five minutes, one of you gets into trouble."

Gav laughed, which came out like a wheeze, one that made him wince. "Thanks, Joe. Remind me to crack jokes next time you've got stitches."

Yablonski stood. "My days of action are over. They should have been, at least. Thanks to you, I was able to enjoy

one last hurrah. I'm just glad it turned out as well as it did."
He gripped Gav's shoulder on his way out. I watched his
fingers tighten momentarily. "You take care of yourself."

"I'll be okay. Ollie will look out for me."

He flashed me a smile. "I know she will." He held onto
Gav's shoulder a moment longer than necessary. "I can't
imagine . . ." He blinked and blew out a long breath. "I
mean, if you . . ." His mouth twisted and he didn't finish.

Gav patted his mentor's hand. "I know, Joe."

The raw emotion on both their faces was too much to
handle. I looked away.

A moment later, Yablonski was gone. I locked the door
after him and returned to the table. "Can I get you anything?" I asked.

"Sit with me awhile," Gav said, looking at me with an
intensity that made my face warm. "I've wanted to talk with
you alone for days. This is our first chance."

"I have so many questions," I said, "but I don't want to
start in until you have time to acclimate yourself. They can
wait."

"I'm fine," he said. "I'm fine because I'm here with you."

"I think it would be better if you rested."

"Ollie." His voice was a warning. "Do not baby me."

I smiled. My Gav was back. "Okay, fine. No coddling."

"Good."

I started in with the question that had me puzzled the
most. "I've been tearing my hair out trying to figure how
you knew to come to Eugene Vaughn's house. You couldn't
have gotten that bogus text. Not during training. And even
if you did get it, what happened? How did you know I was
in trouble?"

He leaned back gingerly, working a smug look onto his
face. "Can't figure this one out, can you, Paras?" For a man
who had suffered a near-fatal injury, he was certainly in a
playful mood. "Remember when Yablonski told you that
you have friends in high places?"

"Yeah . . ."

"He wasn't kidding."

"I don't understand."

"When you didn't show up for your appointment with Josh on Friday, he got worried."

More puzzled than ever, I said, "There's no way he would have known to call you."

"No," Gav agreed slowly, "but he started a chain reaction. He told his mother. When she suggested that you might have simply been delayed, he insisted that you would have called. The kid wouldn't be talked down. He was so insistent, in fact, that he and his mother came down to the kitchen to look for you. According to the agents on duty, Josh pitched a vigorous fit when no one in charge would listen to him. He said he knew you were in trouble. Otherwise you would have come through."

"Josh said that?" My hand flew to my chest.

"You and I both know that Josh and Abby aren't the kind of kids who normally throw tantrums. His mother felt his behavior was off—way off—so she asked the staff to help find you. Imagine her surprise when it turned out that nobody knew where you'd gone."

I sucked in a breath of understanding. "But then how . . . ?"

"They talked to Sargeant."

"What?" I exclaimed.

Gav tried to glare. "You didn't tell me he knew about us."

"I meant to," I said. "He figured it out himself. I just didn't deny."

"Good thing you didn't," he said. "Sargeant suggested they try to find me. Mrs. Hyden couldn't get through, but discovered I was in training. This all took about, oh, thirty minutes. On the high side. At Josh's insistence, Mrs. Hyden called her husband and asked him to get me out of training so they could find out where you were."

"The president of the United States pulled you out of

training because they were looking for *me?*" My mind couldn't wrap itself around that. "Are you kidding me?"

"Not at all. Friends don't get much higher."

"Oh my gosh. It boggles the mind."

"Thank goodness for Josh. Otherwise . . ." He didn't finish the thought.

I reached over and grabbed his hands.

He rubbed my fingers. "You know, I drifted in and out of consciousness for a while. Whenever I woke up, you were there, holding my hand."

"I wasn't going to leave your side. Not until you woke up."

"I know. And that's exactly why I did."

CHAPTER 29

DAYS LATER, WE STILL HADN'T GOTTEN ANY answers as to why Linka had felt the need to have me followed after we'd met with him. We hadn't gotten any word on what happened to him or his henchmen after the federal agents had stormed in and taken them all into custody. Not a word of the story hit the newspapers, the television, or even the Internet.

"Crazy quiet," I said. "Too quiet. There's way more to this story."

Gav concurred. "I'm starting to believe we'll never know what this was all about."

When I finally returned to the White House, my first stop was to see Josh. Doing so required some touchy negotiation on my part with Doug, who seemed inexplicably angry at my request. I didn't understand, but I didn't give it much thought. Probably still holding a grudge because I wouldn't write that letter of recommendation for him.

When I managed my visit upstairs to the First Family's residence, I was shown to the second floor Center Hall, where Josh and Mrs. Hyden waited for me.

I started out with an apology for missing our meeting, but quickly moved to thank Josh, and praise him for his tenacity.

"I cannot tell you how much it means that you had faith in me," I said. "Because of you, I'm okay. Because of you, a lot of other people are okay. We owe you."

"My mom said something happened that we can't talk about. Is that right?"

I admitted it was.

"I had a feeling you were in trouble again. You were, weren't you?"

"Big trouble," I said. "But now, because of what you did for me—for all of us—we're safe. I am so sorry about missing your party, though. How did it go?"

He shrugged. "When you weren't here, I was too worried to think about any party. I asked my mom to postpone it for another time. And it all turned out all right. The twins came down with a sore throat the next day."

Mrs. Hyden nodded. "Strep," she said. "Looks like everything worked out for the best."

"I promise we'll plan another party very soon," I said. "I owe you."

"No, you don't," he said solemnly. "You saved my life once, remember?"

My eyes grew hot. I ruffled his hair. "Yeah, I remember."

BUCKY AND CYAN GREETED ME WITH WIDE-eyed concern when I finally made it to the kitchen. "What in the world happened to you? You've been out for days," Cyan said in a hushed whisper. "Can you tell us?"

I was about to answer when Virgil tossed a comment over his shoulder. "We all had to give up our days off because of you. Next time you want to extend your vacation, how about you give the rest of us a little notice?"

"What's up with him?" I asked.

Bucky rolled his eyes. "Foul mood. There's a rumor going around that Virgil's not particularly happy about."

"What's that?"

Bucky made a face. I looked over at Cyan, who wrinkled her nose. "You're not going to like it, either," she said.

At that moment, Sargeant strolled into the kitchen. "Ah, Ms. Paras, I heard you were back. May I have a word?"

"Of course," I said, eager to talk with Sargeant, too. I cast a wary glance at my teammates as I followed the sensitivity director out of the room. If they'd seemed anxious already, they looked positively alarmed now that Sargeant had interrupted. What had they been about to tell me?

He led me through the long hallway around the kitchen into the ground-floor central hallway. There were tours going on, so we stayed behind the grouping of temporary screens that the uniformed division of the Secret Service erected every tour morning to keep this end off-limits to visitors.

"I'm glad you stopped by," I began. "I wanted to thank you, Peter. I heard you were instrumental in helping locate my whereabouts the other day."

"Hmm, yes," he said. "That's not what I wanted to speak with you about, but I must say that I'm glad they thought to approach me." His brow furrowed. "No one has told me the outcome of your latest adventure, nor do I believe any explanation is forthcoming. I understand this one is a hush-hush operation. I trust everything turned out well enough?"

"It did," I said. "Again, my deepest thanks."

He nodded acknowledgment. The look in his eyes told me I was missing something.

"What else is up?" I asked.

"You haven't heard, have you?"

"Apparently not. Care to fill me in?"

Undisguised amusement flooded his features. He was enjoying this, a situation that immediately put me on edge. "Two things," he said. "The first of which is I wish to extend my thanks to you."

I waited. "For?"

"For informing me about Thora's . . . interest." His cheeks went pink. "Interest in me, that is. Thanks to your intercession, she and I have had the opportunity to share several enjoyable outings together."

Genuinely happy to hear this, I found myself grinning. "That's great. I'm so glad."

"I thought you might be." He waited, eyes narrowing. "The second item may not render you quite so gleeful."

Uh-oh.

"But," he continued, "I must confess to being pleased to discover that I am to be the one to share the news with you."

This wasn't sounding good. "Go on."

"Do you recall when I mentioned that I'd considered consulting you on an unexpected matter?"

"Yes, but you said you couldn't talk about it."

He rubbed his hands together. "Now I can. Through no fault of my own, the secret has been leaked."

"I'm not following you."

"A new chief usher has been chosen."

Oh no. "Please don't tell me it's Doug," I said.

"Worse." With a smile as wide as I'd ever seen on Sargeant, he said, "An official announcement will be issued tomorrow."

"Who is it?"

He held his hands out. "Me."

I felt my jaw drop, knowing instantly that he wasn't kidding. Even as I extended my hand and said, "Congratulations," I put the pieces together: Mrs. Hyden giving Sargeant more responsibility, Virgil's stories about the "insider" having the best shot at the job, and Sargeant's own unsurpassed attention to detail.

"I'm delighted for you," I said, warming to the idea. I shook his hand with gusto. "I really am."

"We've had our differences," he said, shaking with equal fervor, "but I believe we have much to offer the White House. Individually, as well as together."

"I couldn't have said it better."

When I returned to the kitchen, Bucky and Cyan looked ready to bombard me with questions, but just as they started in, Quinn appeared at the opposite doorway. "Ms. Paras, you've been summoned," he said, jerking a thumb. "I'm here to take you to a meeting."

"Where?" I asked.

Quinn was mum. "This way."

"I'll be back, I guess," I said to Bucky and Cyan. The looks on their faces were resigned. "Busy morning. I'm sorry."

Quinn led me into the West Wing, past the Cabinet Room into a narrow hallway that led to the president's secretary's office. Gav was there, leaning on the cane the doctors insisted he use until his muscles healed sufficiently. Instinctively, I rushed to him. "What are you doing here?" I laid my hand on his shirt, just below his rib cage. "You aren't supposed to be out on your own yet."

"I was summoned."

"So was I. What's going on?"

He shrugged. "No idea."

The president's secretary was unruffled by our appearance and appeared to take our quick, bewildered conversation in stride. Quinn said something to her and she nodded. "Go right in."

An aide opened the door. Gav and I looked at each other. "The Oval Office?" I mouthed.

He gave another slight shrug and held a hand out, confused as I was.

"Go on." Quinn opened the door and gestured us forward. "They're expecting you. I'll be out here."

They?

President Hyden was behind his desk. He stood up as I stepped into the room, Gav limping behind me. "Welcome," the president said as Quinn closed the door. Hyden came around the front of his desk to greet us. "I'm sure you're wondering why I've asked you both to be here today."

I didn't know what to say. I turned to Gav, who had drawn himself to attention and was saluting the president. The Commander in Chief returned the salute. "At ease, Agent Gavin."

It was then I noticed Yablonski. He stood in front of one of the two sofas that faced each other at the room's center.

My mouth was completely dry. I didn't know what to say, to do. Fortunately for both of us, Gav had had a lot more experience with the president in such situations than I had. "Are we to assume this meeting has something to do with our recent extracurricular activities?" he asked.

Yablonski almost smiled. "You may assume that."

I finally found my voice. To the president, I said, "I want to thank you for all you did . . ." He started to wave away my gratitude, but I needed to finish. "Especially for listening to Josh. Your son saved my life. He's an amazing young man."

President Hyden beamed. "Thank you," he said sincerely. "I have come to realize that he's learning more from you during your sessions in the kitchen than I had anticipated. I hope you'll continue to look out for him, as long as we're here in the White House."

"It would be my great honor," I said.

President Hyden gestured toward the sofa closest to the door as he and Yablonski took seats on the one opposite. As we sat, the president said, "I've called you here for a specific reason." Making eye contact with us both, he went on, "But first I need to get assurances—from both of you—that whatever you hear in this room today stays here."

I glanced at Gav. We answered, "Of course," simultaneously.

Yablonski cleared his throat, pointing to the file on the low table between us. "The documents in front of you are classified. Only certain very high-ranking members of federal authorities are allowed access."

The president picked up the story. "It has come to my attention that your recent altercation came about because you, Olivia, were searching for answers about your father." He pointed to the folder. "Until you brought your concerns to Mr. Yablonski's attention, he had no knowledge of the dangers your father faced protecting this country. Nor had I."

My breaths were coming in quick, anxious gasps. What was going on here? I tried my best to focus on what the president was saying.

He hefted the thick folder. "I have a meeting I'm already late for, but I've offered the office to you and Mr. Yablonski for as long as you need." He smiled. "Well, until my meeting is over—at least an hour. The folder cannot leave this room with you, but you are welcome to read through any or all of it as long as I have your solemn word that you never share its contents with anyone."

"I won't," I said.

Gav nodded.

"That means," Yablonski warned, "that you can't tell your mother, either. Not a word of what you learn here."

"I understand."

The president placed the file on my lap. He stood and we did, too, me grasping tightly to the bundle as though afraid he might suddenly change his mind. He shook our hands, wished us the best, and within seconds was out the door opposite the one we'd come in.

"Oh my gosh," I said, unable to help myself as we resumed our seats. "We're actually in the Oval Office? Reading a classified file? What could be in here?"

I placed the folder on the table and opened it. The first sheet inside didn't offer much, simply a giant red-stamped warning not to proceed without appropriate authorization. Pages were bound and impossible to remove.

Yablonski pulled in a deep breath. "There's a lot to get through, certainly more than you would be able to digest in an hour. May I offer assistance?"

I turned the file to face him. He flipped a number of pages before finding what he was looking for. "First, I want you to see this." Twisting the folder to face me once again, he pointed a fat finger. "Your father's authentic military record."

I pulled the entire book to my lap and took a look at the Department of Defense form he indicated. "Joint Message Form?" I read, puzzled. My fingers traced the computer printout, running down the numbered list like a three-year-old learning to read. "This is dated right after he was killed. Why would this be in here? He wasn't still in the service when . . ." Pieces of the puzzle began to fall into place. "Wait . . ."

Yablonski wiggled his fingers in a "give it to me" gesture. I complied. He paged through further. "Take a look," he said.

He turned the book to face me and I read another Department of Defense form: "Report of Casualty." It listed my dad's name, rank, and pay grade among other pertinent information. My breath caught when I reached the box where the circumstances of my father's death—two forty-five caliber shots to the head—were recorded there in black-and-white. "My dad . . ." I began, "he never left the service?"

"Your father was working as a military operative at Pluto. He was brought in when—"

I couldn't stop myself from blurting, "They've been selling tainted products all these years? No one's stopped them?"

Gav placed a restraining hand on my knee but it was too late. Yablonski graced me with one of those "quit interrupting" grimaces he was so fond of. "Perhaps you'd care to hear the entire explanation before you jump to conclusions?"

"I'm sorry," I said, inching forward. "I really am. Please go on."

"You can read the notes, all the orders, the background, and the reports, but what it comes down to is this: Pluto never sold tainted products. That was an allegation Fitch made and there is no truth to it whatsoever."

I wanted to express my surprise aloud, but held my tongue.

Yablonski continued. "Years ago, Craig Benson discovered that Harold Linka was using his company, Pluto, as a front to smuggle contraband—drugs, weapons, you name it—to enemies of the United States. He discovered this quite by accident. Instead of firing him on the spot, however, he made a shrewd move. He called a friend at the Pentagon."

He tapped the pages where preliminary reports explained Pluto's initial contact and the authorities' enthusiastic response. I then read Eugene Vaughn's glowing recommendation of my father for the undercover job. He praised him as "tenacious, resourceful, and utterly trustworthy."

"Because your father was active military and had prior success in other undercover operations," Yablonski went on, "the decision was made to have it appear as though he'd been dishonorably discharged. The idea being that Linka would be more likely to trust a man who held a grudge against the United States. Your father agreed to everything. He went into Pluto with the mission of taking Linka down. And in a way, he did."

I paged further, not really knowing what I was looking for. The folder was thick, mostly with reports and forms. I could spend all day reading and not get through it all.

Apparently, however, Yablonski had memorized the book. "Linka believed your father was about to tell Pluto what was going on under their noses. He had no idea your dad was an undercover agent working for the government.

Linka had him killed just as he was to deliver key evidence that would have closed up the illegal operations."

"But if the authorities knew about Linka," I said, risking Yablonski's wrath yet again, "how was he allowed to continue? I mean, it's been more than twenty-five years. Couldn't they have sent in another operative?"

"That's where the story takes an unusual twist," he said, "and why your father's records could never be released."

Gav was way ahead of me on this one. "They *did* send in another operative, didn't they?" He tapped a finger against his lips and stared as though seeing the story unfold before him. "There has always been an undercover agent at Pluto since then, hasn't there?"

Yablonski beamed at his star pupil. "Absolutely correct." To me, he said, "Your father gave us a great gift. He managed to keep his undercover mission secret from Linka, even after his death. This left the door open for authorities to send in more agents."

"But Linka was injured on the job," I said.

"An accident." Yablonski nodded. "The powers that be worried that he'd disappear so deep they wouldn't be able to find him and keep tabs on him the way they had, but they scrambled and came up with another idea. Pluto offered Linka continued employment working from home. This kept the lines of communication open and allowed the FBI and CIA to monitor his dealings all these years."

"Why didn't they just stop him?"

"Sometimes," Yablonski said, "you have more control when your subject doesn't realize you're the one pulling the strings. Linka was a small fish in the realm of war supplies, but he had connections to some of the deepest, biggest cells across the globe. By using Linka's network without his knowledge, we were able to shut down terrorist pods all over the world. And we've been doing so for years."

"Wow," I said.

"Indeed. Your father was a hero."

I turned to Gav. "I knew it."

He put an arm around me. "I know you did."

Facing Yablonski again, I said, "I'm just sorry my mother will never know the truth."

The man looked alarmed. "You gave your word."

"I know I did," I said with a little asperity. "I'm certainly not going to go back on it." I had a thought, though. "Can I tell her that we—Gav and I—know the truth, without actually telling her what it is? I know that will be enough for her. I'll tell her to trust me that everything is okay now."

"No specifics?"

"No specifics. I promise."

"Very well. Do you have any other questions right now, before you read through?" He glanced at his watch. "I have to stay with you until you're done. I've been entrusted with the responsibility of returning this file to its proper home."

"Just one," I said. "What role did Michael Fitch play in this saga? Linka was convinced he'd told me something, but all Fitch claimed was that Pluto was selling tainted products. Linka thought I knew much more than I did and he believed I'd learned it from Fitch."

Yablonski sighed. "Fitch," he said.

We waited.

"Fitch was a terrified, suspicious man who got in over his head. Back when your father worked there, Fitch began nosing around. Your dad warned him off. Apparently he was only partially successful because after your dad was killed, Linka began feeding Fitch the tainted supply story—warning him not to go to the police because then Pluto would have them killed, like they'd killed your dad."

"So Fitch died for nothing?"

Yablonski hesitated. "Fitch wasn't killed. We were careful never to announce his death to the media. He and his wife are in protective custody until we figure out the best way to debrief them without telling them the entire story."

"He's alive?" I put my hands over my face in relief. "I'm so glad. Such a poor, sad man."

"He broke down after you visited him," Yablonski said. "He saw your inquiries as his wake-up call—his chance to make things right for once in his life. He thought that by confronting Craig Benson, he'd be able to make his years of living in fear worth the sacrifice."

"I feel responsible."

"We all make choices," he said, "and we must be willing to take responsibility for them. Fitch learned that late in life. The paradox here is that if he'd come forward with his allegations sooner, we may not have had control over Linka for as long as we had."

Gav, Yablonski, and I spent the rest of our allotted time going through the folder. "You did this for us," I said to the older man as we wrapped up. "You spent time learning what was in this file because you knew we wouldn't have the opportunity to digest it all. Thank you."

"It was the least I could do."

When the president's aide came in and announced it was time for us to leave, we did so with me feeling better about my dad than I ever had. "He was a true hero," Yablonski repeated as he saw us out. "You can tell your mother that, too."

Gav gripped my hand as we were escorted out of the West Wing. "You know," he said, "Yablonski is right."

"About what?" I asked.

"About making our own choices."

I looked up at him, trying to understand where he was going with that, but he didn't say anything more. We followed the page into the residence where the young man left us to make our own way through the Family Dining Room into the Butler's Pantry. From there we took the elevator down to the ground floor in deference to Gav. With that cane, he wasn't ready for stairs yet.

When we reentered the kitchen, my team turned to us expectantly.

"Let me guess," Bucky said with an indignant head wiggle. "You can't tell us anything."

I held out my hands and tried to look sheepish. "Sorry."

Cyan studied Gav for a long moment, surveying us with an odd expression. I could tell she'd noticed how close together we stood. "I think you owe us at least a little explanation."

I felt warmth in my cheeks. "Maybe I do," I began.

"Wait," Gav interrupted. "Ollie?" Something in his voice was different. A little shy, a little bold. Was he trying to tell me he preferred we hold off spilling the beans about our relationship?

When I turned to him, he reached for me, clasping my hand. His gaze was warm, not at all White House appropriate. "Remember when you were hanging the shower curtain?"

My face flushed. Of course I remembered. "I do."

He started to get down on one knee.

"No, don't," I said, grabbing both his arms, pulling him back up.

He straightened. "No?"

I swallowed, giddy now. "Not no. Definitely not no. I just don't want you to hurt yourself."

He wrapped his free arm around me and tugged close. "Always thinking about others, aren't you?"

"What in the world is going on?" asked Virgil.

Cyan and Bucky knew; I could see it in their eyes. I eased out of Gav's embrace, ran my fingers down the inside of his arm and gripped his free hand in mine. Together we faced my team. "You all remember Special Agent Leonard Gavin?"

I waited for them to nod.

"It seems that Gav and I have a little paperwork to take care of this afternoon," I said. "I'll be back in a bit. And, oh one more thing." I grinned. "I'll be taking a personal day off."

"Another one?" Virgil grumbled. "When?"

My fingers laced through Gav's. His eyes twinkled as I gazed up at him. I would love this man until the day I died.

"Three days from now?" I whispered.

Gav smiled down at me. "Three days."

RECIPES

Spring Greens and Berries Salad

Goat Cheese and Mushroom Bruschetta

Garlic Chicken Pasta with White Sauce

Panna Cotta

Hearts of Romaine with Craisins and Raspberries

Savory Dinner Rolls

Tournedos of Beef with Mushroom Ragout

Roasted Baby Red Potatoes with Rosemary

Pumpkin Cheesecake

Cheese Fondue

SPRING GREENS AND BERRIES SALAD

(Makes 1 salad)

> 1 cup mixed spring greens
> 6 fresh raspberries
> 5 fresh blackberries
> 3 fresh strawberries, hulled and quartered
> ¼ cup toasted pecans
> 2 tablespoons gorgonzola
> 2 tablespoons balsamic vinaigrette (recipe
>   follows)

Place spring greens on a chilled salad plate and spread to make a nice bed. Scatter berries across top, followed by the toasted pecans and the gorgonzola. Drizzle balsamic vinaigrette over salad and serve.

BALSAMIC VINAIGRETTE

(Note: Vinaigrettes are typically 3 parts oil to 1 part vinegar)

> ¼ cup high-quality balsamic vinegar
> Herbs to taste (recommend ½ tablespoon dried
>   basil, ½ teaspoon dried cilantro, and ½
>   teaspoon dried tarragon; can use a com-
>   parable amount of fresh herbs instead but
>   unused vinaigrette won't keep as long)
> ¾ cup high-quality extra virgin olive oil

Pour balsamic vinegar into a mixing cup and add herbs. Slowly drizzle in extra virgin olive oil, whisking constantly until mixture is combined. Vinegar and oil should combine into an emulsion, but if the mixture separates simply whisk again immediately before serving.

GOAT CHEESE AND MUSHROOM BRUSCHETTA

TOMATO TOPPING

> *5–7 Roma tomatoes, diced*
> *3–5 green onions (white and pale green parts
>   only, thinly sliced 3–4 tablespoons extra virgin
>   olive oil*
> *Splash of balsamic vinegar*
> *Approx. 1 tablespoon dried basil*
> *Approx. 1 tablespoon minced garlic*
> *Sea salt and freshly ground pepper, to taste*

In a bowl, combine tomatoes and green onions. Pour on olive oil and balsamic vinegar (use enough olive oil to make it slightly soupy, and balsamic vinegar to taste). Add in basil and garlic, then sea salt and pepper, to taste. Toss to coat evenly. Cover and allow to marinate at room temperature for a couple of hours.

(Note: This mixture also works added to freshly tossed let-tuce salads—the oil and vinegar works as a vinaigrette, and should be added like a salad dressing—at the table, not in advance.)

GOAT CHEESE AND MUSHROOM SPREAD

> 8 ounces button mushrooms, cleaned and halved
>   (I have not tried this with other varieties)
> Sea salt and freshly ground pepper, to taste
> 1 tablespoon extra virgin olive oil
> 1 tablespoon unsalted butter, plus more as needed
> 8 ounces goat cheese, softened

Season the mushrooms with salt and pepper and sauté in oil
and butter over medium high heat until golden brown, adding more butter if pan becomes dry.

Meanwhile, cut the softened goat cheese into cubes. Combine mushrooms and goat cheese in food processor (at this
point, you could add a clove of garlic, minced, and a splash
of lemon juice). Process to desired consistency (I like small
bits of mushrooms).

FOR THE BRUSCHETTA

> 1 loaf French bread, sliced approximately 1 inch
>   thick (for this, I cut straight across, not on the
>   bias)
> Sea salt and freshly ground pepper, to taste
> Extra virgin olive oil
> Goat Cheese and Mushroom Spread (see above)
> Tomato Topping (see above)
> ½ pound Parmesan cheese, coarsely grated

Preheat oven to 350°F.

Arrange bread slices on cookie sheet. Brush with olive oil
and season lightly with salt and pepper. Bake in center of
oven until golden brown and crisp, approximately 12 to 15
minutes.

Remove from oven. Spread with Goat Cheese and Mushroom mixture. Spoon Tomato Topping over goat cheese mixture. Sprinkle with Parmesan cheese and serve warm.

GARLIC CHICKEN PASTA
WITH WHITE SAUCE

(Makes 6 servings)

1 pound penne or rigatoni pasta
1 teaspoon dried basil
½ teaspoon sea salt
1 teaspoon minced garlic
½ teaspoon fresh ground black pepper
1 teaspoon crushed red pepper
1 pound boneless, skinless chicken breasts,
  sliced (as for stir-frying)
4 tablespoons olive oil
1 cup fresh mushrooms, brushed free of dirt and
  quartered
½ cup green onions (white and light green parts
  only), thinly sliced 6 cloves garlic, minced
½ cup freshly grated Parmesan cheese

WHITE SAUCE

8 ounces nonfat or light sour cream
1 tablespoon minced green onions (white and light
  green parts only)
1 tablespoon minced onion
½ teaspoon freshly ground black pepper

1 tablespoon finely snipped fresh parsley
½ tablespoon garlic powder
Dash cayenne pepper sauce, or to taste
2–3 tablespoons fat-free milk

In a medium bowl, prepare sauce by whisking together sour cream, green onions, onion, black pepper, parsley, garlic powder, and hot-pepper sauce. Thin mixture with milk. Refrigerate until ready to use.

Cook pasta according to instructions on package.

While pasta is cooking, combine basil, salt, red pepper, and black pepper. Add chicken. Toss to coat evenly.

Heat oil in a 10-inch skillet. Add garlic and sauté for 2 minutes, or until golden brown. Add chicken. Sauté for 5 minutes. Add mushrooms and green onions. Sauté for 4 to 5 minutes or until everything is cooked through. Add sauce and cook for 2 minutes or until heated through.

Drain pasta. Toss with chicken mixture.

Serve with Parmesan cheese and breadsticks, garlic bread, or fresh Italian bread with dipping oil.

 **PANNA COTTA**

Makes 8 servings

> 1 envelope unflavored gelatin (about 1 tablespoon)
> 2 tablespoons cold water
> 2 cups heavy cream
> 1 cup half-and-half
> ⅓ cup sugar
> 1 teaspoon vanilla extract
> Berries, for garnish
> Caramel sauce, butterscotch sauce, or chocolate
>   sauce, for serving (optional)

In a very small saucepan, sprinkle gelatin over water and let stand about 1 minute to soften. Heat gelatin over low heat until gelatin is dissolved and remove pan from heat. (It's best to do this shortly before cream mixture is ready so gelatin is still dissolved when needed.)

In a large saucepan, bring cream, half-and-half, and sugar to a boil over moderately high heat, stirring. (This should be a full boil, not a simmer, but be careful that it doesn't boil over.) Remove pan from heat and stir in gelatin mixture. Add vanilla. Divide cream mixture among 8 five-ounce ramekins and cool to room temperature.

Chill ramekins, covered, at least four hours or overnight.

To serve, dip ramekins, one at a time, into a bowl of hot water for a few seconds. Run a thin knife around the edge of each ramekin and invert ramekin onto center of a small plate to remove panna cotta. Garnish with raspberries, sliced strawberries, or other fruit, and serve with caramel, butterscotch, or chocolate sauce, if desired.

HEARTS OF ROMAINE AND CRAISINS SALAD

(Makes 1 salad)

> *1 cup Romaine hearts (full leaf can be used, but*
> *the hearts provide a crisper salad)*
> *6 fresh raspberries (golden if in season)*
> *1 tablespoon craisins*
> *¼ cup toasted walnuts*
> *2 tablespoons raspberry vinaigrette*

Place greens on a chilled salad plate and spread to make a nice bed. Scatter berries across top, followed by the toasted walnuts. Drizzle raspberry vinaigrette over salad and serve.

SAVORY DINNER ROLLS

	2 Loaves	4 Loaves	8 Loaves

In a bowl, combine:

	2 Loaves	4 Loaves	8 Loaves
*Water**	*½ c.*	*1 c.*	*2 c.*
Sugar	*½ tsp.*	*1 tsp.*	*2 tsp.*
Yeast	*1 tbsp.*	*2 tbsp.*	*4 tbsp.*

Let stand approximately 20 minutes. Mixture should be frothy (if not, then it's possible the yeast is no longer viable). Whisk until blended.

To yeast mixture, add:

	2 Loaves	4 Loaves	8 Loaves
*Water (warm)**	*1 c.*	*2 c.*	*4 c.*
Sugar	*¼ c.*	*½ c.*	*1 c.*
Oil	*¼ c.*	*½ c.*	*1 c.*

Dried spices to taste (recommended combinations include dill and tarragon or basil, chervil, and cilantro)

Stir, then add in:

	2 Loaves	4 Loaves	8 Loaves
*Flour***	*4½ c.*	*9 c.*	*18 c.*
Salt	*½ tbsp.* *(rounded)*	*1 tbsp.* *(rounded)*	*2 tbsp.* *(rounded)*

Allow to rise in warm, humid place until doubled in size (about 1 hour), then punch down and divide into individual rolls. To form individual rolls, tear off an amount of dough about the size of a golf ball, flatten slightly in the palm of your hand, and work the dough slightly, stretching the skin and folding the edges under. Pinch the bottom closed and form into a ball, then set aside to rise. It's simplest to place the raw rolls in rows on a baking sheet lined with parchment paper. Cover loosely and let rise until doubled (about 1 hour). Bake at 350°F for approximately 15 minutes or until done (rolls should be nicely browned). Place on wire rack to cool.

* Note that, as a rule, when working with yeast, water temperature should be no more than 110–115 degrees Fahrenheit, and cooler is actually better. Yeast is a living organism; if the water is too hot, it will kill the yeast and the bread will not turn out. Cool, or even cold, water works just fine, with the only noticeable impact being a slight slowdown in the yeast's rising speed—but since slower rising generally produces better flavor, this is not a bad thing!

** All purpose flour is slightly better for these, but the addition of herbs and spices makes the added gluten of bread flour appropriate as well.

TOURNEDOS OF BEEF WITH MUSHROOM RAGOUT

Makes 4 to 6 servings; 2 cups Mushroom Ragout

TOURNEDOS

> *2 pounds center-cut beef tenderloin roast*
> *Kosher salt and freshly ground black pepper, to taste*
> *2 tablespoons vegetable oil*
> *1 tablespoon butter*

MUSHROOM RAGOUT

> 1 pound mixed mushrooms, such as shiitake,
>   cremini, or white button
> 2 to 4 tablespoons unsalted butter
> 1 medium shallot or ½ small onion, chopped
> ½ teaspoon kosher salt
> Freshly ground black pepper, to taste
> 3 sprigs fresh thyme, leaves stripped
> ½ cup Madeira, vermouth, or white wine
> ⅓ cup heavy cream

Preheat oven to 400°F.

Heat a large ovenproof skillet over medium-high heat. Season the beef all over with salt and a generous amount of pepper. Add the oil to the skillet and heat until shimmering. Add the butter and swirl to melt. Add the beef and sear until nicely browned on all sides, about 8 minutes total.

Transfer the skillet to the oven. Roast until an instant-read thermometer inserted in the center registers 125°F for medium rare (about 25 minutes). Transfer the roast to a cutting board, tent it very loosely with aluminum foil, and let it rest for 10 to 15 minutes.

FOR THE MUSHROOM RAGOUT:

Brush dirt from mushrooms. Remove the shiitake stems and discard. Trim the dry ends off the cremini and white mushroom stems. Quarter all the mushrooms and put in a bowl.

Heat 2 tablespoons butter in a large skillet over medium-high heat. Add the mushrooms and spread evenly in the pan. Increase the heat to high. Let the mushrooms cook undisturbed until they brown, then shake the pan to turn them over. If the pan seems very dry as the mushrooms cook, add the additional butter along the sides of the pan. Continue to cook until nicely browned, about 5 minutes. Add the shallot and cook until softened, about 2 minutes. Season the mushrooms with the salt and pepper and add the thyme. Pull the pan off the heat and add the Madeira, vermouth, or white wine. Return pan to the heat and scrape up any of the brown bits that cling to the bottom of the pan (a wooden spoon is best for this). Add the heavy cream and bring to a boil. Remove from heat and serve.

Slice beef into 1-inch-thick rounds and serve with the Mushroom Ragout.

ROASTED BABY RED POTATOES WITH ROSEMARY

Yield: 4 to 6 servings

> *2 pounds baby red potatoes, quartered*
> *4–5 rosemary sprigs*
> *1½ tablespoons olive oil*
> *Salt and freshly ground black pepper, to taste*

Preheat oven to 500°F. In a jelly-roll or large baking pan, toss the potatoes with the rosemary and oil, season with salt and pepper, to taste, and roast, stirring once, for 30 minutes.

PUMPKIN CHEESECAKE WITH CARAMEL SWIRL

Makes 10 servings

CRUST

1½ cups ground gingersnap cookies
1½ cups (about 6 ounces) toasted pecans
¼ cup firmly packed brown sugar
¼ cup (½ stick) unsalted butter, melted

FILLING

4 8-ounce packages cream cheese, room
*   temperature*
1 ⅔ cups sugar
1½ cups canned solid-pack pumpkin
9 tablespoons whipping cream, separated
1 teaspoon ground cinnamon
1 teaspoon ground allspice
4 large eggs
1 tablespoon (approximate) purchased caramel
*   sauce*
1 cup sour cream

Preheat oven to 350°F. In a food processor, finely grind
ground cookies, pecans, and brown sugar. Add melted butter
and pulse until combined. Press crust mixture onto bottom
and up sides of 9-inch-diameter springform pan with 2¾-
inch-high sides.

Using an electric mixer, beat cream cheese and sugar in large bowl until light and fluffy. Transfer ¾ cup of the mixture to a small bowl; cover tightly and refrigerate to use for topping. Add pumpkin, 4 tablespoons whipping cream, ground cinnamon, and ground allspice to mixture and beat until well combined. Add eggs 1 at a time, beating just until combined. Pour filling into crust (filling will almost fill pan). Bake until cheesecake puffs, top browns, and center moves only slightly when pan is shaken, about 1 hour and 15 minutes. Transfer cheesecake to rack and cool 10 minutes. Run small sharp knife around cake pan sides to loosen cheesecake. Cool. Cover tightly and refrigerate overnight.

Bring remaining ¾ cup cream cheese mixture to room temperature. Add remaining 5 tablespoons whipping cream to cream cheese mixture and stir to combine. Press down firmly on edges of cheesecake to create an even thickness. Pour cream cheese mixture over cheesecake, spreading evenly.

Release pan sides from cheesecake. Slice and serve with caramel sauce.

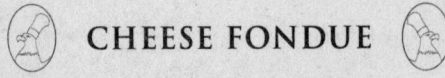

CHEESE FONDUE

½ pound imported Swiss cheese, shredded
½ pound Gruyère cheese, shredded
2 tablespoons cornstarch
1 garlic clove, peeled
1 cup dry white wine
1 tablespoon lemon juice

1 tablespoon cherry brandy, such as kirsch
½ teaspoon dry mustard
Pinch nutmeg
Assorted breads, vegetables, and fruits, for
*   dipping*

In a small bowl, coat the cheeses with cornstarch and set aside. Rub the inside of the ceramic fondue pot with the garlic clove, then discard.

Over medium heat, add the wine and lemon juice and bring to a simmer. Gradually stir the cheese into the simmering liquid. (Melting the cheese gradually will encourage a smooth fondue.) Once smooth, stir in cherry brandy, mustard, and nutmeg.

Arrange an assortment of bite-sized dipping foods on a lazy Susan around fondue pot. Serve with chunks of French and pumpernickel breads. Other suggestions include Granny Smith apples and blanched vegetables such as broccoli, cauliflower, carrots, and asparagus. Spear with fondue forks or wooden skewers, dip, swirl, and eat.

FROM NATIONAL BESTSELLING AUTHOR
JULIE HYZY

BUFFALO WEST WING
A WHITE HOUSE CHEF MYSTERY

With a new First Family moving into the White House, executive chef Olivia Paras can't afford to make any mistakes. But when a mysterious box of take-out chicken shows up for the First Kids, she soon finds herself in a no-wing situation . . .

INCLUDES RECIPES FOR
A COMPLETE PRESIDENTIAL MENU!

Praise for the series

"A must-read series to add to the ranks
of culinary mysteries."
—*The Mystery Reader*

"A gourmand's delight."
—*Midwest Book Review*